CW00358244

Rhianna King has spent more than two decades working as a communicator for state government environmental agencies and an Aboriginal-led not-for-profit organisation.

During Melbourne's long lockdowns of 2020–21, Rhianna craved the company of people other than those in her locked-down household and so created characters to spend time with instead. The result: her first novel, *Birds of a Feather*.

Rhianna lives in Melbourne with her husband and two children.

RHIANNA
KING

BIRDS of a FEATHER

affirm
press

First published by Affirm Press in 2024
Bunurong/Boon Wurrung Country
28 Thistlethwaite Street
South Melbourne VIC 3205
affirmpress.com.au

Affirm Press is located on the unceded land of the Bunurong/Boon Wurrung peoples
of the Kulin Nation. Affirm Press pays respect to their elders past and present.

10 9 8 7 6 5 4 3 2 1

Text copyright © Rhianna King, 2024
All rights reserved. No part of this publication may be reproduced without prior
written permission from the publisher.

 A catalogue record for this
book is available from the
National Library of Australia

ISBN: 9781922992901 (paperback)

Cover design by Louisa Maggio © Affirm Press
Typeset in Garamond Premier Pro by J&M Typesetting
Proudly printed in Australia by McPherson's Printing Group

*To my two grandmothers – Teresa 'Tessie' Croft (nee Morton)
and Gertrude 'Louie' Mooney (nee Walder) – who were both writers,
both remarkable women and both adored by their families.*

Chapter 1

Beth

I spent much of my childhood fantasising that I was adopted. While other kids were pretending to be princesses and superheroes, I was using my stuffed toys to play out a scenario where I found out there had been a mix-up at the hospital when I was born. It was the only way I could make sense of how I came to be a member of my family.

Now, at thirty years old, I no longer played with my toys, of course. But I was still searching for an explanation for my progeny.

My parents exuded an unbridled magnetism that made people want to be around them. Mum – an artist – had recently been commissioned to paint a mural on a toilet block in a park near their place. So many people stopped by to see her while she was working on it that the council received traffic complaints. They rigged up lights so she could paint at night, but then traffic issues became after-dark noise infringements when her friends and contacts descended for a party in the park. For Dad – a musician – a trip to the local shops to run even the most banal errand usually turned into a roaming street party, which, more often than not, involved an impromptu jam session.

Our surname – Dwyer – was used more as a descriptive noun than a proper one.

'Jarrah has such charisma; she's such a Dwyer,' they'd say.

'Did you see Elijah perform? He was amazing; he's such a Dwyer,' they'd gush.

'Have you met the *other* child? She's not a typical Dwyer at all,' they'd remark.

To be fair, I didn't know where 'they' ended and my inner dialogue started, but the sentiment rang in my ears like a case of unrelenting tinnitus. Being the filler foliage in a bouquet of blooms meant people who knew my family related to me in one of two ways. They'd either forget me entirely (I'd lost count of how many times people had said 'I didn't realise Rosie and Thorn had *three* children'), or they'd treat me like I was popular by proxy.

Even from a young age, I knew that when classmates asked for a playdate at my house, they were not seeking out my company (playing with ant farms and DIY crosswords has a limited appeal, apparently). They were hoping for a 'Dwyer experience'. A few times (and most likely out of obligation) my classmates would return the invite, and I got an insight into how their families lived.

I loved that they ate 'normal' food for dinner, not cocktail snacks, takeaway or 'Rosie's surprise', which was a bowl of cereal. I loved that when you rang their doorbell, a tinny chime sang through the house to signal a visitor had arrived. Our doorbell was an old bicycle horn covered in spider webs that sounded like it signalled the punchline in a slapstick circus performance. I loved that their parents wore 'normal' clothes and had 'normal' jobs. And I loved when their parents announced it was time for bed and then read us a story and tucked us in. My parents had raised us with a focus on self-determination and left it to us to choose when we went to sleep. (It wasn't nearly as much fun as you'd think.)

Fortunately, I had Gran – Elise Evans, nee Simpson. And, on the day that changed the trajectory of my life, I drove to Gran's house to collect her for Saturday lunch with my family, as I did every week, feeling grateful to have her as an ally. I was also pleased I'd be able to use her bathroom to wash my hands and rid them of the greasy, smelly petrol film that had coated them since I'd filled up my car – a white 1990 hatchback which was older than me.

My car had a few cosmetic blemishes and mechanical quirks but, more often than not, it got me from point A to B and back again without incident. The lock on the driver's side was broken, which meant I had to climb across the passenger seat to get in and out. Mostly, this was just a mild inconvenience, although, once, I did accidentally disengage the handbrake as I manoeuvred my legs into the footwell. I managed to stop the car before it rolled too far down the hill it was parked on, and perfected the act of scissoring my legs over the centre console so it wouldn't happen again. A few months earlier, on a particularly wet day – the sort when the ability to see out of one's windscreen was crucial to safely navigating the road – the windscreen wiper lever snapped off in my hand. Fortunately, I still had a screwdriver in the car from when the rear-view mirror fell off, so I jimmied it into the cavity and developed a technique to manually activate the wipers. It often took a couple of attempts to engage, so it wasn't ideal for sudden downpours, but it did the job.

Gran's house – specifically, her garden – was one of my favourite places in the world. Well before local councils gave cash incentives for people to plant native gardens, or gardening for wildlife was in vogue, Gran had established a spectacular native haven in an otherwise suburban concrete jungle.

At first (and maybe second and third) glance, the front garden looked haphazard and unorganised. Chaotic, even. But Gran had thoughtfully introduced every plant and arranged every log and stone to provide a sanctuary for birds, reptiles, amphibians and insects. Carpets of pigface, with their pretty pink flowers and plump green leaves, sprawled over the ground, while the dainty white flowers of creeping boobialla scented the air in spring and summer. Bronze rambler and other creepers wound up a retaining wall made from quarry stones, which served as a multistorey apartment building for a thriving population of lizards.

The sharp spines and prickly leaves of the grevilleas and hakeas might have looked inhospitable, but they offered birds a refuge from prowling neighbourhood cats. The bottlebrush and banksia shrubs along the fence served as an all-you-can-eat buffet for birds and bees.

The birdbath in the centre of the garden attracted local magpies, willie wagtails and honeyeaters that splashed and ruffled in the water and fed on the insects it lured. After rain, the pond at its base was a stage for motorbike frogs that performed like an unruly orchestra in which every member vied for a lead part.

After dark, when the diurnal creatures had turned in for the evening, a southern boobook owl that my Gran had named Liber (the Latin word for 'book') emerged from the shadows. It would quietly announce itself with a 'boo-book' call, before assuming its position as nighttime sentinel in the firewood banksia.

The pièce de résistance of Gran's garden was the three-armed grasstree, or balga, as it's also known, which she'd salvaged from a development site. It was impossible to know exactly how old it was, but given the species grows as little as two centimetres per year, it could have been up to 600 years old. Its vibrant green spines contrasted with the charred black trunk; an ode to the hundreds of years it stood in its fire-prone environment.

As I made my way along the path, stepping carefully over a trail of ants and spotting a honeyeater overhead, I could feel my shoulders relax. Gran's house was one of the few places where I felt I could be myself.

My happiest childhood memories were of Wednesday afternoons, when Mum taught art classes and Gran collected us from school. While Jarrah and Elijah lounged on Gran's mid-century settee watching cartoons and eating her delicious cinnamon twists or the Iced VoVos she bought especially for us, Gran and I could be found in her garden, or with our noses in natural history books.

One year, Gran gave me a flower press for my birthday. I carefully selected suitable specimens, which I gently placed between the cardboard sheets like other girls my age might tuck their dolls into bed. Then I would fit the top and bottom boards, replace the wingnuts and begin the excruciating wait for them to dry. After about ten days, I would open the flower press, and lift off the cardboard to reveal the perfectly preserved specimens. Gran – a botanist with the state's herbarium – would help me tape the specimen into a flower journal, describe its features, document its origin, and record its scientific and common name. By the time I had finished primary school, I had created an impressive botanical reference library.

Gran continued to collect me from school long after I was old enough to walk home by myself. By then, I had the whole batch of twists or the entire packet of Iced VoVos to myself because Jarrah and Elijah had given up afternoons with Gran in favour of hanging out in the local park or shopping centre with their friends. When I left school, I scheduled my university and work timetables so I could still visit her on Wednesday afternoons. It was the highlight of my week.

I reached Gran's front porch and called out to her as I opened the front door.

'Hello, darling.' She poked her head into the hallway. 'I won't be a tick.'

'No rush, Gran. I'm just going to wash my hands.'

I walked down the corridor towards the bathroom and breathed in the smell of the house – of Gran. Her house was perfumed by a subtle hint of dusty books, a whiff of her homemade (and sworn-by) vinegar cleaning solution and a trace of the Pond's Cold Cream that she'd used since forever. It used to smell like Grandpa's cigarettes, too, but that smell had faded in the months after he died. The shelves, cabinets and mantles in her house groaned under the weight of the ornaments and trinkets she'd collected from op shops, garage sales and on her travels. And her walls were covered in paintings of flowers, birds, seascapes, landscapes, portraits, still lifes and life studies.

My favourite painting of hers hung at the end of the corridor near the bathroom. The painting depicted two adult Gouldian finches perched on a grass plant. The hues of their resplendent yellow bellies, violet throats and green caps had faded a little over the years, but their colours were still striking. A third bird – a comparatively dull-brown juvenile – was sheltering behind the outstretched wing of one of its parents. When I was younger, I would look to that juvenile and wonder if I, too, would transform into a more colourful version of myself as I matured. A glance down at my black jeans, black Converse runners and black T-shirt indicated that I had not.

I washed my hands, dried them on the stiff, sun-dried handtowel and glanced behind me at the tiny bathtub where Gran had told us fairytales as she gave us our weekly hair wash on Wednesday afternoons. I hunched to inspect my reflection in the mirror, which was positioned at the perfect height for my five-foot-one Gran and no one else. I used my still-damp hands to smooth the stray hairs that had escaped the low ponytail I'd tied at the nape of my neck, and performed an inspection of my chocolate-brown hair for any grey hairs that might have appeared since I plucked two out last week.

After leaving the bathroom, I found Gran waiting by the front door. I leaned down to hug her; her tiny shoulders slipped under my armpits and her short-cropped hair gently tickled underneath my chin. She always seemed tiny; I was taller than her by the time I was twelve. But lately she seemed even smaller, and the hunch she had developed through years of looking down a microscope had become more pronounced.

She had a light-pink silk scarf adorned with flowers draped around her neck and was wearing a pair of silver gumleaf earrings from her extensive collection.

'You look nice,' I said. 'I like the earrings.'

She smiled, and jiggled her head to make her earrings dance below her lobes. 'You ready?' she asked.

I shrugged my shoulders defeatedly.

On our way out, we passed by 'Herrick', who Gran had rescued from a garage sale the previous month. Herrick was a jackalope – a taxidermied head of a rabbit, fitted with a large pair of forked deer antlers and mounted on a dark timber plate. Apparently, the myth of the jackalope began when American colonists spotted rabbits with warty growths on their heads and then some crafty taxidermists from Wyoming attached a pair of antlers to a rabbit's head and sold them for a lark. Now they hung in bars and tourist haunts all over Wyoming – and above Gran's fireplace.

'Goodbye, Herrick,' she called merrily.

'Goodbye, Herrick,' I echoed.

As silly as it was, I was a little jealous of him. He didn't have to deal with my family.

Chapter 2

Beth

'Hola!' my father bellowed as he threw open the front door.

He was wearing a sombrero and a multicoloured poncho. I recognised the poncho as the one he'd bought when he and Mum travelled to South America for four months when I was in primary school. They'd left my siblings and me with Gran and Grandpa.

'Como estas? Come 'ere.' He grabbed for me, pulled me into a big hug and kissed me loudly on the cheek. 'How's my girl?'

'I'm good, Dad,' I replied breathlessly; most of the air had been squeezed from my chest.

I pulled back to survey him. His sombrero was askew, having been displaced by our embrace. Up close, I could see he had used an eyeliner pencil to draw on a moustache. My first instinct was to call him out for cultural appropriation, but I had enough experience with family lunches to know that they usually went better if conversations like those were saved until after we'd exchanged greetings.

'Hi, Elise.' He turned to Gran with a giant smile. They kissed each other's cheeks.

'Darling, you look FAB-U-LOUS,' she gushed. 'If I'd known it was a Mexican-themed lunch, I would have dressed up too.'

'Oh, it was a little last-minute. We accidentally drank all the wine in the house last night,' he chuckled, turning to walk back inside. 'But we had some tequila and Cointreau. So, I figured, when life gives you lemons ... you make margaritas. So, it's a Mexican fiesta – isn't it, Rosie?'

'Ohhhh ... they're here,' my mother cooed as she appeared from the kitchen. She was wearing a Frida Kahlo-esque floral headdress made from large, brightly coloured flowers. She looked magnificent.

People often described Mum as 'breathtakingly beautiful'. Her eyes were a striking aqua, and her wild curly hair – once a vibrant strawberry blonde, but now a little lighter – was often decorated with coloured paint that had strayed from the paintbrushes she wielded.

'Mum,' she said, wrapping her olive-skinned arms around Gran. 'How are you doing?'

'I'm good, darling.' Gran looked Mum up and down like she was admiring a magnificent piece of art. 'You all look wonderful.'

'Thanks,' she said, through a broad smile, her eyes twinkling. There was no question she was at her most beautiful when she smiled. The lines that had developed around her eyes, down her cheeks and across the bridge of her nose didn't seem to age her, but endearingly animated her smile and added to its warmth. And her laugh was a raucous, joyous, contagious sound that reverberated around even the densest space.

Growing up, I'd found it mortifying.

Mum launched into a lively description of how some neighbours – 'the ones from number fourteen that we always thought were a bit odd' – had seen them in the front yard and suggested they all have a drink. It turned out that they were a bit odd, but they also were a lot of fun. One drink turned into one bottle, which turned into one big night.

'Can you believe they've lived down the road from us for nearly five years, and we've only just discovered them?' Mum mused. 'Think of all the fun we could have had.'

I hoped the odd couple from number fourteen knew what they were getting into. My parents had a habit of becoming fast friends with other couples. They would share an intense friendship, living in each other's pockets, until the couple retreated back into their life of suburban normalcy, completely worn out. My parents had an insatiable stamina for life and a vitality that exhausted most others. Few other couples could keep up for the long haul.

'Who's for a drink?' Dad asked, while waving a blender jug in one hand and three upturned cocktail glasses in the other.

'I'll have one,' Jarrah said, materialising from down the hall.

Like Mum, Jarrah moved with an effortless fluidity, which was made even more graceful by the long, flowing skirts she often wore. The bracelets that adorned one of her svelte wrists softly jingled when she moved, creating an ethereal soundtrack for her journey through life. The closest I had to this was a squeak that had developed in the left shoe of my favourite pair.

She gave Gran a hug, me a wave and made her way to one of the armchairs where she tucked her legs underneath her, sat down and rested her head on one of her slender arms.

'Elise? Beth? You having a drink?' Dad asked while already pouring them.

Elijah emerged from his dark, cavernous bedroom, grunted in my direction, gave Dad a thumbs up and pecked Gran on the cheek. He sat opposite Jarrah, in front of a vase of peacock feathers Mum had collected when she worked as an artist in residence at a winery in the valley. The feathers looked like they were extending out of the top of his head like a riotous fascinator.

Elijah had followed in Dad's footsteps and become a musician. He was in a band called One Girl, Three Lovers with one girl – Olivia – and his high school friend, Sam. The trio had decided on the name without realising what it implied about the nature of their off-stage relationship. They were indeed lovers (being in a band had its perks, apparently), just not with each other. But, by the time someone pointed this out, they'd already had posters made up to promote their first gig, so they decided to keep it. Besides, sexual ambiguity was at the heart of many successful bands, they figured.

'There he is ...' Dad said, handing Elijah a drink. 'How was your gig last night?'

Elijah explained that the gig, which was at a small suburban pub, was a little dull until a twenty-first birthday pub crawl turned up. A gaggle of drunken girls heckled the band with requests for mainstream pop songs, while the birthday girl's mother threw up in a pot plant by the stage. A couple of the attending males were caught trying to pull a condom vending machine off the toilet wall, and someone else jumped the bar and took off with a bottle of vodka. The entire party was escorted from the premises as the band played some new material, which went down well among those sober enough to notice it.

Predictably, Elijah's tale prompted Mum and Dad to recall stories of the good ol' days, when Dad had played at some of the city's shadier venues. Like all their stories, we'd heard Mum and Dad tell these ones hundreds of times before, which meant their delivery was well-rehearsed. They finished each other's sentences, paused at key moments for suspense and even threw in some sound effects while ascending towards a suspenseful climax.

The story we'd heard them tell most often was the one of how they'd met. It happened when they were in their early twenties, at an art auction fundraiser at a posh western suburbs private school. The event supported local artists, by exposing them to members of the school community who had deep wallets and a desire to publicly demonstrate their generosity.

Mum was one of the exhibiting artists and Dad had been hired to

11

play the backing track for conversations about overseas ski trips and property portfolios. It wasn't his usual style of gig, but Dad had hoped it might lead to other bookings for cocktail parties and corporate functions. Unfortunately, the evening's program contained a typo and incorrectly identified him as Thorn Dwyer, rather than Thom Dwyer.

Having noticed Mum from across the room (his overused cliché, not mine), Dad had tried to make a beeline for her between each of his sets. But she had spent the whole evening shrouded by bougie folk who asked her about the origins of her inspiration and whether she'd considered painting in a more conventional style. She hated these types of people, but she indulged their inane conversation, as she was desperate to make a sale. The original-painting-selling business was slow, and, as a vegetarian pacifist, she was reluctant to work any more hours at her job as a casual counter-hand in a butcher to make that month's rent.

My mother's painting was the last lot of the evening. It was an abstract landscape she'd created with bold and textural brushstrokes in rich colours.

Aware he was running out of time to meet her before the end of the evening, Dad decided to bid on Mum's painting. He planned to invest every cent he had – $227.60, including the $200 he was to be paid for the event – to procure the painting and secure an introduction to the artist.

Armed with a numbered paddle and a keenness to buy whatever my mother was selling, Dad started his bidding out strong, confidently committing $60 – $10 over the starting price. As he lowered his paddle on the first bid, he realised he'd been so transfixed on the bewitching artist that he hadn't even looked at the painting he was so determined to buy. Fortunately, he thought it was as magnificent as the woman who created it.

A bidding war ensued between Dad, an elderly lady wearing a fur coat and too much perfume, and the father of the school captain. The bidding bounced around between them, increasing by ten- and twenty-dollar increments. Then, just as Dad was about to bid $240 (he felt sure he could procure the shortfall from the coins that occupied the cracks and crevices of his car), the school captain's father delivered a decisive $20 blow.

Dad was disappointed, but he had no time to lament; he was contracted to play a final set to entertain the masses while they settled their purchases and headed out into the evening and back to their waterfront mansions.

But my father's efforts had not gone unnoticed. My mother had been impressed by his deep sultry voice as he played pared-back acoustic renditions of some of her favourite songs. She'd noticed that he moved his body towards the microphone when he sang high notes. And she liked the way he closed his eyes when he played instrumental guitar solos. She also appreciated that his valiant involvement in the bidding war had driven up the price of her painting well beyond her expectations. Thanks to him, she would be able to pay that month's rent and have some money left over for some new paints.

When she'd finalised her sale, my mother wrote her phone number on a piece of paper and had planned to put it in the open guitar case next to Dad. But as she approached the stage, he stopped mid-song and, with childlike enthusiasm, asked: 'Want to get a drink?'

Startled by the abrupt pause in his stunning rendition of Jackie DeShannon's 'What the World Needs Now Is Love', my mother hesitated for just long enough that the lady in the fur coat called out: 'If she doesn't, I will.'

My mother nodded, my father smiled, and the other lady huffed off into the night.

Mum scrunched her phone number into a ball and tossed it into a nearby bin; she had a feeling she wouldn't need it. She was right. My parents went for a drink that night, and within three months they were engaged; within two months of that my mother was pregnant with Jarrah; and three months later, they were married. They've been inseparable as

'Rosie and Thorn' ever since.

This story had been told to us like a fairytale over and over again. Jarrah – a hopeless romantic – pored over every detail.

'How did you know he was the one?' she'd ask Mum.

'What did you first notice about her?' she'd quiz Dad.

'I wonder if love at first sight happens to everyone?' she'd pose to no one in particular.

I was far more interested in the practical elements of the story.

'What would have happened if you'd won the auction and couldn't pay your rent or afford to eat?' I'd challenge Dad, judging his fiscal carelessness.

'What would you have done with the painting if you'd won it and she'd said no to your invitation?' I'd inquire, appalled that he'd tried to buy her affections.

'Weren't you concerned about starting a family without any financial security, assets or conventional careers to fall back on?' I'd ask them both, knowingly picking at a wound first inflicted by my father's parents, who disapproved of their relationship.

But their answer to my questions was always the same: 'It all worked out, and we wouldn't change a thing.'

Chapter 3

Beth

While Elijah helped Mum finish getting lunch ready and Jarrah and Gran chatted, Dad and I searched through my parents' drawer of 'essential items' for paper umbrellas for the cocktails.

'How's work going, Bethie?' Dad asked as he fossicked in the sideboard cupboard.

'It's good. I've been working on a project to build a rope bridge across a major highway that has bush on either side, so possums can safely cross from one side of the road to the other. The bridges have been installed in other parts of Australia and the data shows that far fewer possums get hit.'

Like so many native species in the local council area where I worked as an environmental officer, possums had been severely affected by urban development. My job was to find ways to help conserve these native species before they became locally extinct. I was particularly excited about this rope bridge – I had researched and suggested it, and my manager had agreed to let me run with the project.

'That sounds great, Bethie. Good for you,' Dad said nonchalantly, before triumphantly producing the umbrellas. 'I think Jarrah mentioned she rescued a baby possum when its mother was hit by a car the other day.'

Irritation prickled at me; I was leading a significant project that would likely benefit an entire species across a vast metropolitan area, and he was likening it to Jarrah driving an orphaned possum to a wildlife carer.

'Luncheous est servo,' Mum announced from the doorway. 'Get ready for a Mexican feast.'

The 'feast' was nachos, cobbled together with some stale corn chips, salsa, a browned avocado and a few flakes of grated cheese that Mum had found up the back of the fridge.

'Did you hear the news about the star signs changing?' Jarrah asked, transferring a pile of corn chips from the communal bowl to her plate and then sucking the cheese residue from her fingers with a pop. 'This could be the most significant thing to have ever happened to humanity.'

'What do you mean the star signs are changing?' Mum asked, offering the plate of nachos to Gran.

'Apparently, NASA has found a new constellation, so there are thirteen star signs, not twelve. This means that everything we know about ourselves could actually be wrong.' Her voice escalated in enthusiasm with every word until it reached a shrill crescendo.

Jarrah often made her decisions based on her 'intuition' and her daily horoscope. When she was sixteen, she registered for a service to receive text messages containing horoscopes and affirmations several times a day. Unfortunately, the horoscopes didn't predict the shock you'd get when you received your phone bill and discovered that each message cost $4.95. By the time the bill turned up, Jarrah had amassed $750 worth of spiritual guidance.

'Really?' Mum asked. 'What's the new one?'

'Let me check,' she said, reaching for her phone and swiping at it until she found what she was looking for.

I rolled my eyes. Jarrah sought the meaning of life in everything from crystals to runes. She was superstitious from an early age; she compulsively avoided cracks in the pavement, dreaded Friday the thirteenths, and was forever searching for wood to knock on. She threw herself into the latest spiritual trend: she wore the red Kabbalah bracelet when it was in vogue; and swore by *The Secret* when it was all the rage. She regularly frequented clairvoyants and hijacked every camping trip and sleepover with her ouija board. She rearranged all the mirrors in the house during a phase with Feng Shui. I wondered what the new constellation meant for the living room furniture.

'Oh, here it is ... Ophiuchus,' she whispered dramatically. '"The addition of Ophiuchus, for people born between 29 November and 17 December, has shuffled the entire zodiac chart." Beth! This means your star sign has changed.'

My birthday – 27 December – was tucked away in the awkward week between Christmas and New Year's Eve when the days are committed to cricket-watching, beach visits and leftover ham. People are usually recovering from their Christmas food coma and haven't yet gathered the momentum that builds in the lead up to New Year's festivities. It was pretty much an annual non-event.

'Listen to this,' Jarrah continued excitedly. 'This is Beth's star sign with twelve zodiac signs: "Capricorns are relentlessly ambitious and are known to be unforgiving, serious and boring. They are disciplined and practical, hardworking and pragmatic. They weigh up all their options before making decisions, which are usually based on reason and not emotion." This is like reading your bio, Beth.'

Dad and Elijah chuckled.

'Nawww, that's not very nice,' Mum offered in attempted solidarity.

'I don't see any of those as a bad thing,' I said. 'What's wrong with being disciplined, practical, hardworking and pragmatic?'

'But, listen. Now you're a Sagittarius. "Sagittarians are optimistic and adventurous with a tendency to be restless. They are independent, honest and philosophical and are always ready to learn and have a spirit of independence and love the idea of finding freedom.'" She beamed. 'This is like an astrological makeover. All those years of being serious and boring, and now you can be your true self – optimistic and adventurous with a yearning for freedom—'

'Jarrah,' I said curtly, 'I am who I am because that's my nature, not because of some nonsense profile in a horoscope.'

'But surely you'd enjoy a bit more adventure in your life? A bit more spontaneity? Leave some things to chance?'

'*A little less conversation, a little more action*,' Dad sang, doing a terrible Elvis impression.

'Thorn – no,' Mum half-heartedly scolded. She turned to me with sympathetic eyes. 'We love you just the way you are, Beth,' she said.

'Thanks, Mum. But I'm not apologetic for the way I am.'

'Of course you're not, darling,' Gran offered. 'We're all different, and that's what makes families, and the world, so great.'

'I'm just saying that you could see what life would bring if you allowed fate to take the reins for a while,' Jarrah continued. 'Like, have you ever trusted in the universe to decide which path you should take? Or placed your faith in a higher power? I mean, have you ever even bought a lotto ticket?'

'I'm thrilled that you're happy living out your destiny and making decisions based on how your tea leaves dry in the bottom of your cup,' I said dryly, 'but that's just not for me. And I've got better things to spend my money on than the lotto. Besides, NASA studies astronomy, not astrology, so I don't know what they'd be doing looking for new star signs. The zodiac signs date back to the Babylonians, who divided the zodiac into twelve segments and then picked twelve constellations, which they aligned to their twelve-month calendar. I don't see how there *can* be a thirteenth one.'

'Okay now,' Dad said, reaching for a sour-cream-laden corn chip, half of which fell to his poncho as he tilted his head and inserted it into his mouth. 'Let's just enjoy this delicious meal. Elise, how's it going at the herbarium?'

He wiped his face with the back of his hand and smeared his moustache over the bottom part of his face. He was a mess, but I was grateful for him shutting down the conversation.

Lunch continued in the typical way – conversations about bands I hadn't heard, books I hadn't read and movies I hadn't seen. Once the last bit of dried cheese had been pried from the casserole dish (which I doubted had ever been used for a casserole for as long as it had been in this house) and the last drop of margarita was slurped from our glasses, I motioned to Gran that I was ready to go. I exchanged hugs and kisses with Mum and Dad and nodded farewell to Jarrah and Elijah.

'I wasn't really having a crack at you,' Jarrah said as she followed me up the hallway towards the front door. 'I just think you'd have more fun if you eased up a bit.'

How would I ever prove to her that I was content? Smile more? Wear brighter clothes? Update social media with #blessed posts? And why would I even want to? Having watched on the sidelines as Jarrah danced her way through party after party, loved her way through a series of passionate relationships and ricocheted through exotic adventures, I knew that her highs were a stark contrast to her lows. Her life wasn't all rainbows and sunshine, and at least I had a reliable forecast.

Chapter 4

Beth

'Urgh,' I grunted as we pulled away from my parents' house. 'Imagine thinking that redefining horoscopes would somehow change who we are as people.'

'I know, darling,' Gran sighed. She seemed tired.

'Are you okay?'

I sometimes forgot that Gran was eighty-two and that slowing down was probably something that came with the territory.

'Oh yes, sweetie,' she responded, her singsong chime returning. 'I'm fine. Just a little tired. Actually, that reminds me. Can we stop at the pharmacy on the way home? I have to get a script filled.'

'A script? Is everything okay?'

'Yes, pet. Everything is peachy.' She swatted the air with her hand as if shooing away my concerns. 'My doctor is just tweaking my blood pressure medication. Nothing to worry about; I'm fit as a fiddle.'

Indeed she was. She'd aged in appearance after my grandpa died, though; her face became gaunter, and her hair greyer. But she made a point of keeping busy. She increased her volunteer hours at the herbarium, made jam from every imaginable fruit and did a short course in silversmithing. She often referenced her favourite author, Gertrude Stein, who said, 'We are always the same age inside.' Based on that, I'd have said Gran's inner self was in her mid-twenties.

I pulled into the car park of the small shopping centre that was halfway between our two houses.

'I won't be a jiffy, darling,' she called back to me as she took off through the automatic doors while I was still climbing out of the passenger seat.

The centre was typical of those found dotted in suburbs all over the country. It had the standard line-up of shops: a bottle shop, pizza shop, bakery, beautician, supermarket, newsagent, chemist, barber and health food shop. It also had a multi-function shop where you could get keys cut, shoes mended or drop off your dry cleaning.

I meandered over to inspect the offerings on the discounted book table outside the newsagent. I thumbed through a copy of *Cooking for One: cuisine for singles*; glanced at *Practising Pilates*, which boasted a free stretch band; and smirked at the stack of untouched street directories. Who was upgrading their street directories these days? Then, the illustrations of zodiac signs and the Grecian-style font on the cover of *Science of the Stars: the 12 zodiac signs* caught my attention. I turned over the book to read the blurb:

Are we the masters of our own destiny? Is our future determined by fate? What does your birth date say about you? This is the must-have guide to understanding the 12 zodiac signs and how the planets impact our lives.

Too bad for all the people who purchased *Science of the Stars*, even at the discounted price of $19.95, as the entire book was now defunct if Jarrah was right about NASA's 'discovery' of the new constellation.

I browsed through the magazines and decided to treat myself to a copy of *National Geographic*. *See, Jarrah*, I thought, *I can be spontaneous.* A magazine hadn't been in that week's budget, but I bought it anyway.

'Do you want a ticket in tonight's draw too?' the elderly gentleman behind the counter asked as I handed the magazine over to be scanned. He pointed to a sign that was emblazoned with '$60 million jackpot' and decorated with streamers and balloons.

My first thought was that surely everyone knew that the higher the jackpot amount, the more people who bought a ticket, so your odds of winning were actually lowered. My second was of Jarrah.

'What the hell,' I said, loudly enough to surprise us both. 'I'll take one.'

I paid, tucked the ticket into a pocket of my wallet and made a mental note to adjust my budget spreadsheet to reflect the unexpected purchases.

~

As I stepped over the threshold of my apartment after dropping Gran home, a wave of relief washed over me. It was good to be home. I felt safe in this space, away from the clutter and chatter of the world, where everything was exactly as I wanted it.

Where my parents' house was eclectic, my house was ordered. Their walls were bestrewn with 'statement' art in various shapes, sizes and colours (some my mother's, and others by artists they admired), while my taste in art was minimalist to non-existent. Their rooms were cluttered with odd bits of furniture from the side of the road; my two-bedroom apartment was sparsely furnished. The fabrics that covered my parents' cushions, bedspreads and windows were a helter-skelter of patterns and colours. In contrast, I had chosen upholstery in neutral, calming tones and with subtle textures.

I'd shared a bedroom with Jarrah until I was about twelve, where I'd lived among her chaos and had a front-row seat to the spectrum of emotions she'd catapulted through daily.

The final straw came when a putrid smell materialised in our room and progressively worsened over several days. Jarrah poked around superficially to find the source of the pungent aroma, but failed to uncover it. After several days, when I couldn't stand it anymore, I delved into her piles of clothes. I found a partially decayed baby possum, which I assumed had been brought in by one of the neighbourhood cats Jarrah had befriended and encouraged to come into our house.

I picked up the possum in one of her T-shirts, stormed into the lounge room and, in between sobs and dry retches, announced to my parents I was leaving home to live on my own. I thrust the putrid possum at Mum, who then agreed to cordon off a section of the enclosed sleep-out veranda at the back of the house. I was delighted. Finally, I had my own room, away from Jarrah, her drama and her dead possums.

This was my sacred space until I answered an ad for a 'clean and neat housemate to live with two responsible and studious engineering students' in my first year of university. The shared house was within walking distance of campus, and I lived there for three years. My housemates – Tamara and Jess – lived up to their advertised promise, and we enjoyed a harmonious home life based on mutual consideration and cleaning schedules.

After I graduated and got a job at the council, I moved into a tiny bedsit. I lived there for five years while I saved for a deposit for my unit. Despite my ample salary, this involved a lot of scrimping and sacrifice; while my peers were enjoying brunches of smashed avo and overseas working holidays, I was living to a stringent budget. Admittedly, being fiscally conservative was made easier because my calendar wasn't exactly overrun with social engagements. Having endured a lifetime of my parents' parties, I was never keen to spend time or money on drunken nights and the inevitable hungover mornings.

In an attempt to pay off my unit as soon as possible, I had continued to maintain a tight financial plan. I budgeted for a monthly catch-up with my friends from university, who knew better than to include me in their schedule of buying rounds. And, occasionally, my colleagues from the council went for a Friday-night drink, but I made my exit after one or two beers, or when the twenty-somethings from waste management started talking about getting everyone to do tequila shots – whichever came first.

I could usually absorb other costs incurred due to socialising (such as dinners for friends' birthdays, or wedding and engagement presents) in the $30 I allowed each week for 'miscellaneous incidentals'. And while it had been eons since I'd dated, splitting the bill ensured I wasn't left shouldering the cost of someone else's meal if they'd opted to stray from the evening specials. Jarrah – whose money trickled through her fingers – accused me of being stingy. But I couldn't have cared less, because when I was in my unit, which I could afford *because* I was stingy, I felt at home in my own life.

Chapter 5

Beth

The Monday after lunch with my family I had a rostered day off, which meant I was able to accompany Gran on a field trip to survey orchids in a nature reserve next to Woodside Ridge – the farm where she grew up. I enjoyed tagging along as a volunteer on these visits. It was an opportunity to get out in the bush, without the responsibility of leading the project. I enjoyed having something planned for my time off; I hated squandering it. And any day I got to spend with Gran was a good one.

Gran had been involved in a project to re-establish a population of the species *Caleana fallax*, or warty swan orchid as it's commonly known, for several years. Each plant grows to about 30 centimetres tall and develops two to three smooth dark-purple flowers in spring. Two fleshy, tear-shaped petals grow out from the stem and curve to meet each other at their tips to create a swan-body-like shape. They are covered in a soft fuzz, made up by thousands of tiny hair-like fibres, while a central petal bends 90 degrees at its tip to create what looks like a head at the end of a long, elegant neck. The result: a swan-shaped flower; hence the name.

Gran had been involved in a survey of the species about twenty years ago, when they found there was only a handful of plants left in existence. So, as an insurance policy against something terrible (such as a fire) wiping them all out, Gran and a group of volunteers collected seed to store for safekeeping at the state herbarium and in the Kew Gardens Millennium Seed Bank in Sussex – a kind of global Noah's ark for plants.

And it was lucky they did.

Two years ago, a fire had torn through the reserve, burnt through three of the four remaining populations of warty swan orchids and caused the native wasp, their pollinator, to disappear.

Fortunately, Gran and her team were able to cultivate some plants from the surviving population and grow new ones from the seed they had stored. But, still, the wasps were nowhere to be found.

Knowing that Mother Nature needed a helping hand, Gran visited the plants several times a week. She tenderly collected pollen grains on a tiny paintbrush from one plant and then delicately brushed them onto another. I think she enjoyed the work as much as she enjoyed being able to describe herself as a botanical sex therapist. Whatever her title, one thing was for certain: without her, the entire species would have become extinct.

'I never get tired of coming out here,' Gran said as we slowed to a stop at the edge of the nature reserve under a giant marri covered in blossoms that were teeming with bees. My car had vibrated violently when we turned off the sealed road and onto the track that ran parallel to the nature reserve, so I was glad to give it a break.

'Did you ever think you might end up taking over the farm?' I asked.

'Not really,' she replied, looking towards the timber 'Woodside Ridge' sign that her father had erected when he was still working the land. 'My parents were determined that we would be educated and that my brother, Henry, sister, Daisy, and I all explored a life beyond these fences.

'In fact,' she continued, 'we were the first family of three with more than one girl to all graduate from the university. They even published a story about us in the university magazine. Mummy kept that clipping in a frame on the mantelpiece until she died.'

'They must have been proud,' I said. While they told me they were proud, I don't think my parents ever thought much about me being university educated.

'They were. But, unfortunately, it spelled the end for the farm that had been in our family for four generations.'

A cow in a nearby paddock mooed loudly, as if confirming her account.

'And it was a risk. Daisy and I didn't know what our careers would look like, especially after we got married,' she added. 'Nowadays it's assumed that you girls will have long and productive careers, even if you choose to have a family too. But it wasn't until the mid-60s that married women could work in the public service. I remember two girls I went to boarding school with – Mary Thomas and Edith What's-Her-Name – got married in secret, so they didn't have to quit their jobs. But that just bought them time; they had no choice but to quit when they got pregnant.'

Gran scanned the horizon and breathed deeply.

'Even though I left this place, it always feels like home,' she said, as much to me as to the landscape.

A trail of dust appeared on the horizon, and the farm dogs in a distant paddock were whipped into a barking frenzy. Emily Lim and Jack Walker, who had arrived from the state's herbarium to oversee the survey, waved from inside the car as they slowed to a stop.

Emily was a botanist in her forties who was capable, diligent, thorough and organised, with little interest in small talk. Gran insisted that Emily reminded her of me, which I took as a compliment.

Jack – a proud Noongar man – more than made up for Emily's reservedness. He spoke at a million miles an hour and radiated warmth.

'Elise!' he bellowed as he strode towards Gran with his arms outstretched. 'How are you going? You keeping well?'

He hugged Gran tightly. They had worked together on and off for the past forty years and enjoyed a productive professional history and a genuine fondness for each other.

'Great to see you again, Beth,' he said, turning to shake my hand.

Once we'd unloaded our equipment from the car, the four of us made our way through the open eucalypt woodland towards the population of warty swan orchids. Emily took deliberate, purposeful strides, while Jack stopped regularly to point out a lizard he'd spotted or to listen for a bird call. Gran seemed to be walking more slowly than usual, especially up the inclines. Admittedly, the small pea-sized rocks underfoot did make it slippery.

The undulating terrain of this patch of bushland was why it was still there; my great-great-grandfather chose to clear the flatter land to the east. It was the easier option by comparison, and now this patch of bush was one of only a handful of natural areas left in the district. The landscape was dotted with powderbark wandoos; their slender creamy, skin-coloured trunks were covered in pockmarks and blemishes. The deepest indents were tinged with a deep red-brown colour, as if blood had coagulated in the wounds.

After about fifteen minutes, we reached the population of warty swan orchids, which was marked out by purple tape and protected under a sheet of fine netting.

'Hello, my little darlings,' Gran cooed.

Jack laughed.

'What?' Gran feigned ignorance. 'Plants that know they are loved grow better, you know.'

Emily rolled her eyes good-naturedly. As a scientist myself, I assumed it was because she disapproved of Gran's anthropomorphising of the plants.

'Well, it seems to have worked,' Jack gushed. 'Look at them all!'

We got to work counting and measuring the plants. The original plants looked healthy, and there were seven new ones. The wasps were still missing in action, but the group was confident in its 'build it, and they will come' approach. It would just take time. And a bit more sexual healing.

By the time we tallied our findings and gathered up our equipment, the sun was directly overhead, which shortened the shadows and hazed the horizon. The hum of the insects had become louder and more shrill.

'Are you okay, Gran?' I asked, noticing she'd stopped to catch her breath as we walked back towards the cars.

'Of course I am,' she replied, slightly breathlessly. 'Any fitter and I'd be dangerous.'

Gran looked to Emily as if to check whether she was making a mental note about her diminished capacity to carry the equipment bags. I knew she feared the day they would deem her an occupational health and safety risk and no longer let her participate in the surveys.

About halfway up the last incline she stopped abruptly.

'Ohhhh! Look what I've found,' she exclaimed, pointing to a long red-and-black feather laying against a rock. 'A red-tailed black cockatoo feather'.

'That's a beauty, Elise,' Jack said. 'We call those cockies "Kaarak", which means "black feather". They were my mother's totem.'

Gran picked up the feather, and rotated it between two fingers. The incandescent orange-red hues of the barbs glowed with the sun behind them.

'When I was young, these birds used to descend on this farm in their thousands, you know,' Gran said. 'You'd hear them well before you'd see them, and then they'd flock to the eucalypts around the place.'

Gran removed her wide-brimmed hat and slid the quill of the feather into the band.

'Their favourite tree was the old marri next to the outhouse. They'd pry open the honkey nuts with their beaks, eat the seed and then drop the shell. It made the ground really slippery. The challenge of getting to the loo without falling over or copping a nut to the head was enough to make you shit yourself. And that was before you checked the underside of the seat for redbacks and the long-drop for snakes.'

We all laughed.

After we said our farewells and Emily and Jack drove off, Gran lingered with the car door open and scanned the landscape, as if adding additional colour and detail to her mind's eye picture of the place she'd known her whole life.

'What a good day at the office,' she beamed.

I couldn't have agreed more.

Chapter 6

Beth

The next day at work, I was typing up meeting notes from a particularly productive discussion about a tract of bush that offered quenda – a species of bandicoot – a stronghold in suburbia, when an email notification appeared in the bottom right-hand corner of my screen.

To: Beth Dwyer
From: Matt Moore
Subject: Proposed road closure for installation of possum bridge

I'd known it was possible I'd hear from him; Matt helped coordinate road closures in our council area. Matt and I had met four years earlier when he coordinated a road closure for a project I managed. We were relocating a mob of landlocked kangaroos from a proposed housing development site next to a nature reserve across a major road. He was extremely helpful throughout the planning and execution of the project, and maintained excellent communication via phone and email.

I had thought this was just a commendable demonstration of

professional attention to detail, but he later told me it took him several weeks to work up the courage to ask me on a date. He would call to ask me out and then lose his nerve, so we'd end up discussing the pros and cons of witch's hats over bollards or the benefits of variable message signage over static communications displays. It was just as well it went that way; I would have declined his invitation if he'd asked me out before the project was complete. It wouldn't have been appropriate for us to date while we were working together.

He wasn't good-looking in the traditional sense, but I found him attractive. His lips were upturned at the corners, even when he wasn't smiling, which made him look friendly. Having repeatedly been told I had a steely 'resting bitch face', I found this feature admirable.

Matt was pleasant enough company and was a competent lover. He enjoyed many of the same interests as me – hiking, birdwatching and nature documentaries – and he didn't probe when I dodged his questions about my family. However, he compulsively bit his nails and the skin around them, which I found irritating. And he craved physical touch (his 'love language', apparently) and constantly entered my personal space without any prior invitation, such as to initiate hand-holding. Occasionally, I tolerated short periods of time spent with our digits entwined (on the upside, it served to stop him biting his nails). But I generally preferred to keep my hands to myself.

After about four months, we agreed that our relationship had run its course and we'd be 'better off as friends' (his words, not mine; I wasn't under any illusion we would seek out each other's company for a platonic relationship).

I opened my inbox and clicked on Matt's email.

'Hi Beth,' the email began. 'I hope you've been well.'

I'm getting in touch to make plans to close Banksia Highway so you can install your possum bridge. What dates did you have in mind? It sounds like a terrific project. I look forward to hearing more about it. Cheers, Matt.

I reread the email to scout for any hidden nuances or implied innuendos that suggested our ongoing work relationship would be impacted by our history. But it seemed completely innocuous. Friendly, even. Perfect.

I clicked reply.

Hi Matt,
Good to hear from you.

The curser blinked impatiently as I paused to consider the greeting. It was too familiar, I thought, for professional correspondence between two interagency colleagues, regardless of their history. Besides, I hated the unnecessary salutations people used at the beginning of emails like 'I hope you had a terrific weekend' or 'Happy Fri-Yay'. They're a waste of everyone's time.

I backspaced over the words and continued typing.

Please find the project plan attached, which outlines the expected timeframe. The bridge is currently being manufactured and will likely be completed in the next couple of weeks, so we're looking to install it in the second week of next month. We understand the installation will need to occur overnight, to minimise disruption to traffic. Perhaps we could set up a time to meet when you've had a chance to look over the project plan?
I look forward to working with you again.

I deleted the last line immediately. I didn't want to appear overly friendly or imply any unintended eagerness to reconnect on any level other than professional.

It will be good to see you again.

Nope. That was worse. I held down the backspace key to erase it and then simply typed:

Beth

I attached the document and sent the email.

Matt was not the first man I had been with. I was with Isaac Seth for eighteen months while we were at university. Isaac and I were both keen for our relationship to be free of expectations. We agreed our undergraduate university years were not the time to be serious about anything but our studies, so our time together was spent without pressure. And, as Jarrah had kept reminding me, I could never have a long-term relationship with someone whose surname was Seth; Beth Seth would be ridiculous, should we ever get married. Of course, I had no intention of changing my surname to that of my husband, but it remained true that we were not compatible long-term.

It had been convenient to have someone to navigate the unknown seas of university with. Isaac and I mixed in the same circle of friends and had similar ideals for our study-to-play ratio, and I was glad my first sexual encounter was with someone kind and respectful. Our relationship drew to a natural close when he left to spend twelve months travelling overseas.

The ends of my relationships were nothing like the finales of Jarrah's affairs. Finishing things with Matt and Isaac had felt like a gentle receding of the tide, whereas Jarrah's break-ups resembled a vat of boiling oil after someone had thrown water into it: the two combusting into a spitting inferno before claiming untold collateral damage and ending in an expensive repair bill.

While I was in no rush to jump into a relationship for the sake of it, being single for as long as I had been required an annual readjustment to my five-year plan. At thirty, I was aware my biological clock was ticking, even if the alarms weren't ringing quite yet. A uni acquaintance had recently posted to social media that she had begun the process of freezing her eggs. I got the impression from the number of typos in the post, and the fact she deleted it shortly after, that she was still under the effects of the anaesthetic from having her eggs harvested when she shared it. But it had given me food for thought. If having a baby was something I wanted, then surely I could do it without a partner. And preserving my healthy, thirty-year-old eggs made sense from a medical and reproductive perspective.

However, I wasn't completely sure I even wanted to have a baby of my own. Since the day I'd learned about overpopulation in primary school, I'd despaired at how the human race was reproducing at an unsustainable rate. Now the impacts of climate change, and our lack of immediate and effective actions to mitigate the causes, made bringing a child into the world seem almost negligent.

Besides, I knew I just wasn't that maternal. Whenever someone from work who was on maternity leave visited the office with their baby, all the women gathered around the infant like it was a sun-god and passed it around like a prize. If anyone tried to hand it to me, I would politely refuse and busy myself doing something else.

I was once invited to a cousin's baby shower where one of the activities was to write down a piece of advice we'd like to give the baby, which was then collated into a book. As my cousin read out messages of wisdom such as 'always remember how much you are loved', 'trust your instincts' and 'there's no such thing as perfect timing', I realised I had misunderstood the assignment. Although I still maintain that 'if your gums bleed when you floss, it usually means you don't do it enough' is sound advice.

I also couldn't ignore that if I had a baby of my own, I risked opening a Pandora's box of issues that stemmed from my own upbringing. I didn't even want to think about that.

I continued scrolling through my inbox. While I may not have felt my biological alarm clock ringing, I certainly felt my stomach rumbling. A check of my watch confirmed it was, indeed, lunchtime.

'I'm just going to pop out to the shops,' I said to Alannah, the council's other environmental officer whose desk adjoined my own. 'Do you need anything?'

I asked this as a courtesy; Alannah's diet primarily consisted of coffee and biscuits from the staff tea room.

'I'm all good, thanks,' they replied. 'See you soon.'

~

I arrived at the nearest supermarket, which regrettably was located deep in the bowels of a large suburban shopping mall. The alternative retail option was an independent store that sold expensive organic nuts by the kilo and other overpriced groceries. There was little variation between the tins of tuna available at both retailers, except for the price. So I navigated inadequate parking, tolerated the crowded aisles and dodged the salespeople handing out skincare samples and promises of improved beauty, all to save 37 cents per can, which adds up over a year.

Once inside the supermarket, I selected my tuna in a variety of flavours (it is important when you're eating the same thing each day to include *some* variation) and made my way to the self-serve checkout to avoid Pam on register four. Pam was nice enough, but she always tried to engage in small talk. The last time I went through her checkout she offered her unsolicited observations about what she described as my 'limited taste in cuisine'. I didn't feel like Pam's insights.

As I scanned the last tin and went to place it in my bag, it slipped from my hand and dropped onto the big toe of my right foot. I winced in pain and, as I looked up, I met Pam's eyes. She shot me a warm, sympathetic smile, which made me regret having deliberately avoided her. The world probably needed more Pams.

Hustled by the automated voice that instructed me to 'Please place item in the bagging area', I put the tin in the bag, tapped the buttons to finalise my purchase, and removed a $20 note from my wallet (I found it easier to budget when I dealt in cash). As I did, a small folded piece of paper flicked onto the ground.

'You don't want to lose that.' A rotund middle-aged man stopped scanning his haul of 'frozen meals for one' to bend down and pick up the lotto ticket I'd bought two days before. 'It might be the winning one.'

'Ha,' I snorted, taking the ticket from his sausage-like fingers. 'I doubt it, but thanks.'

I gathered my bag, vowed to always go through Pam's checkout in the future and hobbled out of the supermarket.

A large shiny gold cat statue sat next to a 'Lotto here' sign on the counter of a newsagent kiosk ahead of me. It stared blankly into the mall, waving its mechanical arm up and down. Next to the cat was a sign that promoted an app for 'easily managing your lotto'. I guess it made sense they'd try to make it as easy as possible for people to part with their money. But I wasn't going to waste the data needed to download it; this was the one and only lotto ticket I'd ever buy.

'I'd like to check this, please,' I said, offering my ticket to the bespectacled man behind the counter.

'No worries. Just scan it in that machine,' he replied, gesturing to an electronic box on the counter.

I orientated the ticket so the barcode faced the machine and held it under the fluorescent green light.

After a moment, a tinny dinging sound chimed loudly from the machine and the word 'CONGRATULATIONS' flashed on the small screen.

'Holy fucking shit!' the newsagent blurted as he baulked at the screen facing him.

'What?' I demanded. 'Have I won something?'

'Yes! You fucking have,' he said with a laugh. 'You've won second division.'

Chapter 7

Beth

I walked away from the newsagent booth feeling completely discombobulated. After a few steps, I turned back to check I hadn't hallucinated the whole thing. But the bespectacled newsagent, whose name I had learned was Eric, and the gold, counter-dwelling cat were waving at me in unison in a way that assured me I hadn't.

I clutched the winning ticket and the piece of paper on which Eric had scribbled the Lottery Head Office address to my chest. I could feel my heart thumping against my hand.

Winning the second-division prize isn't like winning at the pokies; dollar coins do not spew from a machine. In fact, Eric had informed me there would be no cash transaction at all. After he'd scanned my ticket, he called the Lottery Head Office to clarify the next steps.

Eric was animated and exuberant, while I was utterly speechless. I had received a smattering of academic accolades and a couple of encouragement awards for turning up for sport, but this was the first time I had won something that was completely random.

Eric relayed that I was to report to the Lottery Head Office where I would hand over my ticket and my bank BSB and account number. Then, in ten business days, $264,412.51 – my second-division haul – would be deposited into my account.

I was told to call the number on the piece of paper when I arrived at the Lottery Head Office car park and someone would meet me at my car and escort me to the building (a security precaution). Once inside, I would be given a booklet about financial planning, information about tax, a box of chocolates and possibly a bottle of champagne if there were any left in the cupboard (they had a habit of disappearing, apparently).

Eric had looked over his shoulders to make sure no one was listening and leaned towards me as he whispered what he said were 'the most important two pieces of information'.

'Think carefully about who you tell until you've had a chance to get your head around it,' he whispered. 'And guard the ticket with your fucking life.'

I looked at my watch. I needed to get back to the office for a meeting with my manager. I hurried through the centre towards the exit nearest my car. As I reached the automatic doors, I passed a patisserie, which had cakes and pastries I had often admired.

What the hell, I thought. *Surely this deserves a celebratory cake.*

I selected a fruit tart with kiwi fruit, strawberries and mandarin segments, arranged artistically under a layer of shiny gelatine on a bed of yellow custard in a chocolate-filled pastry case. It looked delicious. And $4.75 didn't seem outrageous for a post-lotto-win splurge.

I made it back to my car, opened the passenger-side door and climbed into the driver's seat. I decided I would get the driver's side lock fixed as one of my first priorities. It wasn't until I had pulled out of the car park and driven halfway back to work that it occurred to me that I could buy a new car altogether.

~

Back at the office, I sat down at my desk. I wondered how I would focus on my work as thoughts spun inside my head.

What should I do with all the money? Who should I tell? Should I go on a holiday? How much should I give to my family? What charities should I support? Should I pay off my mortgage? Or should I invest it?

'You sure you're okay?' Alannah asked, gesturing to the blank computer screen I'd been staring at for the past few minutes. 'You seem a million miles away today.'

I determined that sharing the news of my win with Alannah contravened Eric's advice about withholding the information until I'd had a chance to digest it.

'Yes. Sure. Absolutely,' I lied, tapping at my mouse to wake up my computer.

Alannah narrowed their eyes at me. We had worked together for about four years; I knew they sensed something was amiss.

'Well,' they started slowly, 'if there's anything I can do, just shout out.'
'I will, thanks.'

I stood up from my desk and made my way towards my manager's office, steeling myself at his door and attempting to gather my thoughts; updating Geoff Kinsman about the progress of the possum bridge was too important to be distracted.

I knocked three times.

'Come in,' he called out without looking up from his computer. Typing did not come naturally to Geoff; he employed only his two pointer fingers and searched for every letter as though he had never seen a keyboard before. I stood silently to avoid breaking his concentration.

'Ahh, Beth,' he said finally. 'Take a seat. How's your week going so far?'

I instinctively clutched the employee ID card that hung from a lanyard around my neck where I had tucked the lotto ticket. At first, I

41

had put the ticket in my wallet for safekeeping. But it seemed foolish to store it in the object most likely to be targeted by a thief, should one enter the office. So I folded it into a small rectangle and tucked it into my bra. Then I had worried the heat of my body would compromise the thermal paper and make the print fade. Next, I placed it under the stationery tray in my desk drawer. I left it there for about two seconds before I decided that was the least safe place in the office, given the regularity with which my colleagues pilfered my office supplies. I imagined their surprise when they came to 'borrow' a bulldog clip or a highlighter, and discovered a winning lotto ticket. In the end, I had decided that it was safest tucked away in the plastic sleeve hanging from my neck.

'My week's going well, thanks, Geoff,' I replied, taking a seat opposite his desk. 'I've been in touch with my contact to coordinate the road closure for the bridge installation ...'

I managed to hold my focus for each of the twenty minutes I was with Geoff, except for the one moment I was distracted by a photo of him and his family at Machu Picchu. I made a mental note to prepare a list of places I wanted to visit. Peru would certainly be in my top five.

'There is one more thing,' I said, as our meeting was drawing to a close. 'I need to head off early today. I'll be leaving just after three.'

'Of course,' he replied, dipping his head slightly to study me over the top of his glasses. I was usually the last to leave and rarely took time off during the day, so it was understandable my request was met with surprise. 'Go whenever you need to. Unless it's for a job interview, in which case I'll need you to stay till six.'

He laughed at his own joke. If only he knew.

Chapter 8

Beth

I pulled up to a large grey building in an industrial suburb east of the city and dialled the office number, as per Eric the newsagent's instructions. There were few people around, apart from a pair of panelbeaters smoking outside the workshop to the left of the Lottery Head Office, and a middle-aged woman wearing an impossibly frilly apron stacking chairs outside the cafe across the road. There was no obvious sign of any would-be lotto ticket thieves.

The office door opened, and a short, slightly built woman with waist-length dark, shiny hair and a huge smile emerged.

I unfurled from my car.

She laughed as she approached me. 'I'll bet a new car is at the top of your shopping list.'

I shrugged my shoulders.

'It's so great to meet you, Beth,' she said, shaking my hand with a vigour that seemed at odds with her tiny frame. 'I'm Amarita Patel. You can think of me as your lotto win concierge, if you like.'

I wondered how a person found themselves in such a career. I didn't remember seeing 'Lotto win concierge' in our careers guide handbooks at school.

'You must be so excited,' she continued, grinning so enthusiastically that the veins on her neck ribboned from her jaw to her shoulders.

'I'm ... I'm ... I guess I'm still in shock,' I stuttered. 'This was actually the first lotto ticket I've ever bought. I don't even enter the office syndicates. So it's all come as a bit of a surprise.'

'Your first ticket? My goodness. No wonder you're in shock. Well, let's get you inside where we can talk it through and get all the paperwork sorted.'

We walked towards the building, and Amarita used a swipe card to open the heavy front door. The young woman behind the reception desk, who was wearing a headset that made her look like a 90s pop star performing on stage, looked up from her computer and beamed at me.

'Welcome,' she said, bringing her hands together in a dainty applause. 'Congratulations.'

'Th– thanks,' I stammered awkwardly.

I followed Amarita down a corridor lined with photos of smiling people holding oversized novelty cheques and standing next to cars festooned with giant red bows. Every third or fourth office door was open and, as we passed, the occupants called out offerings of 'congratulations' and 'good for you'.

When we arrived at a boardroom at the end of the corridor, Amarita gestured for me to enter.

'I'll just run and grab our CEO, Leo, so that he can authorise the transfer of funds,' she said. 'You make yourself comfortable.'

I sat on one of the twenty-or-so chairs that surrounded a giant mahogany board table. Like the hallway, the boardroom walls were adorned with photos that captured the moments when peoples' lives had changed.

One of the photos showed an elderly couple holding a cheque for

$2.76 million made out to 'Mary and William Finkelstein'. Mary balanced her half of the cheque on her walking frame while William clutched his half with hands disfigured by arthritis. I wondered what motivated Mary and William to buy lotto tickets at their advanced age. How many years would they even have to spend their new-found fortune? Based on my experience, the shock of winning might have actually reduced the amount of time they had to enjoy it.

In a frame to Mary and William's right, 'Simon Black' was giving a thumbs up to the camera with one hand, while clutching a $3.8 million cheque with his name on it with the other. To his right, 'Barry Furnish' was poking his smiling face over the top of a cheque made out for $30.5 million. His dirty, high-vis work gear gave the impression he'd come straight from work. I wondered how long he'd waited after the picture was taken to hand in his notice.

Amarita reappeared with the news that Leo would be along shortly, and explained that she was responsible for coordinating the handover of funds. She also provided post-win support, such as dealing with the media and carrying out long-term wellbeing checks. She explained that wellbeing checks were recommended for winners of large amounts, to avoid the effects of 'Sudden Wealth Syndrome' – an affliction that can lead to anxiety, guilt and isolation, as well as poor personal and financial decisions.

'Some of the stories are truly heartbreaking,' she said sadly. 'Couples fight over the money in divorce courts; families and friends turn on each other; people develop drug and alcohol problems or gambling habits; and some end up broke after they buy houses they can't afford to maintain and cars they can't afford to insure.'

I scanned the beaming faces of Mary and William, Simon and Barry in the pictures on the wall. Their smiles conveyed feelings of joy, relief, excitement and optimism; I wondered what had become of them and their fortunes.

However, I was comforted by my ability to make rational and measured decisions, no matter how much money was involved.

'Hello, hello.'

Leo Phillips's voice reverberated around the room before he stepped over the threshold. He was about seven feet tall and muscular, with spectacularly white teeth. He reminded me of a basketball player. Or a game show host.

'You must be Beth. Welcome,' he boomed. He shook my hand and then sat down and placed his right foot on his opposite knee. His feet were enormous. 'Why don't you tell me a bit about yourself?'

'This is the first lotto ticket Beth has ever bought,' Amarita said.

'That's true,' I said. 'To be honest, I subscribe to the theory that we create our own luck. So I didn't think in a million years that I would win lotto.'

'You know, Beth,' Leo started, his brow furrowing slightly. 'Mark Twain said: "Fortune knocks at every man's door once in a life, but in a good many cases the man is in a neighbouring saloon and does not hear her."'

'I guess I did pay attention to fortune knocking this time,' I said, wondering whether deciphering the proverb of a famous eighteenth-century author was a condition of receiving my winnings. 'Or maybe she used the doorbell.'

Leo laughed, and then he got to work finalising the paperwork and funds transfer.

~

I stared at the spreadsheet titled 'Lotto funds distribution', which was open on my laptop in front of me. I had set up a formula to experiment with different scenarios of how to divide the money between seven columns: gifts, donations to charity, short-term investments, travel, long-term investments, miscellaneous purchases and incidental expenses. It was the third consecutive night I'd spent adjusting and readjusting it.

The days since I'd found out I'd won lotto were much the same as any other; I got up, went for a run, went to work, came home, cooked dinner and went to bed. But the knowledge of my win nagged at me like an earworm. Mainly, thoughts of the money and what it meant for my life existed as a soft background hum. But occasionally, they rivalled an entire orchestral symphony, complete with a choir, and left me with ringing ears, a spinning head and a stomach full of knots and butterflies.

I had accepted that winning $264,412.51 would be 'life-adjusting', rather than 'life-changing'. I was certainly not about to quit my job, buy a house in the golden triangle and never think about money again. However, I suspected my life would forever be different. And certainly a little easier.

Before I left the Lottery Head Office, Amarita gave me a pamphlet, which I had read so many times I could recite it verbatim. It cautioned winners against making rash decisions and implored them to scrutinise new or returning 'friends' and anyone with opportunistic investment proposals. It also suggested winners withhold the exact amount they won from anyone they gift money to, to avoid discussions about fairness and entitlement. 'Instead, consider using statements such as: "I've come into some money" or "I've recently had some good luck, which I'd like to share"', the pamphlet advised.

I felt like I'd been preparing for this my whole life. I was hardly likely to make rash decisions, and withholding key details about my personal affairs was my modus operandi. It helped that my family never seemed interested in my life anyway; they were too busy oversharing the details of their own adventures. Settling on what I would actually do with the money was proving a bit trickier. Of one thing, I was sure: I had no intention of moving house. I had accrued some equity in my apartment, so I committed to paying whatever was left after I'd divided it between columns A1 to A6 off my mortgage. This would free up my income to invest elsewhere over time.

The pamphlet had a blank space for jotting down some 'luxury splurge items'. So far, I had listed new shoes (leather Derby shoes with punch hole detailing) – $179 – and two new bras (one black and one flesh coloured, without fussy lace or bows, to replace the ones I had worn to death) and matching knickers (four pairs) – $185.

While it pained me to do so, my altered financial position forced me to reconsider the long-term viability of my car. I had to admit that it had become a liability. Any money I spent on repairs – cosmetic or otherwise – would only prolong the inevitable. And now that I had the means to do so, it made financial sense to invest in a more reliable vehicle with better long-term prospects and fuel economy. After I conducted a comprehensive analysis of the new car market, and synthesised consumer reviews and expert articles, I settled on a hybrid hatchback and made an appointment for later in the week for a test drive.

After confirming how much holiday leave I had (nine weeks), I turned my mind to travel and made a list of places I was keen to visit. Topping the list was the UK; I had a guilty fondness for the royal family, and was keen to do the Harry Potter studio tour.

Unlike many of my peers, I'd never taken a gap year. Instead, I had travelled to the UK and Europe for a few short stints and used some money Gran gave me as a graduation present to travel to South-East Asia. Shortly before I was due to leave for that trip, Leah Knight – a friend from uni – said she was keen to tag along. I decided it would be good to share the cost of a double room, and the company would be nice too, I thought.

Two days into our trip, Leah convinced me to attend a Full Moon Party on a Thai island. Parts of the island were absolutely beautiful; warm turquoise water lapped gently at magnificent beaches that were fringed with lush green jungle. But the tourists who visited the island to enjoy its beauty ruined it with the vulgar behaviour they brought with them and the rubbish they left behind. Shortly after we arrived at the party, Leah spent the equivalent of two days' food budget on a mango-flavoured mushroom shake. I spent the next eight hours following her around while she sang in colours, stared at lights, giggled uncontrollably and professed her love to anyone and everyone in her vicinity. After the effects of the mushrooms had abated and I was sure she was safe, I told Leah I didn't think our travel styles were compatible. I retreated back to the mainland, and my meticulously planned itinerary, to enjoy the rest of my trip alone.

I had to admit, it would be nice to travel to the UK without needing to stay in a hostel, or to take seven connecting flights via Narnia to save on airfares. With travel, a new car, and new shoes, bras and knickers locked into my spreadsheet, I redirected my cursor to the 'Gifts' column, and the conundrum of what to give to my family.

Amarita's pamphlet had recommended that 'any money you gift to friends and family, you do so without any expectation or condition'. 'Any' was bolded and underlined for emphasis. Winners needed to accept that not everyone would spend the gift in ways they approved of.

'Consider how you would feel if you gave money to a relative to pay off a student loan and they used it to fund a holiday instead,' it urged. 'What you would do if you gifted a friend the opportunity for a fresh start and they used the money to perpetuate destructive behaviours or activities?'

This had certainly provided cause for pause. Jarrah's fiscal habits had always driven me crazy. She was frivolous with her spending, impulsive with her employment status, and she never sacrificed anything to save for the future because she never planned for anything. The real kicker: somehow, she ended up with everything she wanted anyway.

When I was about ten, I'd collected a twelve-part magazine series about animals of the world. The first issue was $2.95 and included a free binder to hold the collection. Subsequent issues came out each month and cost $4.95. There was a shortfall between the recommended retail price and the $1 I earned each week by unstacking the dishwasher and feeding the pets. So I negotiated with my parents for a pocket money pay rise – an additional 20 cents a week to take out the rubbish as well.

I looked forward to the first Tuesday of each month when Mum would take me to the newsagent. I would hand over my money, take possession of the next issue, and spend much of the following week poring over its contents.

I was so proud the day I went to collect the final instalment. I had worked hard to earn the money and was excited about the bonus magnifying glass that was promised with the edition that profiled insects of the Amazon.

While we were in the newsagent, Jarrah spotted a copy of *The Complete Guide to Arts and Crafts* – another collectable series. Because she'd spent what little allowance she did earn (her approach to chores was unreliable, at best) on mixed lollies from the milk bar, she had no money. She swooned over the series and told Mr Altemura – the newsagent owner – about her ambitions to become an artist.

Mr Altemura disappeared into his storeroom and reappeared a few moments later with the complete series of *The Complete Guide to Arts and Crafts*, which he handed to her with a smile.

Mum made a half-hearted effort to pay for the series, but Mr Altemura insisted on supporting Jarrah's dream, in exchange for a signed painting when she became a famous artist one day. To make matters worse, he made me pay for my copy of *Animals of the World* and he'd run out of magnifying glasses.

Would gifting Jarrah a huge cheque just reinforce this pattern of getting things without earning them? And could I actually hand it over without 'expectation or condition'?

Chapter 9

Beth

By the time Saturday lunch came around again, I had drawn and redrawn the distribution lines of the lotto win several times over. I had settled on what I would give my family: $10,000 each for Jarrah and Elijah and $15,000 for my parents, and I had rehearsed the speech I planned to deliver. I considered holding off my announcement until the money had landed in my account so I could present them with a cheque as well as the news. But I figured it was probably good to give them a few days to digest the information before handing over the money.

Gran was a different kettle of fish. Of course, I wanted to share my good fortune with her, but I suspected she would refuse cash; she had the means to buy whatever she wanted or needed. Instead, I planned to offer to upgrade her camera or pay for a trip. Or maybe I could track down a taxidermied unicorn head to go with her new jackalope? I decided it was best to ask her what she'd like.

I pulled up at Gran's house to collect her for lunch, climbed out of the car and made my way to the front door. Since I had decided to purchase a new car, I had become increasingly irritated by the need to climb over the passenger seat. I had put up with this exit method for years without feeling inconvenienced. In fact, I became defensive when people ridiculed my car's quirks. But I looked forward to having a vehicle that I could get into without performing an acrobatic manoeuvre and that had 'reliable' as one of its key features. When I test-drove the hybrid car, I had decided to buy the model with a leather interior and tinted windows. They were modest luxuries, I told myself, and ones that would aid resale. But since then, the fabric seats that often gave me a static zap and lack of sun visors in my current car had suddenly become unbearable.

'Gran,' I called out, opening the front door. 'It's just me.'

'Darling,' she cooed, appearing from the kitchen. 'How are you?'

'I'm good,' I answered, bending down to hug her as she arrived in front of me and then recoiling when I saw a large, multicoloured bruise on her arm.

'Jesus, Gran! What have you done to yourself?'

'Oh, it's nothing,' she replied dismissively. 'I'm on a new blood pressure medication that can cause me to bruise easily. It doesn't hurt, it just looks bloody awful.'

'How did you do it?'

'It was silly, really. I knocked my arm at the herbarium when I was putting away a new specimen.'

When she wasn't traipsing around the bush checking on orchids, Gran volunteered in the state herbarium to catalogue new species records. She and a team of volunteers gathered in a lab to attach newly collected specimens to special parchment, using dental floss – a hardy and trusted material. They applied barcodes, details of when and where it was found, and a label with whatever name it had been given. Then they put it in a special plastic container, inside a climate-controlled, fireproof vault alongside records that were collected on early European expeditions by the likes of Bruni D'Entrecasteaux, Nicolas Baudin and Matthew Flinders.

As we got into the car and drove towards my parents' house, Gran told me that the specimen she'd been working on was a new species of mistletoe. A softly spoken botanist whom I'd met on a field trip a few years back found the plant while he was surveying for wattles. He had an encyclopedic knowledge of plants in the north-west and figured that if he didn't recognise it, it was probably new to science. He was right.

'You should have seen his face when he saw the specimen carrying his name,' Gran recounted. 'He was absolutely chuffed. And so he should be; it's a great honour.'

'I've always thought botanists are lucky they get plants named after them,' I mused. 'I feel for the entomologists, who have their life's work honoured by the naming rights of a newly discovered cockroach or dung beetle, or the parasitologists who work with parasites.'

She chuckled.

With only a few minutes' drive left until we arrived at my parents' place, I sought to steer our conversation away from whether the naming of a North American slime-mould beetle *Agathidium bushi* – after George W Bush – had been intended as an honour or insult, and instead towards my recent financial windfall.

'Gran,' I began, seizing a brief moment of pause. 'Do you want for anything? I mean, is there anywhere you wish you'd gone? Anything you wish you'd bought? Anything you wish you'd done? Or anything you'd like to have another go at?'

'Goodness me, darling. That's a deep question for a Saturday morning. What's brought this on?'

'Oh, nothing,' I lied. 'I'm just curious if there's anything you regretted not doing. Or seeing. Or buying.'

'No. Not really,' she said, her head tilted slightly in thought. 'I have all I could possibly need. I'm happy and healthy and comfortable. And I'm surrounded by a loving family and good friends. I've enjoyed a rich, full life …'

Her inflection went up, and the sentence hung as if incomplete.

'Go on,' I encouraged, braking at a set of red traffic lights and taking the opportunity to study her face for clues.

'Oh no,' she said with a little shake of her head. 'It's nothing.'

'Please, Gran. What were you going to say?'

She fiddled with the dangly beaded earring that hung from her right lobe.

'Well ... since you've asked. I've always wondered what happened to my first love.'

I snapped my head around to look at her. I had expected her to say 'I've always wanted to see the Amazon' or 'I'd rather fancy a grand piano', which I would have satisfied with an all-expenses-paid trip, or a surprise delivery of a Yamaha. Tracking down a long-lost lover was not what I had anticipated. I doubt I would have been any more shocked than if she'd told me she wanted to try heroin.

'Your first love? Who was *that*?'

It had never occurred to me to ask if she had been with anyone before Grandpa, and she'd never volunteered it. I wondered if Mum knew anything about this mystery relationship.

'Gerry Burnsby,' she replied, her voice slightly breathy.

'You've never mentioned him before,' I said, doing my best to keep my eyes on the road now the traffic had started moving again.

'Of course not, darling. It's ancient history. We studied botany together at university and lived in the same college. Gerry was from the UK but was studying on a government-sponsored exchange in Australia. We were so in love.'

'So what happened between you?'

She sighed deeply. She was stroking her thumb on the back of her opposite hand, which she routinely did when she was reading or when her mind wandered elsewhere.

'Gerry went back to London. We promised we'd write to each other, and even made plans for me to visit when I finished my degree. But I wrote, and wrote, and wrote, and never received a reply.'

'My goodness, Gran. I'm so sorry. Did you ever find out what happened?'

'Our relationship was ... complicated,' she replied tentatively.

'Complicated? How?'

'It was a different time back then, darling. You couldn't just "hook up" with whomever you wanted.'

She used her fingers to create air quotes around 'hook up' to indicate it was a concept that was not familiar to her generation.

'Gerry's family was noble, and there were certain ...' she paused to search for the right word, 'obligations that came with being born into a world of such extreme wealth and privilege. They would not have approved of our relationship at all.'

'What did your family think?' I asked. 'Surely they would have been keen to welcome an aristocrat into the family.'

'No one ever knew we were together,' she said wistfully. 'It was just the two of us, in our own little bubble. Just Gerry and me. It was lovely, actually. But it meant that no one understood how utterly devastated I was when it ended.

'Anyway,' she chirped after a moment, with a little shudder of her head, as if shaking off the memories. 'About six months after Gerry left, I met your grandpa. Then we got married and lived happily ever after.'

She smiled at me, but I could tell she wasn't telling me the whole story.

'Did Grandpa ever know about Gerry?'

'No. Well ... no, not really.' She paused. 'Anyway, it's all ancient history now. I probably shouldn't have even brought it up. I don't know what made me think of it.'

As I put my indicator on to turn into Mum and Dad's street, I wondered if I could use my winnings to help resolve the mystery around Gerry. I could hire a private detective to find him and arrange a reunion.

Or perhaps I could enlist the help of a historian to work out whether there was an explanation for why he never wrote.

'You've been to the UK lots of times since you were at uni,' I said. 'Did you ever try to get in touch?'

'No. I never did. I thought about it a lot and spent many nights planning what I would say if we ever saw each other again. But it wouldn't have been fair to your grandpa while he was alive, and I haven't been to the UK since he died.'

We pulled up outside my parents' house and made the journey up the front path. As we reached the front door, Gran turned to look at me.

'I know you don't believe in fate, Beth,' she said earnestly. 'But if things had worked out with Gerry and me, none of you would exist. And I wouldn't change that for anything.'

I exaggeratedly squinted my eyes at her, partly in gest, and partly because I hadn't heard Gran – a trusted voice – speak of fate like that before. It was unnerving.

The front door opened, revealing my dad standing in the doorway wearing one of Mum's old kimono dressing gowns, white socks and thongs.

'Konichiwa,' he said, with his hands in a prayer position, bowing his head. 'Anyone for sushi?'

Chapter 10

Beth

I didn't think Jarrah did it intentionally, but somehow, she always seemed to trump my news and special occasions with a drama or announcement of her own.

I used to think it was because she was older, so her news sat higher on the scale of significant life events than my milestones. But, as I got older, I grew to realise that Mum, Dad and Elijah just seemed more interested in her announcements than mine, so it wasn't hard for her to pull focus. Additionally, her lack of self-awareness meant she often rushed up on the stage to steal the mic while I was gearing up for a rare moment in the spotlight. Metaphorically speaking, of course; I wouldn't be caught dead on stage.

My earliest memory of this was when I was elected school environment captain in Grade Six – a position I had dreamed of holding from my first day of school. I had convinced my peers to vote for me during a stirring campaign speech when I promised to create a wind farm to power the school by buying up all the surrounding houses. It was an ambitious policy platform that, unsurprisingly, never came to fruition. Nevertheless, the news of my appointment was usurped by Jarrah's joy that the school principal had decided not to expel her after she was caught stealing cinnamon buns from the tuckshop.

The day I received my Year 12 score, which earned me a place in my preferred university course, she interrupted Dad's celebratory toast to declare she planned to get bangs. She sobbed through dinner at an Italian restaurant to celebrate me getting a job at the council after her boyfriend of two months texted to say he wanted to 'slow down'. She made such a spectacle that a waitress brought her a piece of complimentary tiramisu to cheer her up. It didn't. The tiramisu ended up coating the outside of Dad's car after she threw up the dessert, and the two bottles of champagne she'd washed it down with, on the way home.

I hoped this announcement would be different.

'Family,' I planned to start, 'I have some news. Someone recently told me that Mark Twain said "Fortune knocks at every man's door once in a life." As you know, I don't believe in fate or luck. And I certainly don't believe that "fortune" is an entity capable of knocking on anything. However, something surprising and completely unexpected has happened.'

At this point, I would pause for dramatic effect.

'I have come into some money,' I would continue. 'It's not a huge amount, but it is enough to make a difference to my life. And I would like to make a difference to yours too.'

Then I had planned to announce that I would gift $10,000 to Jarrah and Elijah, $15,000 to my parents and buy Gran whatever she wanted. I would tell her that I had been researching taxidermied wolpertingers – a construct of a rabbit head, squirrel body, antlers and wings – as a mantle ornament for underneath her jackalope. There was one available on eBay, which had a decorative pipe hanging from its mouth. The current bid was at $594.43, plus international postage.

But it did not play out that way.

'Family,' I began after we had finished the last of the California rolls, and the dining table was littered with tiny fish-shaped soy sauce containers. 'I have some news.'

'Ohhhh,' Jarrah squealed so loudly that it startled us all. 'So do I. Sorry Bethie, we'll get back to you in a sec. I almost forgot to tell you that I made the bold and, might I say, brave decision to quit my job yesterday.'

'What?' Mum, Dad and I responded in unison. Elijah raised his eyebrows, and Gran sat quietly, seemingly withholding judgement.

'At the florist?' Dad asked, pouring himself another glass of sake.

'No, Thorn. That was her last job. This one was at the frozen yoghurt place,' Mum said, holding out her glass for a refill.

It was impossible to keep up with Jarrah's jobs; she changed them every few months. In the past few years, she had hosted kids' tie-dye parties; sold popcorn at the drive-in; posed as a life model; walked dogs; delivered singing telegrams in a bear costume; sold raffle tickets at the footy; and waitressed in a 'cat cafe' – a place where patrons go for coffee and to pat the resident felines.

Typically, she cited 'irreconcilable differences' between her and her employer, or her and the customers, as the reason for why she decided to leave a job. In some cases, her employers beat her to it. One notable example was when she worked as an elf at a year-round Christmas shop until a young boy had asked if they sold 'the special pens that made Santa's handwriting look like his Mum's'. Jarrah decided the boy was old enough to be told that Santa's writing *was* his Mum's. He was six. Her elfing days ended well before Santa had started making his lists.

'You're both wrong,' Jarrah said, rolling her eyes. 'I was a secret shopper. But it just wasn't ... nourishing me.' She put her hand to her chest, closed her eyes and shook her head soberly. 'It was so lame,' she sighed. 'Going from shop to shop ... pretending to have questions about styles of clothes I would *never* wear and items I would *never* buy ... reporting back about whether the sales assistant was helpful or not, if the ambient lighting was too harsh or if the music was too loud. Urgh. I just want something that *inspires* me and where I can make a difference.' She paused. 'But I need something that pays well and has flexible hours so I can pursue my other interests too.'

I snorted. 'What are you going to do for money while you're waiting for this well-paying, flexible, soul-nourishing job to land in your lap?'

'I always manage,' she responded sheepishly. 'There's always JobSeeker. And Dad might spot me a loan, if things get really dire. Right, Daddio?'

Jarrah turned to Dad, clasped her hands under her chin, and gave him her best 'charm will get me everywhere' smile. Dad rolled his eyes playfully. I had never turned to my parents for a loan, and here she was, just expecting them to bail her out. Again. I was right to be doubtful about giving her the money. If she couldn't hold down a job for more than a month just because it wasn't 'nourishing', how could she be trusted with $10,000?

'You can't expect people to bail you out when you just don't want to work,' I said, my voice raised. 'That's not how the real world works.'

'It's not that I don't *want* to work,' she replied defensively. 'It's just that I haven't found a job I really want.'

'Oh, right. That clears it up,' I said sarcastically. 'Jarrah: they are the same thing.'

'Okay now,' pleaded Mum. 'That's enough. Why does it always end up with you two arguing? Can't we just enjoy a nice lunch?'

'Why?' I asked rhetorically, turning my frustration on my Mum. 'Because I can't sit back and watch this anymore. You and Dad enable her. She still lives with you at thirty-two – rent and board free. She takes no responsibility and doesn't face any consequences. There's no incentive for her to grow up or make any adult decisions.'

I looked at Jarrah. 'Don't you want a career? Aren't you sick of floating from one thing to another? You're so capable and competent. But you never stay with anything long enough to give it a real go.'

'Beth,' Jarrah said tersely, her frown betraying that my words had hit a nerve, 'You were saying only last week that we're all entitled to live the way we want to—'

'Yes,' I interrupted. 'But we shouldn't expect other people to bankroll it.'

'Bethie, just because we're supportive of our kids, doesn't make us enablers,' Dad said. 'Jarrah is welcome to live here while she works out what she wants to do – and afterwards, too, if she wants. The same goes for you and Elijah. We love having you all around, job or no job. And this will always be your house; no one *made* you leave.'

I united my chopsticks into a straight line on the table in front of me and then reached for a spare set and repeated the action. It soothed me to have order in my immediate vicinity when my family felt so chaotic.

There was no point in arguing: Dad had clearly missed the point. Besides, I would never move back to my parents' house, even if I needed to. I'd never felt like I belonged there in the first place.

'Now. I think that's enough of all that,' Dad said with an infuriating optimism that we could all just move on. 'What was your news, Bethie?'

He held out his hands, palms up, offering me the floor to share my news. I looked to Jarrah, expecting her to interrupt again. But she was folding a paper napkin into an origami hat. Her face was sullen.

Who was I kidding? I wasn't capable of gifting the money without 'expectation or condition'. In fact, I felt that by giving her the money, I would be perpetuating her behaviour. Once again, someone else would be providing a solution so she didn't have to face the consequences of her careless decisions.

'Nothing,' I mumbled. 'Never mind.'

I endured the rest of lunch and managed to bite my tongue long enough to help clear the table and wash the dishes. Later, as we drove away from Mum and Dad's place, my knuckles were white as I gripped the steering wheel.

I might have been silly, but I was looking forward to being the hero of my family for once and witnessing their excitement from the centre rather than watching it from the periphery. I had looked forward to seeing their faces as they contemplated what the money meant for their lives and I wanted to be able to share the secret of my win.

But Jarrah had hijacked my moment. Again.

'You shouldn't let her get under your skin, darling,' Gran said. 'I know it's easier said than done, but Jarrah will do as Jarrah will do; there's really nothing you can do or say to change that.

'You can be a little set in your ways too, you know,' she continued.

Even without taking my eyes off the road, I knew the look she was giving me; it was the one that encouraged me to take responsibility for my role in my relationship with Jarrah.

'You're just two very different people. And, while she can be a bit ... directionless, you know if you ever needed anything, she'd be there for you in a flash.'

She was right. I thought back to high school, which wasn't the easiest time for me. While Jarrah was the 'it' girl of the school, I'd spent my lunchtimes sheltering in the library from Nadia Ktasia and her henchwomen. When Jarrah found out I was the subject of an entire chapter of their *Mean Girls*-style 'Burn Book', and they were the ones who shoved a mandarin into the bell of my trombone on the night of the jazz concert, causing a terrible mess, she launched into action. She told them that if they didn't stop bullying me, she'd mobilise the entire school against them. And they knew she could.

'I know,' I said to Gran. 'But I just can't sit around watching her wasting her life. I mean, she's still living at home, while leading a completely self-indulgent lifestyle, without any foreseeable prospects.'

'But aren't they her issues to work out?' Gran offered rationally. 'I mean, it's her life.'

In usual circumstances, this might be sound advice. But Gran wasn't armed with all the information. And I'd be damned if I was going to give Jarrah money to skulk around doing nothing.

Chapter 11

Beth

After I dropped Gran off and drove home, I checked over my meal plan for the following week. I had allowed myself a bought lunch on Wednesday *and* Friday, and takeaway Thai on Saturday night. By my standards, this was a splurge.

I walked back into the lounge room, placed my coffee on the table and slumped on the couch with my laptop in my lap. I double-clicked on the file icon of the latest version of my lotto spreadsheet. It opened, and Jarrah's name was highlighted; a record of the last edit I had made. I sighed deeply and closed the file again.

At least the day wasn't a total loss – there was Gran's surprising revelation about the 'one who got away'. I had no idea if it would be possible to track down Gerry Burnsby, but I figured a Google search of his name was a good place to start.

The search engine boldly declared there were twelve exact results. The first one – a paper on the metabolic rate of vascular plants native to central England – was written by Gerry Burnsby et al. *Could it be that easy?* I wondered. Gran and Gerry had studied botany together, so it seemed plausible that he would write a paper on English vascular plants.

I clicked on the link, and a scientific paper popped open. The paper was presented in the typical way: title at the top, followed by the authors' names. I scanned the list of authors – Frederick E Forsyth, William K Lee and Gerry M Burnsby. A superscripted 'three' annotated the 'y' at the end of Gerry's surname, which correlated to a list of tertiary institutions below. Gerry was associated with the University of New London. I found the university's website, but paused after typing Gerry's name in the website's search bar.

Was searching for Gerry a violation of Gran's privacy? What if I found him? Would Gran want to know? Of course, I'd have to tell her if I found him. But then what? If she really wanted to find him after all these years, wouldn't she have done it herself by now? And why did this feel like a betrayal of Grandpa?

I took a sip of my coffee and steadied myself. While it would be an uncanny coincidence if it wasn't, there was no guarantee that the Gerry Burnsby who authored the paper on vascular plants was the same one Gran fell in love with all those years ago.

I hit enter, and the search results filled my screen. I hovered my mouse over the first entry: 'Meet our team – staff profiles: Department of Botany (Plant Sciences)'. I clicked on the link, and twelve smiling faces appeared. I scanned their faces, looking for someone who might be Gerry Burnsby, but there were only four men on the team, and they were all too young to have been at university with Gran.

Just as I was about to back out of the page, I spotted the name 'Burnsby' under a photo of woman with a warm, broad smile and cropped white hair. If I had to guess, I would place her in her late seventies or early eighties – roughly the same age as Gran.

The caption read 'Geraldine "Gerry" Burnsby – Adjunct Professor'.

My mouth fell open, and I lurched towards the screen for a closer look. My eyes darted between the woman's photo and her name. It couldn't be the same person, could it?

Was Gran's first love a woman?

I clicked on the photo, which enlarged the picture and brought up a biography advising Geraldine had graduated with a Bachelor of Science (Botany) from Fisher University in Perth in 1959. Gran had said Gerry was from the UK and studying on a government-sponsored exchange. If she had graduated in 1959, she would have been at Fisher University at the same time as Gran.

'Our relationship was ... complicated,' Gran had said. 'It was a different time back then.' There was a heaviness to her words as if they still weighed on her.

Indeed it would have been nearly impossible for Gran and Gerry to be open about their relationship in the 1950s without risk of prejudice and persecution.

'We were so in love,' she'd reminisced.

I scanned Gerry's biography. She'd specialised in plant sciences and worked at the United Kingdom Herbarium. She was now retired from full-time work but still held tenure as an adjunct professor at the University of New London.

I clicked back to the tab with the search engine and scrolled down the page. I reached one from *Trove* – an Australian database for journals and newspapers – and double-clicked on an article from the *Western Weekly* dated 27 February 1956. A grainy, pixellated photo of a man kissing a young woman on the cheek was positioned underneath a headline that announced 'LOCAL BOYS PLANT ONE ON ENGLISH BOTANY STUDENT'.

Eighteen-year-old Londoner Miss Geraldine Burnsby might be a long way from home, but she's finding her way around Perth, thanks to some very willing tour guides.

Miss Burnsby has travelled from the UK to study botany at Fisher University as part of an exchange with the University of New London. She is one of two lucky girls who began their undergraduate degrees in the School of Plant Sciences this year.

Was Gran the other one? I continued reading.

On the day we met her, Miss Burnsby wore a fetching floral blouse and navy slacks, which showed off her svelte physique and alabaster complexion.

'A lot of people think botany is all about pretty flowers and assume that's why I'm drawn to it,' Miss Burnsby said.

'But I have always been fascinated by the natural world and dreamed of studying somewhere abroad where I could meet new people and explore new places.

'Western Australia is a treasure trove of native plants, and I am delighted to be studying somewhere where I'm surrounded by such rich biota, including countless species that are yet to be described.'

While Miss Burnsby said her number one priority since arriving had been settling into her studies, the local gents are hopeful it won't be all work and no play for this English rose.

I closed the article and rolled my eyes. It shouldn't have surprised me this was the way women were reported on in the 1950s, even intelligent, highly educated ones. English rose, indeed. The next article in the search result was titled "'Elizabeth Gould: watching from the wings" by Gerry Burnsby'. I clicked on the link, and it opened on an image that featured an illustration I had seen a million times before. Two resplendent adult Gouldian finches together with a little brown juvenile sheltering behind its mother's wing – the same painting that hung in my Gran's hallway.

Gerry's by-line and the article title sat above a blurb that read:

'Bird Man' John Gould is credited for highlighting the beauty and uniqueness of Australia's animals through his magnificent and comprehensive works. His wife, Elizabeth Gould – talented artist, naturalist and mother – played a pivotal but often overlooked role in his success.

The painting cemented it for me. This had to be the same Gerry.

I closed the document and continued down the list of search results, looking for more evidence it was the same person, not that I needed it. I clicked on a link for 'Branch' – a networking platform for the scientific community. Gerry's photo was the same as the one on the University of New London's website, and her bio contained most of the same details. But this page had a 'message' function. I could contact her directly right now if I wanted to.

I snapped the lid of my laptop shut. I needed to speak to Gran before I did anything else. I didn't want to invade her privacy any more than I already had, no matter how intrigued I was. I needed to tell her that I'd found Gerry. Then, if she was open to it, I could help her reach out.

Chapter 12

Beth

'Hello, pet,' Gran said warmly as she opened the front door.

I had messaged her during the day to tell her I would be dropping past after I'd finished work and run some errands. I probably should have just left work early again; I had been distracted the entire day with thoughts of Gran and Gerry, and how Gran would react to the news I had found out about their relationship and discovered a way to connect them. But, over the course of the day, my sense of hesitation had evolved into full-scale anxiety, so I was happy to defer telling her for a couple of hours.

I dipped into her open arms for a hug.

'How was your day?' I asked as I nodded to Herrick en route to the kitchen. I noticed Gran had draped some beads across his antlers since I was last at her house.

Gran removed two beers from the fridge and handed one to me. My grandparents had drunk a beer at seven o'clock every single night they were at home. The crack of the ring pull, the hiss of the air escaping the can and the slurp as they captured the froth that escaped from the top was usually set against the trumpet fanfare that heralded the beginning of *ABC News*.

I found myself deliberately avoiding her eye contact as Gran chatted away about the cuttings of Geraldton wax she'd helped herself to from a house down the road.

'Are you okay, darling?' she asked. 'You seem a million miles away. And it's not like you to fidget.'

She gestured to the ring pull of the can that I had twisted and bent until it snapped into four satisfyingly even segments.

'Sorry,' I replied, trying to refocus on what she was saying while collecting the metal pieces into a pile. 'Go on. What were you saying?'

'Never mind, it was nothing. I was just chatting. Tell me, what's going on with you? You seem a bit ...'

As she searched my face for clues to help inform the next word of her sentence, my stomach lurched. I knew I had to tell her now, or I would completely lose my nerve.

'It's just ... well ...' I took a deep breath to steady myself. 'I have a bit of news, actually.'

She sat forward in her chair and nodded her head as if to encourage me to go on.

'Do you remember at lunch the other week, when Jarrah was talking about star signs, and she gave me a hard time about not believing in fate or ...' I wiggled my fingers to convey the frivolity of the whole conversation, 'leaving anything to the universe?'

'Yes, darling. Although sometimes it's hard to keep up with all the things you two disagree about,' she said.

Usually I would prickle at this, but I had bigger fish to fry.

'Well,' I continued, 'do you remember we stopped at the shops on the way home so you could fill your prescription?'

'Yes, darling,' she said guardedly, her eyes narrowing.

'While you were in the chemist, I bought a lotto ticket to prove her wrong.' I felt the words rush out of me. 'I wanted to prove that we make our own luck and that things don't just land in our lap because they're predestined to.'

I took a big sip of my beer.

'Except I didn't. Prove her wrong, I mean,' I continued eventually.

I paused, waiting for a sign that the penny had dropped. The room was silent until the kitchen wall clock ticked over.

'Do you mean ...?' she began. 'I'm sorry, darling. I don't know what you mean.'

'I won lotto,' I blurted. 'Second division! I won $264,412.51.'

I slapped my hand across my mouth.

'Oops, I wasn't meant to tell you how much I won,' I mumbled from behind my fingers.

'Beth!' Gran gasped. 'Good heavens. Congratulations!' She pushed herself up off her chair to embrace me over the table. 'When did you find out?'

I told Gran about checking the ticket, driving to the Lottery Head Office and the excruciating days that had followed when I'd deliberated over what to do with it.

'What *are* you going to do with it?' she asked. 'Goodness, Beth. This could set you up for the rest of your life.'

I'd had a few days to get used to the idea of my win, but seeing Gran's reaction renewed my sense of shock about the whole thing.

'Well. I'm still deciding. I've bought a new car, and I plan to buy a couple of other bits and pieces, and then I'll pay a chunk off my mortgage, and I might go on a trip somewhere.'

'A new car,' Gran exclaimed excitedly. 'That *is* good news.'

I couldn't ignore that her reaction to my getting a new car was more animated than her reaction to the win itself.

'I'm also planning on giving some to Mum and Dad, and Jarrah and Elijah,' I continued. 'I was going to tell them on Sunday, which is why I got so annoyed when Jarrah told us she'd quit her job. I know this money was never mine to begin with, but I just couldn't bring myself to hand over a cheque for her to fritter away on living expenses while she works out what job will "nourish her soul".

Ahh.' Gran nodded her head in realisation. 'I see.'

'So, I think I'll just sit tight until I've had some more time to think.'

'Well, sweetie,' she said, reaching for my hand. 'I'm absolutely thrilled for you.'

'Thanks, Gran,' I said, my stomach tightening at the thought that sharing details about my lotto win was just Act One. 'But that's actually just the start of it.'

I let go of Gran's hands and took another sip of beer.

'Do you remember when I asked you whether there was anything you wish you'd done, or somewhere you'd wished you'd been?'

Gran nodded.

'Well, that was actually a fact-finding mission. I was trying to work out how I could share some of this win with you in a way that you'd enjoy. I figured handing over a cheque would be a bit meaningless.'

'Oh, darling,' Gran tsked. 'I insist you don't give me a penny; I want for absolutely nothing.'

'Except that's not 100 per cent true,' I replied, knowing that there was no going back from here. 'Is it? You told me you wanted to know what happened to Gerry Burnsby.'

Gran flinched slightly.

'What happened to Gerry Burnsby,' she repeated slowly. 'Oh pet, that's ancient—'

'I looked her up,' I blurted.

'*Her?*' she reiterated cautiously.

'Yes, Gran. *Her.*' I emphasised the feminine pronoun to demonstrate my complete understanding of its implication. 'I found her online.'

'But how did you ...?' Her eyes widened and she sat up a little straighter.

'I googled her name, Gran. You can find anything or anyone on the internet. I hope you're not mad.'

Gran stood up quickly, her chair squeaking across the floor. She walked to the sink where she filled a glass of water and gulped from it hurriedly. Even with her back to me, I could see her hand was shaking.

'I'm sorry, Gran,' I said, panicked that my fears had been realised and she was mad at me or that I'd upset her. 'I just wanted to do something nice for you. You said you wanted to know ... so I thought ... and once I found out ...'

She put her hand to the bench but misjudged its proximity and re-righted herself on the draining rack. A cascade of cutlery cluttered onto the floor.

I guided Gran back to her seat, refilled her water and then gathered up the utensils and put them in the sink.

She looked pale and definitely seemed rattled. She was usually so pragmatic and calm, it was unsettling to see her so vulnerable.

'Are you okay?' I asked, afraid of her answer.

'I should never have said anything,' she said, as if scolding herself. 'What was I thinking? Speaking about Gerry after all these years ... I must have been out of my mind.'

I reached for her hands but she retracted them quickly and placed them in her lap.

'I don't know what to tell you, Beth,' she said finally. Softly.

'You don't have to tell me anything,' I said. 'The way I see it, we have a few options. You can tell me to drop it, and I will never mention it again. You have my word that I will never tell a soul. Or, I can tell you what I know, and you can decide what to do with that information. I don't even have to tell you now, if you're not ready to hear it. I could tell you tomorrow, or next week, or next month. Either way, you can tell me as much or as little as you want.

'But I want you to know,' I added, 'that I didn't mean to pry and I never wanted to hurt you.'

73

Silence hung between us, but I noticed some of the colour had returned to her face. She was fiddling with her wedding band on her right ring finger; she'd moved it there a year to the day after Grandpa died.

'When it comes to Gerry, I ...' she started, before shaking her head and abandoning that train of thought. I imagined her mind was racing. 'It was just so complicated. I still don't know what to call our relationship, or my feelings for her. And, until you, until now, no one else has ever known about it.'

I allowed a few moments to pass, to create space for her to add more, if she wanted to.

'As I said, Gran, you don't owe me, or anyone else, an explanation,' I said finally. 'But if you are interested, I think I've found a way to contact her.'

She sat forward in her chair and, for the first time since she'd sat down again, she made eye contact with me.

'She's alive?' she blurted. 'I mean, I didn't think she wouldn't be. But we're both getting on. And, after she left, I guess it was just easier for me to stop imagining her life without me in it.'

I nodded, waiting for her cue that I should go on. She was stroking her thumb on the back of the opposite hand.

'Okay,' she said finally. 'Let's hear it. Where is she? And what the hell has she been doing all these years?'

I told Gran about Gerry's tenure with the University of New London and recounted the article from the *Western Weekly*.

'Oh, that,' Gran said with a soft chuckle; it was so good to see her smile again. 'She was outraged about that article. She hated that the journalist was more interested in her clothes and hair than her academic endeavours. So, naturally, I teased her about it mercilessly.'

I handed her a printout of Gerry's article 'Elizabeth Gould: watching from the wings'.

She scanned the article, which described Elizabeth Gould's life. She was a skilled artist who had married John Gould in 1829 and become his trusted professional collaborator. They travelled to Australia in 1838 where, for two years, she feverishly illustrated the plants and animals her husband and his team collected and described. Her work from the expedition was immortalised in the acclaimed series *The Birds of Australia*, which was still an eminent resource for Australian ornithology. But almost a year to the day after they returned to England, Elizabeth died from childbirth complications. Devastated at the loss of his wife, John named what he thought to be the world's most beautiful bird species after her – the Gouldian finch.

'Gerry gave me that print, you know,' Gran said, gesturing to the illustration of the trio of birds that featured in the article.

'I suspected that.'

'We admired Elizabeth Gould, so much,' she continued. 'We first learned of her when we found a copy of a book released in the 1940s, which contained a collection of letters she'd written and sent back to her family in London.'

She sat back in her chair, her shoulders slumped.

'Gerry was so many things to me,' she continued, her eyes filling with tears. 'She fulfilled me intellectually, emotionally and physically. We would spend hours discussing philosophy, politics and feminism ...' she gestured to the article – it went on to give credit to all the other female scientists whose contributions to their fields had been overlooked in favour of men, or stolen outright by them. 'She was a wonderful confidant and companion. We had so much fun together, and shared such tenderness and intimacy.'

Her voice crackled. 'It was a confusing time. But it was such a happy one.'

'I suspected that too.'

'How did you say we could get in contact with her?' she asked tentatively.

'We can message her through a networking platform for scientists,' I replied. 'Do you want to see a picture of her?'

She sat forward again, this time with such force that she knocked the table and caused our drinks to wobble. 'Do you have one?'

'There's a photo on her bio page.'

I pulled my phone from my bag and swiped and stabbed until I landed on the photo of Gerry. I turned the screen to face Gran.

She took the phone and gasped. I watched her eyes flit over the screen.

'Her hair was strawberry blonde when I knew her,' she said wistfully. 'And it's shorter. But she's still got those beautiful blue eyes. And I see she still doesn't leave the house without her "touch of lippy", as she used to say. She's still so beautiful.'

She startled and thrust the phone back at me. 'She can't see me, can she?'

I laughed. 'No, of course not.'

She exhaled quickly.

'I need to think about all this,' she said.

'Of course,' I said, slipping my phone into my bag. 'Do you want me to stay with you for a bit?'

'No, darling,' she said, shaking her head decisively. 'I'm fine. It's just a lot to ... it's been a long ... I'm fine.'

'Honestly, I can stay if you—'

'No,' Gran said. 'Actually, I had planned to get an early night tonight anyway.'

I suspected she hadn't thought about what time she would be going to bed before that moment, but I understood her keenness to be alone.

'Okay,' I said, rising from the table. 'But if you need anything, just let me know.'

'I will, love,' she replied before adding: 'I'd rather not tell anyone about any of this, so please don't—'

'Gran, I would never,' I replied assertively. 'I won't tell a soul. And I won't do a thing until you tell me to.'

I walked to her side and wrapped my arm around her shoulders, giving her a side hug.

'I'm just sorry it was so difficult for you to love who you wanted to back then, Gran,' I said. 'I can only imagine how hard it must have been to hide your relationship from everybody.'

'Thank you, pet,' she replied, her voice cracking again. 'Are you okay to let yourself out? I'm just going to pop to the loo.'

'Sure,' I replied, releasing her from my grip. 'I'll talk to you tomorrow.'

As I reached the front door, I turned back and saw her stop in the hallway to look at the Gouldian finch painting. I watched as she reached up and tenderly touched the birds and then wiped beneath her eyes.

Chapter 13

Elise

After she'd splashed some water on her face, Elise made her way into the spare room, where she probed her hand around the back of the top shelf of the wardrobe, searching for the box she'd hidden there on the day she and John had moved in. Eventually, her fingers made contact with the cool metal, and she shimmied the box towards her.

She manoeuvred the box off the shelf and then carefully climbed down off the chair, exhaling deeply when her feet reunited with the carpet. She was well aware that balancing on a dining chair, while home alone, could result in a broken hip and mark the end of her independence. She'd seen it happen to many of her friends.

The box, which had held Elise's most fiercely protected secrets since university, was about the size of a tissue box and had a heavy black combination lock. A thick layer of dust – a measure of how long it had been since she'd last retrieved it – coated its lid. As she wiped the dust from the top of the box, she tried to shake the feeling that Beth had betrayed her privacy. But it wasn't Beth's fault she'd discovered Gerry was a woman and unearthed the secret of their relationship, Elise reasoned.

It was, after all, Elise who had volunteered her name. After sixty years of keeping their relationship hidden, she had become careless.

Elise had no trouble remembering the combination: 0–5–0–2 – the fifth day of the second month; Gerry's birthday. However, the dial was difficult to manoeuvre; it had been years since she had last opened it, and her hands were stronger then. She jiggled the shackle until it popped open, then twisted off the lock and opened the lid. A thick musty scent escaped like a genie from a bottle.

Over the years, Elise had taken refuge in the box's contents when she and John had had a fight, or when she felt irritated or melancholic. Fingering through the contents had felt like a silent rebellion; an escape to another life, without any real-world consequences.

She had thought often about destroying the contents to avoid the risk of John or Rosie opening it and drawing conclusions if she wasn't around to explain. But she had never been able to bring herself to throw any of it away.

Elise lifted a small black-and-white photo from the box and ran her fingers along the scalloped edges. The image depicted Gerry looking directly at the camera, with her mouth smiling and slightly ajar as if captured mid-laugh. Elise was to her left, her face turned in profile as she gazed up at Gerry, partly because she adored her, partly because she was a full foot shorter.

Elise and Gerry first met during university orientation week at Camelot House. Elise was in the dining hall with her brother, Henry, and sister, Daisy, when Miss Turniss – the bristly house mistress – brought Gerry over to introduce her as the only other girl enrolled in botany.

'It makes sense for the two of you to stick together,' Miss Turniss said, glaring at Henry, whose body language suggested that he too would appreciate the opportunity to spend time with Gerry.

Elise didn't need any encouragement; she had been instantly captivated by Gerry.

Gerry spoke the Queen's English and oozed sophistication and refinement, but she enjoyed dropping a well-timed 'fuck' into a sentence, which always garnered raised eyebrows from people who didn't expect it. She was quick-witted, well-read and could hold an informed conversation about almost anything. But she also reveled in salacious gossip, and she enjoyed trashy romance novels as much as high-brow tomes.

Her tall, slender figure seemed better suited to a Parisian catwalk than the provincial streets of Perth. And her eyes were a brilliant sky-blue. Elise thought she was absolutely beautiful. And she wasn't the only one.

Men fell all over themselves to invite her to dances and to join them at the pictures. They would often ask Elise to put in a good word, or for advice on how to woo her. Despite their valiant efforts, Gerry swatted away their advances. She told them she planned to stay focused on her studies and respectfully suggested they do the same. Occasionally, they recycled their failed pick-up lines on Elise, but once you locked eyes on Gerry, it was hard to turn your attention elsewhere.

As the only two females in the course, it was assumed that Elise and Gerry would sit together in lectures and be lab partners. They soon became inseparable outside of their coursework too. Their bedrooms at the college were side by side. They ate together and studied together. They spent their spare time playing cards, watching TV in the common room, exploring the bush on the city's fringes or taking the bus to the beach where they would tan and swim until they looked like lobsters. Most days, Gerry was the first person Elise saw in the morning and the last person she saw in the evening.

Elise's sister Daisy teased her relentlessly about it. She would sing:

Gerry had a little lamb, little lamb, little lamb
Gerry had a little lamb, she didn't have a beau
'Cos everywhere that Gerry went, Gerry went, Gerry went
Everywhere that Gerry went, Elise – the lamb – would go.

It irked Elise that Daisy's taunts had some truth to them; she did follow Gerry around like a little lamb. She hung off her every word when they were together, and she thought of her endlessly when they weren't. Elise often felt the urge to pinch herself that someone like Gerry – beautiful, dynamic, interesting and intelligent – would want to spend time with her. She was infatuated.

A few months after they met, Elise travelled home for the mid-term break. Elise had pleaded with Gerry to come too – she was dying to show her Woodside Ridge – but Gerry had insisted she didn't want to intrude on their family time. Gerry later confessed that she had indeed wanted to come, she just couldn't bear spending a week with Daisy.

Despite having the opportunity to soak in the country air and take long walks in the nature reserve, Elise spent the trip home in a state of irritation. She blamed the stress of university when her mother asked her what was wrong. But the truth was, even though she was home, she was homesick for somewhere else. Or, rather, someone else.

By the end of the week, Elise was aching to get back to the city. Back to Gerry. The journey back to Camelot House felt excruciatingly long. Even though Daisy and Henry had agreed to take an earlier train, they had to persuade Elise not to hitchhike the rest of the way after a delay added an hour to the journey.

When they arrived back at the college, Elise ran up the driveway and then flew up the stairs, two at a time, towards their rooms. She rapped on Gerry's door and waited impatiently for her to open it. But there was no answer. As she knocked again, Miss Turniss (or Miss Too-Priss, as Elise and Gerry had come to call her) rounded the corridor.

'Elise, were you away so long that you forgot which room is yours?' she asked, nodding her head towards Elise's door, her lips pursed like a cat's anus.

Elise laughed awkwardly.

'Actually, I was looking for Gerry. Have you seen her?'

'I thought as much,' she replied coolly. 'I think she went into town. She's been having a wonderful time this week, so who knows when she'll be back.'

There was a mean smugness to her delivery.

Disappointment prickled Elise's core. She had been counting down the seconds until she saw Gerry; it had not occurred to her that her eagerness might not be reciprocated.

Once inside her room, Elise set her suitcase on the floor and launched herself theatrically on her bed. Moments later, there was a banging on the door.

'Elise!' Gerry cried, as she flung open the door. 'You rat. You're back early.'

Gerry rushed over to Elise and planted rapid-fire kisses all over her cheeks.

'Oh, how I missed you,' she said, lying down next to her. 'Never leave me again! Life here is awfully boring without you around.'

'I missed you too,' Elise replied in a whisper; seeing Gerry again had made her breathless.

'Miss Too-Priss said you'd had a wonderful week,' she continued, despite not wanting her disappointment validated.

'Oh, ignore her,' Gerry scoffed. 'She's a horrible woman, and her head is so far up her arse she wouldn't know what I'd been up to. I've been moping around all week just waiting for you to get back.'

'Here,' she said, as she repositioned her body and thrust a small, wrapped box into Elise's hands. 'I got you something. That's what I was doing when you beat me back.'

Elise propped herself up and carefully pulled off the gold ribbon and pried open the black-and-white herringbone paper. Inside the wrapping was a luxurious silk lipstick case with her initials – 'ES' – embossed in gold. She undid the tiny clasp and flipped open the lid. A gold Estée Lauder lipstick shone up from the case.

'What's this for?' she asked, her surprise reflected in the tiny mirror on the inside of the lid.

'Because you're always admiring my lipstick. I saw the colour and thought it would look beautiful on you. Here ...' Gerry took the lipstick from the case, removed the cap and twisted the bottom to reveal a stunning watermelon-coloured tint.

'Allow me,' she said with mock formality as she repositioned herself so their bodies were facing each other. 'Hold still,' she said with a chuckle.

Elise took in the warmth of Gerry's breath, which smelled of tea and her last cigarette, and the sensation of their legs touching. She hoped Gerry couldn't hear the butterflies thrashing around in her stomach.

Gerry cradled Elise's chin with one of her hands and dragged the lipstick across Elise's bottom lip with the other. She moved back slightly to inspect her work and examined Elise's face in a way that made her feel exposed. No one had ever looked at her with such intensity before.

'Do this,' Gerry said, flattening her top lip.

Elise laughed nervously and copied her. Gerry slowly traced her top lip. Elise wanted desperately to lick her lips, to know how Gerry's tasted.

'Now do this,' Gerry said, pressing her lips together and then releasing them in a fluid, rolling motion to even out the colour. Elise copied her, unable to take her eyes off Gerry's mouth.

'Beautiful! I knew that colour would be perfect on you,' Gerry said, shifting her hips down the bed. Elise instantly missed her closeness.

'I can't believe you got me a gift,' she said, resisting the urge to pull Gerry back towards her. 'Thank you.'

'I'm just glad you're back. Now, there's no point in looking as good as you do if you don't have somewhere to go.'

Gerry jumped off the bed, reached into her bag and produced two tickets to *All About Eve*, which was playing as part of a Bette Davis festival at one of the cinemas in town.

'But luckily, we do.'

Sixty years later, alone in her house, Elise lifted the movie ticket stub from the black box, reading the faded text. She made a mental note to rewatch the movie; she had been meaning to since someone suggested a few years ago that the character of Eve was queer. Perhaps, she had thought then, she wasn't the only one who hid her sexuality in plain sight. Besides, she had left the film having no idea what it was about – she had spent the entire time focused on Gerry's hand in hers.

Chapter 14

Beth

Despite being elbow-deep in the environmental assessment of a proposed road that, if built, would likely wipe out a population of a particularly rare and fascinating moth, I jumped for my phone when I saw it was an incoming call from Gran.

I hated the thought that my actions had rattled her and had spent the night interrogating everything I had said and done. Should I have chosen a different way to tell her I'd found Gerry? Should I have made contact with Gerry myself? Should I have asked Mum for advice before telling her? Or should I have just bought her a skvader, which I had learned was a relative of the jackalope made from a hare and a wood grouse, rather than delve into her deep, unresolved issues in the first place?

'Okay,' she said when I answered, skipping over our usual exchange of pleasantries. 'I've waited six decades to find out what happened to her. Let's not wait another second. Do you have a profile on this networking site she's on?'

'Yes, I do,' I replied.

'Good. Can you come around tonight, and we'll send her a message?'

'Yes, of course. I'll come after work.'

'We'll need your computer. Mine's only good for solitaire.'

'Yes, I'll bring it with me.'

'Excellent. Brilliant,' she replied. 'I love you.'

She hung up before I could respond. The knot in my stomach loosened slightly.

'That was a short call,' Alannah said sheepishly from over their computer. They leaned in conspiratorially. 'Are you up to something dodgy? Is that a burner phone?'

I laughed loudly, expelling twelve hours of anxiety as I did.

'It was my gran.'

'Is your gran up to something dodgy?' Alannah hypothesised in a mocked, hushed whisper. 'Is she a drug dealer? I mean, you've mentioned she takes trips out to the bush to visit her "special plants". I should have guessed.'

I laughed again. 'No, not exactly.'

Gran's only brush with the drug-dealing underworld had been when she worked at the herbarium and was called as an expert witness to identify marijuana in a criminal case against one of the city's most notorious drug lords. Her boss decided the task exceeded his own personal risk threshold, so he delegated it to her. Fortunately, the accused was found guilty and received twenty years; Gran was hopeful he wouldn't hold a grudge for that long against the botanist who identified his prize crop.

'It would be the perfect cover, though,' Alannah continued, closing one eye and holding up their hands in a square to capture my face in a frame as they imitated a newsreader. *'Nerdy council worker teams up with green-thumbed Gran to grow drugs.'*

They put their hands back down and examined me through a sidewards squint.

'No one would ever suspect. It's genius. Next, you'll be turning up to work wearing gold bling and an over-the-shoulder bag, and driving a new car.'

'Oh! That reminds me,' I blurted. 'What's the time?'

'Three-thirty,' they said after glancing at their watch. 'Why?'

'Because I have to go and pick up my new car.'

'Really?' they snorted.

'Yep. I pick it up this afternoon.'

'Well, I never,' they said, shaking their head and looking back to their computer. 'Drug dealers ... you can never pick 'em. It's always the ones you least expect.'

~

The car dealer handed me the keys to my new car like he was presenting me with a Nobel Prize. He told me it had a full tank of fuel and then he handed me a picnic rug with the dealer logo on it – a gift, apparently. It felt odd to accept free fuel and merchandise when the car itself was paid for by my lotto winnings, but the rug felt like it was good quality, and I'd been meaning to get a new one ever since a dog had cocked its leg over mine at a sunset cinema. And it was good I didn't have to stop at a petrol station on the way home and endure the midweek price spike. I was thoroughly pleased.

I couldn't help but reflect on how this experience differed from when I'd bought my other car. Dad and I had driven to east of the middle of nowhere and taken possession of the vehicle from a man wearing a singlet that told the story of his last few meals, who was selling it because he'd lost his licence. Again.

Once in my new car, I adjusted my mirrors and seat, each with the simple press of a button, and without the need for a wrench. I lowered the sun visor to reveal a small, lit mirror; the last time I'd done that in my old car I had discovered a spider had taken up residence there. And,

I had to admit, the new car smell was indeed an improvement on the odour of mould.

I glanced in the rear-view mirror to see my old car in the parking lot, which I'd traded in for not much more than the cost of the complimentary picnic rug. I felt irrationally disloyal to it, but was chuffed to have my first-ever new car.

I pulled out my phone and opened the Dwyer family chat. I didn't usually contribute much to the conversation – my family had a habit of talking even more rubbish in the messenger chat than they did in person. And while I was happy to share information with my family on a need-to-know basis, I felt uneasy about not having told them about my lotto win – the biggest thing to have ever happened to me – especially since I was now the beneficiary of Gran's secret too. But they had ribbed me so much over the years about my old car that I thought they would be pleased to know I finally had one that didn't have a leaky roof. So I decided to share the news.

I scrolled back over the unread messages.

There were a few back and forths between Mum and Elijah about whether he'd used the last of the almond milk. (Yes, apparently.) And there was a message from Dad pleading with everyone to avoid any spoilers about the latest episode of *Farmer Wants a Wife*. (He hadn't watched it yet and was rooting for Amy, whoever that was.)

The last message was from Jarrah.

Hello fabulous family. I don't have any petrol in my car (or moolah to correct the situation). Can I borrow someone's wheels for a couple of hours tonight?

Underneath the message was a thumbs up from Dad.

I was outraged. Again, her financial mismanagement was someone else's problem to solve. And, again, Dad was bailing her out. I threw my phone a little too roughly onto the passenger seat. I certainly wasn't going to share the news of my car with my family now. I wouldn't put it past her to ask to siphon some petrol out.

~

When I arrived at Gran's and smelled my favourite dinner – pork in mustard sauce, served with rice and green beans – which she made for me on special occasions, wafting from her kitchen, I felt relieved. When she told me she'd made my favourite dessert – rice pudding – I knew for sure she wasn't mad.

She insisted we eat dinner before sending the message to Gerry. This suited me fine; I'd barely eaten all day. By the time my stomach knots had untangled, it was time to pick up my car, and I hadn't had a chance.

'Okay, then,' I said, after we'd eaten and cleared away the dishes, and I had transposed Gran's handwritten draft into Gerry's 'contact me' dialogue box. 'You're sure about this?'

'Wait on,' she said, lifting the handwritten pages towards her face. 'Just let me read it one more time.'

She had filled two sheets of thin, lined paper. The pages were covered with passages that had been crossed out and rewritten, and single words that had been scribbled out and replaced. The paper she'd written on had yellowed in the years it had been stored in the writing bureau in the corner of her lounge room, and the note looked like it could have been as old as the feelings it conveyed.

Gran's handwriting was neat and feminine, but not too flowery. I loved the way her S's began with a severe straight edge but then curved into a soft half-circle, and the way her R's looped at the top. Even the veggies in her garden were identified by little plaques that she'd prepared with as much care as would be given to the little name cards on the banquet table in the state dining room at Buckingham Palace.

Over the years, her writing, like her voice, had developed an ever-so-slight wobble. Her written strokes were lighter and less confident, and her spoken words had a tiny tremble that was almost imperceptible – except to anyone who hung on her every word, like me.

'Dear Gerry,' she read under her breath. 'I hope my getting in touch will be a welcome surprise. It may seem that I'm contacting you out of the blue, but the truth is that I have thought of you often over the past sixty-or-so years.

'I was thrilled, but not surprised, to read about your illustrious career. I always knew you had so much to contribute to science. Elizabeth Gould would be proud. I worked in the state's herbarium for many years and now volunteer there to keep them, and me, on our toes. Coincidentally, I contributed to the Millennium Seed Bank Project in Kew Gardens, which I see you were involved in.

'I married John Evans, and we had one daughter, Rosie. I have three grandchildren, including Beth who is helping me make contact with you.

'I'm so glad I've found a way to reach you, Gerry. I don't expect anything from you but want you to know that I've thought of you often and with fondness.

'With love and best wishes, Elise (nee Simpson).'

'It's perfect, Gran,' I offered.

'Do you really think?' she asked, sitting back in the chair and removing her glasses. She looked apprehensive. 'Maybe I should just—'

'Don't get cold feet now,' I interjected. 'You said yourself you've always wondered what happened. This is your chance.'

'You're right,' she said with a decisive nod of her head. 'Send it.'

I ceremoniously tapped the mouse button before she could change her mind.

'And now we wait,' I said with a nod.

'And now we wait,' she repeated, rapping her hands on the table and then getting up and walking to the stove. 'Do you want more rice pudding?'

'No thanks, Gran,' I replied, rubbing my uncomfortably full belly. 'I couldn't eat another thing.'

After Gran had loaded me up with Tupperware containers of leftover food, I farewelled her with the promise that I would let her know right away if I heard anything from Gerry and the assurance I would return her Tupperware when I next saw her. I effortlessly slid into the driver's seat of my shiny new car, pushed the button on the dash that engaged the keyless ignition and then tapped the button to fire up the seat warmer. The night was crisp but not cold, so I opened the sunroof and welcomed in the fresh night air to mingle with the new car smell.

It was nice to know I would make it home without needing a call-out to roadside assistance.

Chapter 15

Beth

It had been three days since Gran and I had sent the message to Gerry. Quite understandably, her patience for a response was waning.

It wasn't uncommon for us to speak on the phone a couple of times during the week as we arranged transport to and from my parents' house on Saturdays or exchanged work updates. But she'd called me each morning and night to see if I'd heard anything, even though I assured her that I would let her know the second I did.

Despite her agitation, she had an air of sprightliness to her. When I called past on my way home one night to return her Tupperware, I could hear her vocal improvisations before I even reached the front door. She used to always perform operatic acrobatics when she was pottering around the house (occasionally an identifiable tune snuck into her arrangement, but she'd usually moved on by the time you've worked out what it was). It was only now I realised I hadn't heard her do it since Grandpa died. It made me happy to see a lightness to her again. And, for just a moment, I allowed myself to wonder what it would feel like to be so buoyed by the prospect of connecting with someone.

On the fourth morning, I woke to the mechanical chiming of my phone alarm and sleepily looked at the screen to check the time. As I hovered my finger over the snooze button, I spotted a notification of an email received at 2.56am.

I sat up as quickly as I could for first thing in the morning and opened the email from Gerry Burnsby with the subject line: Hello.

Dearest Elise,

I am so sorry it has taken me several days to reply. I rarely use my university email, and in the excitement of receiving your message, I somehow uninstalled the program from my computer and then managed to lock my account. It's taken three days and two patient IT fellows to get me back online.

I tore my gaze away from the screen to stop myself from reading any more. As tempting as it was to continue, it wasn't mine to read.

It was 6.15am – too early to ring Gran. Instead, I decided to forgo my run and head to her house on the way to work.

I quickly showered, dressed and ate breakfast. As I was walking out the door, I sent Gran a text.

I'm coming over. Gerry replied.

A few moments later my phone chimed.

Hurry. Let's see what that new car of yours can do.

When I arrived, Gran was waiting for me on her porch. She was wrapped in her turquoise green robe and had her hiking boots on, which I suspected were the quickest thing for her to put on. She had a coffee in each hand and held one out to me as I made my way up her path.

'Come on, come on,' she said, ushering me inside. 'I'm getting older by the minute. What did she say?'

'I don't know,' I replied as we made our way towards the kitchen. 'I haven't read it.'

'What!' she squawked incredulously.

'*You* should be the first to read it,' I said, sitting down, taking out my laptop and firing it up. Gran paced around the kitchen muttering about how she'd waited sixty years, and now she'd have to wait even longer while the computer loaded.

'Okay. Here it is.' I turned the computer around to face her. She sat down, pulled her glasses out of her dressing gown pocket, took a deep breath and angled her body towards the screen. The laptop screen made small blue reflections in her specs.

I studied her face for clues about the contents of the email or how it made her feel. But, as her eyes tracked from left to right, she was expressionless.

After several moments, she removed her glasses and wiped them on her dressing gown. Her eyes were wet with tears, and the skin on her chin dimpled and quivered slightly.

'Well, there you have it,' she said, returning her glasses to her nose with a sniff.

'Have what? What did she say?'

She turned the computer back to me, stood up and walked to retrieve a tissue from a box on the shelf by the kitchen door. She dabbed her eyes and blew her nose loudly.

I braced myself as I began reading.

Dearest Elise,

I am so sorry it has taken me several days to reply. I rarely use my university email, and in the excitement of receiving your message, I somehow uninstalled the program from my computer and then managed to lock my account. It's taken three days and two patient IT fellows to get me back online. I can't begin to tell you how happy I was to hear from you. I have thought of you many times since we last saw each other all those years ago.

How wonderful that you were part of the Millennium Seed

94

Bank Project – it was such a wonderful initiative and has been
such a great example of the global scientific community working
together.

I have loved my work over the years, although I wouldn't read
too much into my tenure at the university. I think they only invited
me to be an adjunct professor because I kept hanging around and
they needed to find a way to insure me while I was on campus. But
I still love working with the young people; they are so vibrant and
full of energy and enthusiasm. They remind me of us a hundred
years ago.

I never married, but have enjoyed love in my life and have
travelled extensively. I have also had the joy of being an aunt and
great-aunt to my sister's children and grandchildren. It has been
one of the great pleasures of my life to love without expectation or
responsibility.

I would enjoy the opportunity to keep in touch, Elise. Given
my limited aptitude for technology, perhaps we could speak on the
phone. My great-nephew Nick has set me up with a smartphone so
I can make as many calls as I want, to whomever I want. Imagine
if this technology had existed all those years ago. How different
things might have been.

If you send me your phone number, I will give you a call.
London is eight hours behind you, so perhaps I could call when it's
evening here and morning there. Or the other way around.

I am delighted to have heard from you and hope to speak to you
soon.

With love,
Gerry

'What do you make of it?' I asked after I had read the email twice. I
couldn't ignore how different this message was to my recent exchange

with my ex, Matt.

'It's wonderful.' Her eyes glistened with tears and optimism. 'It's really wonderful.'

'Do you want to reply with your phone number?'

'Oh yes, darling,' she replied enthusiastically, as though it should have been obvious. 'Of course.'

Gran dictated an email that detailed her delight at receiving a response, her keenness to keep in touch and her phone number.

I hit send. It was 11.10pm London time, so it was possible that Gerry would call today if she had a habit of checking her emails late in the evening, we agreed.

Irrespective of the time in London, it was definitely time for me to get to work.

'I have to go, Gran,' I said, putting my laptop back in the case and sculling the last of my coffee. 'I'll keep my fingers and toes crossed that she calls soon.'

'Thank you, my love.' She grabbed my arm firmly. 'Thank you for everything. You will never know how much this means to me. I'd given up on ever finding out what happened to Gerry, let alone getting in contact with her again.'

Her voice wavered.

I kissed her forehead and then stood back to admire the look of joy on her face. Despite my current romantic prospects being non-existent, I was glad Gran looked so optimistic about matters of the heart. And I felt oddly proud that I'd played a role in facilitating it.

'I love you, Gran. And I'm really happy for you.'

She dabbed her nose with a tissue with one hand and swatted me away affectionately with the other.

'Now, be gone with you,' she joshed. 'I'm waiting on an important call and I can't have you hanging around to eavesdrop.'

As I pulled away from the kerb outside her house, I wondered how long she would sit at the table waiting for the phone to ring. After sixty years, what was a couple more hours?

Chapter 16

Elise

Elise's kitchen had always been the heart of her house. The table she now sat at alone had hosted competitive card games, countless conquered homework tasks, creative craft projects and philosophical discussions. The kitchen sink had provided the setting for her nightly debrief with Rosie about her day when she was young. The warm soapy water helped to soothe her daughter's teenage angst and there was something about standing side by side, rather than looking directly at each other, that encouraged her to share. John – who prided himself on being an early adopter of gadgets – was keen to get a dishwasher as soon as they were on the market, to make life easier. But Elise resisted until Rosie had left home, arguing it would make life easier, but not better.

Elise looked to the scars etched into the doorjamb to the left of the sink, which provided evidence of Rosie's and then the grandkids' height milestones. Crude markings documented their transitions from toddler, to child, to teen and beyond, when they no longer wanted their height measured and Elise wouldn't have been able to reach the tops of their heads anyway.

Being a grandmother had brought her so much joy. She and John had been apprehensive when Rosie and Thorn were married after only eight months, and when they had Jarrah shortly after that. Elise had worried that their bohemian lifestyle and what she considered to be alternative theories about parenthood were not suited to caring for a baby. But Jarrah had thrived in a world filled with colour and music and, most of all, love.

When Jarrah was about twenty months old, Rosie fell pregnant with Beth. Everyone was thrilled their family was growing. However, towards the end of her pregnancy, Rosie experienced some bleeding. She called Elise to come and look after Jarrah so she could go to the doctor. By the time Elise got to the house, she'd had a major haemorrhage. Elise arrived to find Rosie shaking with shock in the bathroom and Jarrah covered in the blood her mother had lost on the way down the hallway.

Rosie was put on bedrest for several weeks and then delivered of her baby by emergency caesarean under general anaesthetic a few days after Christmas. Elise and Thorn spent hours pacing the hospital corridors waiting for news. Eventually it came: mother and baby were okay. But just. Rosie was very poorly for several days, and Beth was treated in the neonatal intensive care unit. When the pair was reunited, feeding didn't come easily, and Beth was very difficult to settle.

By the time Beth was about four weeks old, Rosie was not doing well. Nowadays, she would have likely been diagnosed with postnatal depression but, in those days, it was usually chalked up to a case of the baby blues that would abate once the baby started sleeping better. One afternoon Elise felt an urge to detour past Rosie's on her way home from work. She could hear Beth's high-pitched screams reverberating through the quiet suburban street before she'd even got out of her car. By the time she reached the front door, she heard Jarrah's wailing and Rosie's sobs too.

She took one look at her daughter and called for John to bring around a suitcase of her things. She spent the next three weeks helping to care for

Beth while Rosie got some much-needed rest.

It was during this time that she began the ritual of bundling Beth into her pram in the early evening, when she was at her most fractious, and walking to the local park. They sat under a giant lemon-scented eucalypt where Beth stared up at the leaves while Elise read *Snugglepot and Cuddlepie* until the local kookaburra issued the final birdcall of the day and indicated it was time for them to go home.

Elise and Beth continued these trips to the park for months; long after Rosie had emerged from her postnatal fog and found joy in motherhood again. No doubt the trips helped lay the foundations for the bond they shared, which grew as Beth matured and she too developed a love of the natural world.

Elise understood the role she played in Beth's life. She provided dependability and stability when it wasn't always available at home, and she allowed Beth the space to be herself. Sometimes she felt like she was the conduit between Beth and the rest of the world and she was aware she was closer to Beth than many other grandparents were to their grandchildren. She was happy for Beth that she'd won the money. And she hoped that by giving her a financial leg-up, it would help ease her self-imposed burden of responsibility.

Elise looked at the clock for the second time in as many minutes. It was 7.25am – 11.25pm London time. She knew the chance of hearing from Gerry today decreased with every second that passed.

She walked into the spare bedroom and retrieved the box from the bottom drawer of the bedside table. She hadn't returned it to its hiding place on the top shelf of the wardrobe; she figured she was much less likely to break her neck revisiting it there, and it seemed like a small, symbolic gesture to inch it out of the closet, even if it was still hidden in the shadows. The combination dial moved more easily this time, and she felt more confident, excited even, about delving beyond the photo and ticket stub into the box's contents, and into her past.

Elise's return from Woodside Ridge during the Easter after she met Gerry had been a turning point; she could no longer ignore that her feelings for Gerry extended beyond platonic. And this had terrified her.

Pastor O'Reilly – the jolly Irish clergyman at the tiny church Elise's family went to – often told the congregation that it was a sin for two men to 'lie together'. And, once she moved to the city, it was hard for her to avoid the newspapers that declared that homosexuality was an epidemic. The hysterical articles celebrated a special law enforcement taskforce that had been formed to rid the community of the 'growing crisis' and named and shamed the young men who were arrested at 'queer' parties or in public toilets.

Those who weren't arrested, charged or incarcerated were treated for what was considered to be a mental illness. Elise had heard whispers that the brother of a school friend had been subjected to behaviour aversion therapy during which he'd been shown same-sex pornography and given electric shocks to his genitals. Others were subjected to drugs, religious interventions, various psychological therapies and even lobotomies.

While the law did not seem to actively target women in the same way as men, Elise had been in her second-last year of high school when two Kiwi teenagers – Pauline Parker and Juliet Hulme – bludgeoned Pauline's mother to death with a chunk of brick in a stocking. Elise and her friends gathered around the wireless at the end of each day of the trial, to hear details of the case, and debate whether the girls were lovers. The general consensus was that women who were attracted to other women were wicked, and needed to be cured of their affliction before they harmed themselves or others.

Elise decided that avoidance was the best way of dealing with her feelings for Gerry, so she pretended she was ill and locked herself away in her room. But her phoney illness did nothing to keep Gerry away. Gerry brought Elise soup and cold compresses throughout the day, and offered to sit with her through the night.

After a week complaining of everything from muscle aches and dizziness to itchy skin and light sensitivity, Gerry and Miss Too-Priss sent for the doctor. The doctor declared there was nothing physically wrong with Elise and that the best treatment would be for her to head home to Woodside Ridge to convalesce in the country air.

While Elise couldn't face seeing Gerry at college, she couldn't bear the thought of being apart from her again either. So the moment the doctor had collected his medical bag and left her room, Elise declared she was feeling much better and turned her acting efforts to convincing everyone she was on the mend.

'I'm so glad to have you back,' Gerry said, when Elise agreed to 'test her strength' with a walk through the university gardens. 'All this time we've spent apart lately has made me realise how much I enjoy your company and how much I love spending time with you.'

The two women gravitated to a park bench inside a fern grotto. The damp green foliage that lined the perimeter cocooned them.

'I want you to know how much you mean to me, Elise,' Gerry started. 'Seeing you so poorly made me realise ...'

She dropped her eyes and stroked the back of Elise's hand.

'... how much I love you.'

Elise felt her heart somersault inside her chest. She yearned to tell Gerry that she loved her too. That she loved her more than she had ever loved anyone. And that her love was so intense and confusing that she didn't have the words to describe it. But the stakes were too high; what if she'd misunderstood, and Gerry didn't love her the same way? But, as Elise searched for what to say, the space between them disappeared and their lips connected.

For the next two years, they debated who kissed whom first. Gerry maintained it was her. Elise insisted it was her. But they both agreed it was one of the most amazing, surprising, exciting things that had ever happened to them.

From that moment, Gerry and Elise's lives became one. By day, they were scholarly study buddies, intellectual equals and college companions. By night, when the college hallways were dark and quiet, they were lovers. The fact that their romance was nocturnal, and hidden from the world, only heightened its intensity.

Early in their relationship, they hadn't been so careful. They assumed that a brush of the arm here or a quick peck there wouldn't rouse suspicion. But they vowed to be more discreet after a mathematics professor rounded a corridor and caught them kissing. Gerry, quick to provide a plausible excuse for why Elise was holding her face and showing such close attention to her mouth, faked a choking episode.

The memory of it now made Elise chuckle. She rummaged her fingers deeper into the box, until she felt what she was looking for – a brooch she had tucked in there after she'd written her last letter to Gerry. She lifted the brooch from the box and oscillated it in her fingers, so the dainty stones glistened in the light.

The Gouldian finch brooch was about the size of a fifty-cent piece. The bird was positioned on a branch, with its head turned in profile to reveal its magnificent colouring. The yellow of its belly, the green of its back and the blue of its lower tail feathers were shiny enamel, while its purple throat and red face were coloured with tiny crystals. It was exquisite.

Elise ran her finger over the letters engraved on the back: *EG*. Elise and Gerry. Or, if anyone had asked, 'Elizabeth Gould'. She clutched the brooch to her chest, just as she had when Gerry gave it to her.

On the last night before Gerry went back to the UK, they had ventured to a spot on the river's edge, not far from their college. They shared a serve of fish and chips and drank bottles of lager from paper bags as the sun set on a perfect February day, and on their time together. They stayed there for hours – well after the other students retreated and the mosquitos emerged – making whispered promises that they would write, and see each other as soon as possible.

Gerry had the brooch made by the only jeweller in the city to carry the Royal Warrant of Appointment. Elise often forgot that Gerry came from such wealth and privilege; she was never flashy or ostentatious. But then Gerry would do something – like commission a stunning hand-made brooch that probably cost as much as a year's lodging – and remind her they were from two very different worlds.

'I wanted to give you something to commemorate our time together,' Gerry had said when Elise insisted it was too much. 'Something you could wear close to your heart.'

Gerry pinned the brooch to the front of Elise's cardigan.

'I chose a Gouldian finch because Elizabeth Gould was such a remarkable woman,' she continued. 'And I know you're going to achieve great things, just like her. But I also chose it because John Gould named the bird after her; he thought it was the most beautiful bird in the world.'

Gerry leaned in and kissed Elise gently.

'But you, my love, are the most beautiful bird in the world, to me.'

Remembering those words now, Elise allowed the tears she'd been fighting to flow freely down her cheeks. As she placed the brooch back in the box, she recalled that the void Gerry left when she returned to the UK had nearly swallowed her up.

She removed her phone from her dressing gown to confirm that the volume wasn't set to silent. It wasn't, just like the four other times she'd checked.

Waiting for her phone to ring reminded Elise of the anxious anticipation she felt in the weeks after Gerry had left. Each day, Elise rushed to the pigeonholes outside Miss Too-Priss's office, hopeful there was a letter from Gerry. Elise's pigeonhole was on the second-highest row, which provided her with a glimpse of its contents as she approached it from down the corridor. The moments after she spotted a letter propped inside the small wooden recess were filled with unbridled hope. The hours after discovering it was from her mother or a friend were filled with crushing despair.

When Gerry first left, Elise wrote every second day. She applied the lipstick Gerry had given her and placed a kiss alongside her name at the end of the letter. She sealed it, gave it another kiss for good luck and put it in the outgoing mail tray under the pigeonholes. After three months of no reply, she reduced the frequency of her letters to weekly as the cost of stamps was eating into her modest student budget. Two months after that, when she still hadn't received a single word from Gerry, Elise wrote her final letter. But instead of adding a watermelon-tinted kiss, she let her tears fall onto the page like big wet punctuation marks. As she sealed the last envelope, Elise closed her heart to ever knowing that kind of love again.

The shrieking ring of her phone, which she still had tucked back into her dressing gown pocket, catapulted Elise from her thoughts.

She gasped in anticipation and fished out the phone.

The phone face illuminated with 'No caller ID'. Elise swallowed deeply.

'Hello,' she said cautiously, holding the cold, flat screen to her face. There was a pause, and Elise wondered if it was one of those scam callers that she'd heard about on *A Current Affair*.

'Elise ...' the voice annunciated in perfect Queen's English. 'It's Gerry.'

Chapter 17

Beth

On my drive to work, I tried hard to refocus on the busy day ahead. First up was a meeting with representatives from the state's environment agency and a local Aboriginal land council, to talk about joint management of a tract of bush.

I walked into the meeting room and selected a chair to Geoff's left.

'Good morning. How's things? How's your day going?' he asked. I had noticed he'd been a little more attentive since my early finish the other day, which I assumed meant he thought I *did* have a job interview.

'Good thanks,' I said as I sat down and poised my pen above my notebook, ready to take notes. 'I've been looking forward to this meeting. This is a special patch of bush.'

The area provided the setting for many older residents' memories of the good ol' days, when they'd spent from sunrise to sunset building forts and climbing trees. Today, people cherished it as one of the last remaining natural areas for miles. The bush also offered refuge to some endearing native animals, such as the honey possum and quenda. And a couple of western grey kangaroos persisted there despite all the odds.

Most importantly, the area had particular significance to First Nations peoples, as it contained a number of plant species that were used for bush medicine. These meetings were an important part of ensuring that the Traditional Owners were central in conserving this natural apothecary. But, as hard as I tried to focus on the numerous 'action items' being captured and promises made to 'circle back', my mind kept wandering to thoughts of Gran and whether she'd heard from Gerry.

'Oh, hi there,' Alannah said, looking up from their screen when I returned to my desk after the meeting. 'You're popular today.'

'What do you mean?'

I had never in my life been described as popular.

'Your phone has been buzzing nonstop for the last hour.'

'Oh, sorry.' I launched my hand into my bag to retrieve it. I loathed it when unattended phones buzzed away or, worse, rang, in open-plan workplaces.

'It's fine. It was a nice distraction from having to listen to that lot dissecting last night's episode of *Married at First Sight*.' Alannah nodded their head towards the group of twenty-somethings from the events management team, who were huddled over a screen trawling through a gossip news site, whispering and giggling.

I tapped on my phone to illuminate the display and gasped. There were sixteen missed calls from Gran.

'Everything okay?' Alannah asked.

'I hope so,' I said. I hurried outside and hit redial. Gran answered after the first ring.

'You took your time,' she huffed mockingly down the line.

'Sorry, Gran. What's wrong?' I asked, slightly breathless from the worry that something terrible had happened and from the exertion of dashing outside.

'Nothing's wrong,' she laughed. 'In fact, everything's great.'

'I take it you heard from Gerry, then,' I said, my breath rate calming.

'I sure did.'

'So?' I probed. 'What did she say? Did she sound the same as you remembered?'

'More or less,' Gran replied pensively. 'A little more ... mature, perhaps. But her voice was still as lovely as ever. I always loved the way she said my name. *Elise. Elise. Elise.*' Gran repeated her name in a plum English accent, emphasising different syllables each time as she experimented with the sound.

'What did the two of you talk about?' I asked.

'Oh, you know,' she said coyly. 'This and that.'

I hmphed down the line. Normally I wouldn't dream of probing for information from someone who was clearly not willing to share. I hated when Jarrah pressured me for what she irritatingly referred to as 'the 411'. But this felt different; I felt completely invested.

'We're speaking again tonight.'

'It must have gone well, then,' I said. Geoff appeared at the doorway and nodded to indicate he wanted to speak to me. 'I have to get back inside for another meeting, but give me a call tonight after you've spoken to her.'

'I will, pet. Wish me luck.'

~

That night, after I had washed up from dinner, folded my clean washing and selected my outfit for the next day, I settled down on the couch with my phone close by.

I watched a documentary about a woman advocating for better food labelling regulations in hospitality venues after her son suffered a fatal allergic reaction. Then I sat through a debate between a conservative white male politician and a drag queen about the need to invest in the arts. I started a detective show set in a tiny English county with a worrying rate of crime per capita, but I must have dozed off before the handsome cop figured out whether the priest had been murdered by the loyal parishioner or the creepy publican. I started awake when my phone chimed with a message from Gran.

It's late. I'll call you tomorrow. It went well. xx

I typed a reply: *I'm so glad, Gran. I can't wait to hear all about it. x*

Another message quickly followed with a smiley face emoji.

I smiled broadly at my phone, aware of the lunacy of grinning at an inanimate object. I then checked the doors, turned out the lights, changed into my pyjama shorts and top, brushed my teeth and slipped into bed.

The sheets were cool against my bare legs. On nights like this, when it was crisp but not quite cold enough to use the flannel sheets or my winter pyjamas, I had to admit it might be nice to climb into the bed with someone else. It also might have been nice to have someone to debrief with about what a big week it had been.

The next morning, I set off for work ten minutes ahead of schedule. I planned to call Gran from the road and wanted to allow for extra time to hear how it had gone with Gerry.

I was enjoying the modern conveniences of my new car. Beyond being able to get in and out without performing a yoga manoeuvre, I was enjoying the radio that played AM and FM, the connectivity with my phone, and the ease of opening and closing the windows with the touch of a button.

'Hello, darling.' Gran's voice filled the space of my new car via bluetooth.

'Soooooo?' I wasted no time on pleasantries. 'How did it go?'

'Oh, love,' she sighed euphorically. 'It was wonderful. We spoke for hours and hours. And I'm sure we could have spoken for many more.'

'You do have sixty years to catch up on.'

'Indeed,' she chuckled.

'Has she changed much?'

'Yes and no,' Gran replied thoughtfully. 'It sounds cliché, but it feels like no time has passed, and yet like I'm getting to know someone for the first time. She still has a lightning-quick wit, and she's incredibly clever and accomplished, so nothing's changed there. But her rosy view of the world has tarnished. She carries scars from navigating a world that hasn't always been willing to accept her.'

Gran paused before continuing in a more upbeat tone. 'But she's fit and healthy, and she's led a full and rewarding life, which is all any of us can ask for.'

'Did you find out what happened to her after she returned to the UK?' I asked.

'No. I didn't want to get into it when there was so much else to catch up on,' she said. 'It didn't feel like the right time. And I'm still not really sure I want to know.'

Gran explained that Gerry had become the eminent authority on English vascular plants and had enjoyed a long and illustrious career with the University of New London. Her work with plant fossils had been revolutionary and had earned her widespread accolades.

Gerry told Gran that as well as providing her with immense personal satisfaction, her career had also offered a socially acceptable justification for why she hadn't married or had children. Her unwavering dedication to her work was more readily accepted than her sexual preference for women, apparently. She also shared that she had enjoyed love in her life, including for many years with an internationally known thespian whose name Gran was 'not at liberty to share'.

'We've got a date to speak again tonight, too,' Gran finished as I pulled into my office's car park.

'Wow!'

I shut off the engine, gathered my things and began the walk to my office.

'Sweetie, at our age, there really is no time like the present,' she said, obviously sensing my surprise that they were speaking again so soon.

'Fair enough. Well, keep me posted.'

'I will, pet,' she replied. 'And thank you again.'

'Morning,' Alannah said when I arrived at my desk, gesturing to the phone that was still in my hand. 'Was that my favourite drug dealer?'

I laughed. 'Yes, it was. She's just reconnected with someone she'd lost touch with years ago, and she was keen to tell me about it.'

'That's nice,' they said, looking back towards their screen. 'It's so nice that you're close to your gran. I really miss both of mine.'

Alannah's maternal grandmother had passed away last year, six months after their mother had succumbed to cancer. They said what upset them most was knowing how much fun the two of them would be having 'upstairs' without her. Their family was Irish, and the tales of family gatherings were legendary.

'Just make sure you make the most of her while you've got her. She won't be around forever,' they said tenderly.

Alannah was right.

This whole business with Gerry had started because I wanted to use my lotto winnings to make Gran happy. Admittedly, this had catapulted us both on a journey I did not anticipate. But sixty years after they had been separated by a chasm of distance – geographic and sociopolitical – they had the opportunity to cross the abyss and reunite properly. And I had the means to make it happen.

I picked up my phone and hastily typed a message to Gran.

Is your passport valid?

I waited as three dots danced on the screen.

Yes. What have you got in mind?

Chapter 18

Beth

Gran had, in principle, agreed to a trip to London to see Gerry, but was oscillating between being giddily excited and wanting to call the whole thing off.

'What was I even thinking?' she said to me days later, only hours before I was planning to book the tickets. 'It's lunacy. Fancy thinking that I could just pop over to London to catch up with her after all these years. Women my age don't simply jump on a plane and traipse halfway around the world on a whim. How would I even explain it to people?'

'You don't have to explain it to anyone,' I replied emphatically. 'It's no one else's business. You're quite entitled to go on a holiday any time you want to.'

'But I don't even know if she wants to see me,' Gran responded. 'What am I meant to say to her? "Hey Gerry, you know how sixty years ago we fell in love and carried on a secret relationship? Well, what's say I put my wrinkly, arthritic eighty-two-year-old body on a flight to London and we can pick up where we left off. Next Tuesday work for you?" She'll probably assume I have frontal lobe impairment caused by dementia or a stroke.

Goodness. Maybe I do.'

'Well, if she doesn't want to see you, then we'll just make the most of a trip to London. Are you planning on speaking to her tonight?'

'Yes. She's calling at eight.'

'Well, just talk to her,' I urged. 'Tell her you're thinking of coming over. If she reacts well, tell her you're planning to come sooner rather than later. If she seems unsure, then we'll go anyway, and she'll be none the wiser. We can tour the palaces, wander through galleries and see a show or two. We don't even have to stay in London the whole time. Don't you have family in the country? We could go and visit them.'

'Maybe,' she said. I imagined she was stroking her thumb on the back of the opposite hand. 'It just all feels very rushed. Maybe we don't need to cancel it. Perhaps we should just delay it for a while.'

'But this is the only time we can both go, remember,' I rationalised. 'I've got the installation of my possum bridge, and you've already locked in the dates for your orchid field trips. You said it yourself: there's no time like the present.'

'I hate it when you use my words against me,' she groaned.

'Besides,' I continued, 'you're hardly rushing into this. This reunion has been sixty years in the making. And somehow I don't think any amount of warm fuzzies would see you through a northern hemisphere winter, so it has to be this time of year.'

She emitted a loud *hmmmmm* down the phone.

I had to admit, encouraging someone else to be bold and supporting them to step bravely into an uncomfortable situation wasn't my usual role. But hearing Gran talk about Gerry, having Alannah remind me she wouldn't be around forever, and the idea of using the lotto money to travel to a city I loved, propelled me to continue.

'And don't you want to catch up with Gerry properly?' I continued. 'A phone call here and an email there isn't going to bridge all the years you've spent apart.'

'Yes, yes. You're right,' she conceded.

'We'll leave next Tuesday and be back a fortnight later,' I said assertively, hoping my pragmatism would help solidify her decision to go.

'Okay. But I won't have you paying for the whole thing. I don't care how much money you won.'

After some debate, we agreed that I would play for flights, she would pay for accommodation and that we were both as stubborn as each other.

About an hour after we hung up, Gran sent a text.

I spoke to Gerry. She's excited. London here we come.

I set about booking the flights and accommodation immediately. As far as I knew, airlines did not offer flexibility to accommodate matters of the heart, and travel insurance policies did not cover cold feet. Once the trip was locked in, she wouldn't be able to change her mind again.

~

'I'm sorry,' Mum said incredulously down the phone. 'You and Gran are going where? And when?'

I realised when Mum called later that afternoon that neither Gran nor I had told her about our trip. Now the trip had been booked, sharing our plans seemed pertinent.

'We're going to London. Next Tuesday.'

'O-kay,' she said, emphasising both syllables in the way people do when they're processing information en route to forming a judgement. 'When was this decided? And whose idea was it?'

It was impossible to answer this without providing the backstory, which I was under strict instructions not to do.

'Well ... we just kind of agreed, I suppose. I can't actually remember whose idea it was in the first place.'

Not entirely true; I had suggested it. Nevertheless, I didn't feel the details of our decision-making process had any bearing on our ultimate choice to go.

'What about work? I thought you had some projects on the go. What about the possums?'

I hadn't thought she'd been listening when I talked about the bridge project.

'It's fine. Geoff has okayed me taking a fortnight off. This was actually the only time I could go for the next couple of months. So we just sort of jumped at the chance.'

'Oh my God,' Mum said. I heard the slap of her hand against her mouth. 'Is Gran okay? This isn't one of those end-of-life trips, is it? She's dying, isn't she? Is she going somewhere to have euthanasia? I've read about this, where people travel to places overseas where it's legal.'

Her words tumbled out of her uncharacteristically. She was usually annoyingly calm when it came to sombre or serious situations. When Grandpa died, she took on an almost ethereal calmness, which she credited to daily yoga and meditation. I suspected the half-smoked joint I found in her bedside table had something to do with it too.

'She's not—' I started.

'Fuck!' she said, cutting me off. 'She was talking about her blood pressure medication the other day. She'd just been to see the doctor, and she'd changed her medication. Or had she increased her medication? I think she said she had been dizzy too. Or tired? Or both. I can't remember what she said.' Her tone was becoming more urgent with each word. 'I should have known something was wrong. I told her she should have been taking lemon and turmeric tea, but you know what she's like.

'What is it, Beth?' she implored. 'Tell me. Is it cancer? Heart disease?'

'Mum, she's—'

'Come to think of it,' she interrupted again, 'she was saying some odd things about righting the wrongs of the past and second chances, or something. She must be making amends with her life before she dies. Fuck.'

'Mum!' I said, loudly enough this time to demand her attention. 'She's not sick. I promise. We've just decided to go on a trip together.'

'But ...?' The word, loaded with questions, lingered down the line. I had to admit, Gran having an incurable illness was probably more plausible than my decision to take an impromptu holiday.

'Besides, assisted dying is legal in Australia now,' I added, in an offer of further assurance.

'Oh,' she replied. 'Yes. Yes, you're right. It is. Although I'm not really sure if that's a comfort.'

'It's just a holiday,' I promised. 'I thought you'd be pleased I'm being more spontaneous.'

'Is that what this is all about?' she asked, sounding exasperated. 'Proving that you're capable of spontaneity?'

'No,' I scoffed. 'I have no interest in proving anything to anyone. But everyone is always telling me to seize the day. And now, here I am "seizing the day", and you're freaking out.'

'I'm not "freaking out", Beth,' she replied defensively. 'It's just taken me by surprise, that's all. I've seen you spend more time planning what movie you'll see at the cinemas.'

'Where will you stay?' she asked, changing the subject in what I recognised as a deliberate gesture of amnesty.

'We've booked a hotel in Kensington, just near the gardens,' I said cheerily – my own olive branch.

'Oh, it's lovely there. Such a pretty area. Your Dad and I stayed there when we spent a night partying with the lead singer of ... Ohhhh!' she exclaimed suddenly. I could picture the way her shoulders had risen with a little shimmy when she had an idea. 'I've got an idea! Maybe I could come too? Three generations travelling together.'

I was grateful to be on the phone, so she couldn't see my face contort into a look of horror.

'Um ... I ... ah.' I scrambled for reasons to dissuade her. I grasped at the most obvious one. 'Wouldn't Jarrah feel left out?'

'Maybe she could come too? She's not working at the moment so doesn't have anything tying her here,' Mum posed enthusiastically. 'It could be a girls' trip.'

A wave of anger rose from my stomach. I was furious that Mum just assumed she could invite herself along, and then twisted it to revolve around Jarrah. The fact she had used Jarrah's self-imposed unemployment as a reason for her to come only made it worse.

'Except that you've forgotten the bit where Jarrah has no money because she chooses to focus on finding employment that "nourishes her soul", rather than saving money for a rainy day, or a trip to London,' I said curtly.

'Well ... maybe she ...' She paused, searching for a way to solve Jarrah's problem of having no money for a trip that never involved her in the first place.

'We're flying business class,' I interjected before she could continue.

It was true; we were flying business class. I had booked the tickets to make the flight more comfortable for Gran. I'd gawked at the price; two return tickets had cost nearly as much as my new car. But I had purchased them on a credit card with a loyalty points scheme linked to the airline, which meant I would get two free domestic flights from the frequent flyer points I would accrue.

'Business class,' Mum repeated, her surprise palpable. 'Wow. You two do have it all sorted out. Don't worry about us, then.' Martyrdom hung on her every word. 'Perhaps you'll take another trip together sometime, and you won't mind us tagging along. If we won't cramp your style, of course.'

There was a sting in her words.

'Mum, it's not ...'

I didn't know how to explain we weren't deliberately excluding anyone from the trip, without revealing our motivation for taking it.

'It's fine,' she snapped.

I picked at a few pills that had assembled on my jumper.

'I just wish sometimes ...' she said eventually, but her voice trailed off.

'What?' I prompted.

'It would have been nice to go on a trip with you, that's all. But maybe we can do it another time.'

I was surprised; she hadn't suggested we travel together since she'd proposed a girls' yoga retreat with Jarrah and me. It had been impossible to coordinate our calendars so I told them to go without me. I'd also passed on the rebirthing seminar she went on to celebrate her sixtieth birthday; I couldn't think of anything worse than re-enacting a descent of the birth canal with a room full of strangers. And I'd deliberately planned a hiking trip to avoid a two-day art workshop that she and Jarrah had attended where they'd made models of their vaginas and written letters to their 'inner goddesses'.

'What time do you leave on Tuesday?' she asked, her voice soft again.

'We fly out at midday, so we will need to be at the airport at about 10am. I'll drive to Gran's and leave my car in her garage.'

I had been thinking about the schedule for Tuesday since we'd booked the tickets. I found the morning of any trip stressful, so I planned for every eventuality. I made a habit of leaving early for the airport to allow for traffic and always allowed plenty of time for check-in.

'I can drop you off, then.'

'Well ... actually,' I began self-consciously. 'The airline will be sending a car to pick us up. It's one of the perks of flying business class, apparently.'

'Ohhhh. La-di-da,' she mocked, but not unkindly. 'Goodness me. Did one of you win lotto, or something?'

'Ha!' I exclaimed, louder than I'd intended. 'Can you imagine?'

Not telling my family about my lotto win had been weighing on me, but after my first failed attempt at sharing the news, I wasn't in a rush to try again. I couldn't tell Mum and Dad, but not Jarrah and Elijah. Nor could I give money to one of my siblings but not the other. So I'd decided to wait until we returned from London to tell any of them. I hoped that Jarrah would have found a job by then, so I wouldn't be funding her Bikram yoga and coconut water smoothies while she looked for her next soul-nourishing appointment.

'It sounds like you've got it all sorted,' Mum said. 'Maybe we can do dinner the night before you go then.'

'That sounds great.' I was pleased I would have an opportunity to give them the perishable food from my fridge, so it didn't go off while I was away. I would hate to see any go to waste.

Chapter 19

Beth

I spent the next few days washing and packing, finishing any work that couldn't be passed to Alannah or shelved until I got back, and worrying about whether we were doing the right thing. When I arrived at Gran's house on the morning we were due to leave, I was hoping she might provide me with some reassurance. Instead, I found her in a complete tizz. It was unnerving, to say the least; Gran was usually a pillar of calm who I relied on to coax me in off the edge. But, instead of hearing her melodic trills as I dragged my suitcase up her front path, I heard her ranting to herself.

'Gran?' I called out through the opened front door. 'Are you okay?'

'Come in here, will you,' she called as she bustled into the kitchen. 'Come and see what I've done.'

I hurried after her and found her standing over the kitchen table staring at a sodden pile of papers. Beside them, a potted cyclamen was lying on its side. Water was cascading off the edge of the table and pooling on the floor, where it was mixing with spilled potting mix. I stepped over the slurried mess and grabbed for her passport which was among the papers. Mercifully, only the cover was wet.

'Can I smell burning?' I asked.

'Oh, God!' she lunged towards the toaster and popped up a charred piece of bread.

'Are you okay, Gran?' More than just frazzled, she looked pale and a bit off kilter.

'I'm okay; I'm just a bit lightheaded. I'll be fine in a sec. The pot was slippery so I dropped the ruddy thing.' She gestured to the plant as if it should take its share of the responsibility for the mess.

'Come and sit down.' I guided her to a seat. 'I'll look after this.'

I wiped up the water while I made another piece of toast and boiled the kettle for tea. I righted the cyclamen, scooped most of the potting mix back into its pot and replaced it on the windowsill, then cleaned up the mud on the floor.

'Right,' I said as I washed my hands. 'All better. Are you okay?'

'Yes. Thanks, pet,' she said nodding.

'But are you still dizzy? Should you even be travelling today?'

Mum told me that, after freaking out we were travelling to the UK to take part in an assisted dying program, she'd pressed Gran on her health. Apparently her doctor was monitoring her blood pressure, which was a bit high. I wondered if she'd told her doctor that she was travelling to the other side of the world for a life-altering adventure filled with nervousness and exhilaration. I doubted it.

'Oh, don't worry about that. It comes on sometimes, but it's nothing,' she said dismissively. I looked her up and down for signs she was okay, or otherwise.

I set her tea down in front of her and watched as she put three heaped teaspoons of sugar in it.

'Sweet tea. My mother's cure for nerves,' she said, anticipating my reaction. I hoped her nerves would subside quickly, or she'd likely be battling diabetes as well as light-headedness before too long.

'I'm not surprised you're nervous, Gran,' I offered. 'It's a big deal.'

Gran was fiddling with her wedding band again.

I had been anxious about the trip too, and not just because it was so spur-of-the-moment. (Mum was right; I'd spent more time deliberating on what to have for dinner than I had on booking the trip.) I was worried that Gerry might not be as pleased to see Gran as Gran was to see her. Or that Gerry had changed, and Gran would be disappointed. But, most of all, I worried that Gran would get hurt again, and she'd blame me.

I tried to remind myself about how I had convinced Gran to come on the trip in the first place: we were simply a grandmother and granddaughter going on a nice holiday together. If one of us happened to meet up with someone from their past, then that was just a bonus.

I also couldn't shake the sense of discomfort I had felt since I told Mum about the trip. She was so excited at the prospect of us all travelling together. Had I been too quick to shut it down? I might have been irritated when she suggested Jarrah come too, despite her not being able to afford it, but it would be hypocritical to ignore that the only reason Gran and I were going was because I'd won the lotto. Of course I had savings, but I certainly wouldn't have been digging into them for an impromptu jaunt to the UK. And if I had given my family some of my winnings when I'd planned, Mum and Jarrah could have come as well. The guilt sat in my stomach uncomfortably, but I reminded myself that when we booked the tickets and accommodation, no one else knew about Gerry. Besides, the focus of the trip was on Gran's reunion; the last thing they needed was the entire Dwyer circus arriving to pull focus.

The car that picked us up – part of our business class ticket – was a fancy BMW that smelled like new leather and a hint of the driver's cologne, or possibly the air freshener hanging from the mirror. After insisting that he look after our suitcases, rather than have me lift them into the boot, he ran through all the mod-cons of the car and took our preferences for music selection and ambient temperature. It was the most luxurious car I'd ever sat in. The royal treatment continued when we arrived at the airport and were welcomed into the business class lounge, which provided access to delicious food and free drinks.

'I could definitely get used to this,' Gran said, as we clicked our champagne flutes and ate a selection of cheeses. Calm-looking travellers chatted away in hushed voices or tapped at keyboards, while staff poured drinks and surreptitiously cleared tables around us.

'There's even a spa here,' Gran whispered excitedly when she returned from the bathroom. 'And you should smell the hand soap.'

She held her hands to her face and breathed deeply.

I wished I'd known there were spa facilities in the lounge. As this trip had been so last-minute, there had been no time for my usual pre-holiday personal grooming regime. I always liked to ensure I was well kept before heading abroad, but things were pretty unruly 'downstairs'.

Compared to the pandemonium of the rest of the airport, the lounge felt like a utopia. When our flight was called, I steeled myself to re-enter the 'real world' and endure the chaos of the security queue. But, instead, Gran and I were guided past the long line and straight to the gate.

On board, business class was everything I'd imagined and more. Large, luxurious seats that converted into flat beds, attentive flight attendants and spacious bathrooms made the trip incredibly comfortable. I was disappointed to see all the single-use plastics in the comfort packs waiting for us on our seats, but the bamboo pyjamas were very nice and the lemon myrtle and macadamia hand cream felt amazing.

Midway through the flight, I walked to the galley to stretch my legs and found a woman from a few seats over using every available inch to perform yoga stretches. Gran and I had boarded just after her and had shared whispered speculations about her age. It was hard to pick – her face was unnaturally plumped and smoothed – but, if I'd had to guess, I'd have put her in her early forties. Her travelling companion, whom we assumed was her partner, but could have been her father, was easier to age. We put him in his seventies.

'Hi there,' she said, twisting her torso away from her bent knee. 'How's your flight so far?'

'It's great, thanks,' I replied. 'I even slept. Being able to lie down is a game-changer.'

She laughed, flashing a luminous set of pearly whites that I suspected were as fake as her boobs.

'I know, right. I can't understand why anyone would *ever* travel in economy,' she said with a flick of her diamond-ladened hand. 'It's so cramped and gross. And have you seen the state of the cabin by the end of the flight? Those people are animals.'

I assumed she was referring to the incidental rubbish created by hundreds of passengers who have been jammed in like chattel and serviced by only handful of flight attendants.

'Where are you off to?' she asked. Without pausing for the answer, she switched poses and continued. 'Hubby and I are popping over to Rome for a little vay-cay for our anniversary. He just *lurves* to spoil me. We're away for two weeks. Actually, three if you count the wellness retreat I've booked for when I get home to detox from all those Italian carbs.'

She patted her washboard-flat stomach.

'And the best part: I don't have to see his kids for two whole weeks. Hubby owns a mining company, which his kids work for, so we see them a lot. Unfortunately.' She rolled her eyes but the rest of her face remained completely still. I wondered how much money had gone into crafting her perfectly smooth forehead and angled cheekbones.

'That's how we met,' she continued, answering a question I hadn't asked. 'I used to work at the company. His kids don't really like me because of the way their parents separated.'

I knew I shouldn't make assumptions about her based on the stereotypical relationship between a moderately young attractive woman and her wealthy old male boss, but she wasn't helping. She folded her body over so her chest was on her thighs as I changed my left ankle rotations from clockwise to anticlockwise.

'I need this holiday so badly,' she continued, her voice slightly muffled as she spoke into her knees. 'I've had such a busy couple of months. We're renovating at the moment and it's been a total nightmare. We've been living in one of our other houses, so I've been back and forth each day to keep an eye on the tradies. You know what they're like.'

I did not know what she meant, and I resented being made complicit by association in whatever judgement she was making. Was this what all rich people were like? Or just the second wives of mining magnates? I had the feeling Gerry – who had come from old money and aristocracy – would be different. I hoped she was.

'I was nervous about leaving them alone for this trip,' she continued. 'Last time we went away they laid one of the marble tiles the wrong way round in one of the guest bathrooms. Hopeless. But you've got to take some time for yourself. Am I right? That's why this is our fourth overseas trip this year ...'

As she chattered about flying to Morocco to find tiles for the pool house, spending a week in Bali and travelling to Dallas to see Taylor Swift in concert, I mentally calculated how much they must have spent on airfares alone (not to mention the carbon cost to the environment). I wondered how rich you had to be for four double business class airfares to be inconsequential and how long it took to recalibrate your definition of 'expensive' when you came into wealth.

'Anyway, I'd better get back to my seat,' she said, untwisting her legs from around each other. 'Hubby will be wondering where I've got to.'

She sashayed out of the galley.

I thought back to the photos on the walls of the Lotto Head Office and the smiling faces of the major winners. I wondered if they'd adjusted to a life of international travel and Moroccan tiles. Indeed, my win had changed my life, and I was certainly enjoying some of the upgrades I had made by opening up to the idea of letting a little bit more luxury into my life – but with the exception of this one-off flight in business class, I would be happy to retreat back to my life of middle-class privilege once we were home.

Chapter 20

Beth

Despite all the comforts we had enjoyed en route, and a stopover, we were both exhausted by the time we arrived at Heathrow, 7.30am London time. Luckily, being at the pointy end of the plane meant we disembarked first.

'It's too late to turn back now,' I said to Gran as I took her carry-on luggage from her so she didn't have to carry it. I chose not to react to the distinctive clink of glass on glass, which I assumed came from the haul of complimentary little wine bottles she'd stowed away.

'What's Gerry's great-nephew's name again?' I asked as we collected our luggage off the carousel. Gerry had arranged for him to collect us from the airport. If I'd been travelling by myself, I would have insisted on taking the train or a taxi – the idea of swapping forced pleasantries with a stranger did not appeal to me, especially after a long-haul flight. But Gran looked shattered, so it was probably good that we didn't have to navigate tube lines, or the hordes of jostling tourists in the cab rank.

'Nicholas, I think,' she replied. 'Gerry said he's very tall and should stand out from the crowd. Apparently, he'll be holding a sign.'

As we approached the arrivals gate, the sounds of laughter and squealing from people reuniting with loved ones became louder. It occurred to me we were about to walk into the real-life opening scene of *Love Actually* – a movie that Jarrah and Mum insisted on watching every Christmas. I found it overly sentimental. Although I did appreciate Emma Thompson's character, who prioritised her own dignity and self-worth.

We rounded the corner as a woman dropped her backpack and leapt into the arms of a man who'd pushed through the crowd to get to her. An older woman, who had been using a walking stick, held it in one of her outstretched arms as she loped towards three waiting children holding a sign with 'Welcome Nanna' written in glitter and sequins. Two men who looked like twins embraced each other exuberantly. It was all very touching, but, annoyingly, they were all blocking the exit.

'Can you see anyone holding a sign?' I asked, craning my neck.

Gran grabbed my arm and pointed to a guy who stood a full head taller than everyone around him.

He was searching the crowd expectantly while clutching two foil helium balloons that were bobbing energetically above his head. One – a giant koala – had 'Beth' written in sharpie across its stomach, and the other – an enormous kangaroo in profile – had 'Elise' tracking up its spine. I hated kitsch, and this was next level.

'I guess that's him, then,' Gran said, waving as she made a beeline towards him.

'Nicholas?' Gran asked; the only uncertainty being his name.

'Nick, please. Nick Aitkens.'

Gran held out her right hand to shake. He smiled broadly as he extended his own right hand, which was clutching the balloon strings, towards Gran. Realising that shaking hers would mean letting go of the balloons, he offered up his pinky finger instead, which she shook with good humour.

'It's lovely to meet you, Ms Simpson,' he offered earnestly.

'Please, call me Elise,' Gran replied.

I noted that Gran didn't correct her surname; Simpson had been her maiden name.

'Elise,' he said with a satisfied nod. 'It's lovely to meet you, Elise. Aunt Gerry has been really looking forward to seeing you.'

He turned to me and shot me a grin that disarmed me. The lines that gathered around his eyes gave a genuine warmth to his face, and one of his front teeth overlapped the other just enough to give his smile character.

'You must be Beth. Welcome to London.'

He spared me the awkward handshake, but lurched clumsily towards me to take the carry-on bags I was holding. He grabbed the first in his empty hand.

'Let me help you with—'

As he tried to take the other bag from me, one of the balloon strings slipped from his grasp and Beth the Koala floated towards the soaring airport roof.

Nick's shoulders drooped as he tracked the ascent with his eyes.

'Well, that's that then,' he said, with what seemed like genuine devastation. 'He was on borrowed time, really. The guards at the security checkpoint were not happy about having him go through the x-ray machine. It was hard enough convincing them to forgo the internal cavity search.'

He shook his head solemnly. I suspected he was joking, but wondered: *could his humour really be that dry?*

'Oh, darling,' Gran said compassionately, as he tied the kangaroo string onto the handle of the bag. 'Thank you for bringing them anyway.'

She looked to me with slightly bugged eyes, as if encouraging me to second the sentiment. There was no chance; I wouldn't be entertaining any of this until I had completed my initial assessment of him. I hadn't decided whether he had a quirky sense of humour or was a complete oddball.

'Anyway,' he interrupted abruptly. 'Onwards and upwards – literally in his case.'

He looked to the koala, which had nestled into a cavity in the ceiling, again.

'I'm sure you're tired from your journey, so let's get you to your hotel.'

Gran had told me that Gerry had suggested we stay with her, but she had insisted on getting a hotel room. Understandably, she didn't want there to be any obligation or awkwardness if things didn't go well between them.

Nick's car was an electric vehicle. This was redeeming; even if he was an oddball, at least he didn't drive around the city in a fuel-guzzling four-wheel drive

As he drove, I surreptitiously sneaked a look at him. Nick seemed like the type of quintessential English gentleman who would appear as a love interest in a period piece such as *Downton Abbey* or *Pride and Prejudice*. His skin was fair, and his eyes were a light blue, which, from what Gran had told me about Gerry's, was a family trait. He had fine features, but a strong jaw, and – it had to be said again – a very nice smile. Add to that his height and slim but muscled physique, and he was an attractive package.

While en route, Nick fired questions at us about how often we'd been to London and our plans for our stay. Mercifully, Gran assumed the lion's share of small talk; it had never been my forte. He also asked weirdly specific questions about the climate at home.

'What do you do?' I asked from the back seat after he asked about whether we'd observed an increase in coastal inundation on the west coast.

'I'm a meteorologist,' he replied.

'Oh, how interesting,' Gran said enthusiastically.

'To us Brits, maybe. Do you know, there was a study done a few years back that found that 94 per cent of Brits had discussed the weather in the past six hours?' he said rhetorically. 'Mainly about how awful it is. I worked as a forecaster while I finished my PhD, and it got a bit monotonous telling people it was going to rain day after day.'

I thought back to my last visit to London when unexpected and intense downpours punctuated many of the days. I had indeed cursed the forecasters for not providing more accurate predictions.

'Even my friends and family trolled me every time it rained unexpectedly,' he said dryly. I looked to the rear-view mirror in time to catch him winking at me. 'And then you add climate change into the mix and the grim forecasts for what our planet is going to look like fifty years from now ...' his tone had changed, indicating he felt the burden of responsibility shared by many of our generation.

'So you're no longer a forecaster?' I asked.

'Not anymore,' he responded. 'Now I'm at a private company where I do climate modelling and analysis to inform wind- and solar-power projects.'

'That sounds wonderful. Beth works in environmental management for a local council,' Gran said, a little too enthusiastically.

Nick looked at me through the rear-view mirror again. A gathering of crow's feet at the corner of his eyes indicated he was smiling as if somehow this was good news. 'Really?' he prompted. 'That's great.'

As Nick navigated the heavy traffic, narrow London roads and hordes of bikes and pedestrians, I told him about my local council area and some of the projects I was involved in. He was particularly interested in the possum bridge and asked loads of questions. At first I was worried that I was boring him with unnecessary detail, but he continued to prompt me, as if genuinely interested. Despite being utterly exhausted, I found him easy to chat to.

We were mid-discussion about the difference between English and Australian magpies when Gran issued a loud, guttural snort from her position in the front seat. It startled us both, and caused Nick to swerve out of his lane. He corrected the car and waved to the driver beside us who had responded to our unexpected deviation with a long honk.

Gran mumbled and masticated for a few moments before settling back to sleep and a rhythm of soft snores.

'Good grief,' Nick whispered sharply. 'That was a big noise to come out of a tiny person.'

Gran's snoring was legendary. I remember staying at her house as a child and being woken by what sounded like a wild boar. As I crept out of bed and down the corridor towards her room looking for comfort, I discovered she was the one making all the noise.

'She's definitely greater than her size,' I replied. 'In all respects.'

'It sounds like she's been carrying a lot of baggage for her tiny frame too,' he offered insightfully. 'From what Aunt Gerry has hinted at.'

'Yes,' I replied, my eyes connecting with his again in the rear-view mirror. 'You're not wrong.'

'Have you two always been close?' Nick asked, gesturing with his head towards Gran.

Explaining the nature of our relationship required me to describe the rest of my family for context. But I didn't feel like explaining that I was the boring, awkward Dwyer and Gran was the only person in the world who'd ever seemed to get me.

'Yes,' I replied, without further elaboration.

'You're lucky,' he said earnestly. 'My grandmother died young; before I was born. Aunt Gerry became a kind of surrogate mother to my mum, and a grandmother of sorts to my sister and me. Having a family of her own was never really ...' he hesitated as if searching for the correct word ... '*available* to Aunt Gerry. So our relationship means the world to all of us. And she's terrific. I know you'll love her. But I'm sure Elise has already told you that.'

He took his eyes off the road to smile at me again in the mirror.

'We're nearly at the hotel,' Nick said, turning down a lovely street with a long, walled park. 'Once we've got you settled, I'll leave you to rest and head off to work. Then, Aunt Gerry is hoping to meet up with your gran for dinner. Did you fancy getting a pint and leaving them to it? There's a great little pub a couple of doors up from where you're staying. I can meet you there after I've dropped Aunt Gerry off, so they can reunite without us hanging about.'

I was exhausted and had planned to spend the evening unpacking and realigning my body clock with an early night. And the in-flight magazine I read on the plane advised that drinking alcohol exacerbated the impact of jet lag.

However, as I glanced in the rear-view mirror just in time to catch his gaze I was surprised to hear myself say, 'That sounds great.'

Before I could correct myself, we pulled up in front of a quintessentially London white-terraced building.

'Here we are,' he announced loudly.

Gran responded with a snuffle and groan.

Nick tapped at the screen to turn off the car, and I put my hand on Gran's shoulder and gently squeezed it.

'Gran,' I said quietly, not wanting to startle her. 'We're here.'

She turned around to face me, blinking her bleary, bloodshot eyes as she tried to find focus.

'Here?' she asked, confused. 'Where?'

'We've arrived at our hotel.'

'Oh, God,' she exclaimed urgently. 'Is Gerry here?'

'No,' I laughed. 'She'll be here later tonight.'

'Thank goodness,' she said, rubbing her eyes vigorously. 'Can you imagine? The first time I've seen her in six decades, and I've got sleep in my eyes and my hair is a mess. No amount of that lovely airline hibiscus face mist could stop me looking like something a cat has coughed up.'

I decided not to tell her about the drool that glistened like a snail's track between her mouth and chin.

Nick removed our luggage from the car, an operation made infinitely more precarious by the giant kangaroo balloon, which had spent the journey looping itself around the back headrest. After he'd disentangled the kangaroo, he wheeled our luggage across the narrow footpath and into the hotel lobby.

The lobby area was decorated with blood-red carpet, heavy velvet curtains and wallpaper in dark maroon, and glistening timber panelling around, on and behind the reception desk. It reminded me of a museum exhibition I'd been to as a kid, where you stepped into a giant womb to experience what it was like in utero. A brown leather chesterfield armchair sat in the corner, and a stuffy-looking aristocrat stared down pompously from a large, gilded frame mounted on the wall.

We checked in with the assistance of a helpful receptionist who used a map to point out to us where we would find the best coffee and some must-see landmarks nearby.

'Here, Nick,' Gran said, fishing around in her handbag before victoriously producing her wallet. 'Let me give you some money for petrol or tolls or whatever.'

'Absolutely not,' he responded with a laugh and a dismissive, but not unkind, wave of his hand. 'I wouldn't dream of it. It was my pleasure.'

'Are you sure?' Gran asked. She must have been weary from the flight or she wouldn't have taken no for an answer; she was staunchly independent when it came to paying her way. 'Well, thank you, Nick. We really appreciated it.'

'I'll see you later tonight,' he said, giving me a wink as he made his way to the door. I sensed Gran's gaze on me as if searching for a reaction.

Ordinarily, I despised winkers. I tarred them with the same brush I reserved for people who assigned unnecessary nicknames, or punctuated their statements with a double finger-gun action. Mr Raven – my high school PE teacher – had embraced the trifecta with gusto. Each lesson, he'd wink and give double finger-guns while calling people 'partner', 'big guy' or 'champion'. This had done nothing to improve my enthusiasm for running and team sports, but it did provide some inspiration during boxing and archery.

But there was something a bit endearing about Nick's winks. They seemed genuinely jovial, rather than pretentious. And they were subtle: unless they were directed at you, you wouldn't even spot them. However, since he'd done it twice in the short time I'd known him, I couldn't rule out that he had an ocular disorder or involuntary tic.

~

We made our way along the narrow corridor to the tiny lift and then through another passage to our room. Gran opened the door to a tastefully decorated suite with cream-coloured carpet, heavy chocolate-coloured drapes and two double beds covered in crisp white linen, separated by a bedside table. A chandelier hung from the ceiling, and ornate sconces were mounted above each bed. I stuck my head into the bathroom, which was adorned with marble and contained a bath, shower, sink and toilet. The room was large by normal standards; by London standards, it was palatial.

The last time I was in London, I stayed in a hotel room with a bathroom that was so tiny you could shower, go to the toilet and brush your teeth in the sink all at the same time. The bedroom had been about 30 centimetres wider than the bed on each side, which left almost no space to walk around the room, let alone stow any luggage. I had to sleep with my suitcase at the foot of the bed.

But that tiny room was a vast improvement on the accommodation I'd endured on my first visit to the UK. A repulsive, overpriced backpackers' lodge with a shared unisex bathroom had proved to me that despite his poor aim and lack of consideration for bathroom etiquette, Elijah was far from being the grossest male in the world.

'Not bad at all,' Gran said, the corners of her mouth lifting to a smirk.

'It's gorgeous,' I said, walking over to the compendium of hotel information neatly arranged on a small table. I liked to familiarise myself with the hotel's facilities and amenities, and the necessary emergency procedures, as soon as I arrived anywhere.

For the next few hours, we dozed and read. After an intense few weeks, it was nice to feel like I was on a holiday.

At lunchtime, we wandered down the street in search of something to eat and settled on an outside table at a cafe that had Union Jack bunting in its window.

'So,' I began after the waiter delivered two bowls of steaming pumpkin soup and thick crusty bread to our table. 'How are you feeling about tonight?'

'What's happening tonight?' she joked, adjusting the paper serviette that was flapping in her lap from the breeze created by a red double-decker bus that whooshed past.

I rolled my eyes in jest.

'Oh, love,' she said laughing. 'I think I'm feeling every emotion on the spectrum. I'm excited and nervous and happy and grateful.'

'But, to be honest,' she paused to dunk her bread in the soup, 'I'm a bit pissed off too.'

'Why?' I asked, taken aback by her suddenly sharp tone.

The waiter appeared from nowhere.

'Is everything okay with the food?' he asked, his eyes wide with concern.

'Oh sorry,' I said apologetically. 'Yes, everything is great.'

I deposited a large spoonful of soup into my mouth to reassure him, but the scalding liquid burnt my tongue and irritated the back of my throat. I coughed and spluttered, which did little to appease his concerns.

'Everything is wonderful, darling. Thank you,' Gran said.

The waiter bowed his head and scurried away.

'I'm pissed off,' she said in a hushed whisper this time, 'because it's taken this long. All those years of wondering and wishing.'

I searched for something reassuring to say, or practical to offer. I wanted to say that Gran and Gerry had been at the mercy of time and circumstance, and the distance between them for all these years had been greater than just the oceans that separated their homes. But I didn't trust I could speak without bringing on another coughing fit. So I just nodded.

Chapter 21

Elise

There was a soft knock on the bathroom door.

'I'm going to head off shortly, Gran,' Beth called out.

'Hang on, pet,' Elise replied. 'Just give me a jiffy.'

Elise had one last glance in the mirror. The concentration involved in applying eye and skin make-up for the first time in years had offered her a brief reprieve from her nerves. She rarely wore make-up, save for some lipstick and pressed powder for special occasions, but, before leaving Perth, Elise had ventured to her local department store, where a cosmetologist whose eyelashes reminded Elise of hairy spiders had helped her to upgrade her make-up products to some made this century. (The cosmetologist had also encouraged her to visit the waxing booth to take care of the rogue facial hair, which, until then, Elise hadn't been aware she had.)

Elise had replicated the cosmetologist's application of some BB cream, three tints of eye shadow applied on different areas of her lids, mascara, and a plumping lip-gloss that tingled her lips. She hoped her efforts would lessen the shocking contrast between the last time Gerry had seen her and how she looked now. The rest, she thought, would rely on Gerry's hopefully failing eyesight.

Elise opened the bathroom door and looked to Beth expectantly.

'Gran!' she exclaimed as she stood up from the small table with such haste that the chair rocked behind her. 'You look unbelievable.'

'Is it okay?' Elise asked, suddenly self-conscious that she was overdressed. She smoothed her new black pants, which she had paired with new boots and a charcoal velveteen jacket. 'I haven't got this dressed up to see an Englishwoman since the 1960s when I went into the city to see Queen Elizabeth and Prince Philip. "I did but see her passing by, and yet I'll love her till I die," she added, reciting a Thomas Ford poem, quoted by Sir Robert Menzies.

'It turns out Her Royal Highness wasn't the only Englishwoman you'd love until you die,' Beth added with a dry smile. 'You look amazing. Your clothes, and your face … everything looks great.'

Beth leaned in and kissed Elise on the cheek, careful not to smudge anything.

'Unless there's anything else you need from me, I'll get going and leave you to it.'

Elise looked at her watch. It was 6.45, fifteen minutes until she was due to meet Gerry in the lobby. The butterflies in her stomach were waking from their slumber.

'I'm fine. You go and enjoy yourself. Give my best wishes to Nick.'

'I will,' Beth replied, hurriedly moving towards the door. When she turned back, Elise noticed her eyes glistened with tears. Seeing Beth so sentimental did nothing to alleviate her nerves.

'I'm so happy for you, Gran,' she said. 'I imagine nothing about this has been easy, but I really admire you for … well, for everything.'

Elise marvelled that sixty years ago her family would have disowned her if they knew she was in love with Gerry. But now she was earning her granddaughter's admiration for travelling across the world to see her.

'Thank you, love,' Elise said, shooing her out the door. 'Now get out of here. I have far too much make-up on to get misty-eyed. It took me half an hour to get my eyeshadow to look symmetrical.'

~

As Elise descended to the lobby in the lift, she felt lightheaded again.

'Not now,' she muttered to herself as she put her hand to the lift wall to steady herself. The feeling passed after a few moments, but it reminded her that, with the different time zones and long-haul flight, she hadn't taken her blood pressure medication. She took the blister pack from her handbag and swallowed the pill dry.

As the lift dinged to indicate she'd reached the ground floor, the butterflies resumed their frenzied flapping inside her belly.

Despite having seen Gerry's photo on the internet, she was worried she wouldn't recognise her. And Gerry had no way of knowing what Elise looked like now. *What if I approached the wrong person?* She wondered. It occurred to her they should have arranged to each carry a rose, or a copy of *Wuthering Heights* perhaps.

But she needn't have worried.

As she rounded into the foyer, she spotted Gerry immediately. She was sitting on one of the plush armchairs with an upright elegance; her knees were together and feet to one side. Elise wasn't wearing her glasses, and the lines on Gerry's face were smoothed, so she looked just like when Elise had last seen her.

Gerry looked up and smiled in instant recognition.

'Elise,' she said, rising out of the chair with an ease that couldn't be assumed in a woman of her age. 'It's so good to see you.'

Elise willed her legs to work, but they felt like they were filled with cement. She had travelled halfway across the world, but the ten or so steps needed to reach Gerry felt like the greatest part of the journey.

Gerry approached her and placed a hand on either side of Elise's upper arms. Her grip was warm and firm – confident and reassuring, just like it had always been.

'Oh, Gerry,' Elise said in a whispered gasp as she leaned into her embrace.

Gerry felt bonier than Elise remembered, and her scent, while lovely, was unfamiliar. But Elise felt a familiar tingle down her spine. She'd felt it the first night they were together and every time she touched her afterwards.

The tears that had gathered in Elise's eyes spilled down her cheeks. She pulled backwards and sniffed into her hand.

'Urgh, God. Sorry. What a mess. My face is leaking.'

She rummaged around in her jacket pockets for a tissue but, as it was new, she hadn't stashed any away.

'Aha!' Gerry exclaimed triumphantly, reaching into her handbag. 'Allow me.'

She produced a small folded handkerchief with dainty scalloped lace edges.

'Oh my goodness,' Elise exclaimed, taking the handkerchief and inspecting the tiny coloured stitches that she had shaped into a Gouldian finch in the corner of the hankie sixty years ago. It was dotted with small splotches of discolouration, which betrayed its age, and the fabric had worn slightly in the folds.

She turned the hankie over in her hand. The backside was as neat as the front; her mother would have been proud of her needlework – if she could have looked past the fact it was a gift for her female lover.

'I can't believe you kept it,' Elise exclaimed. 'I had completely forgotten about this until now.'

'Of course I kept it. I've treasured it since you gave it to me. They'll have to pry this out of my cold dead hand.'

Elise pointed to the Gouldian finch brooch on her lapel, which she'd retrieved from the box on the day she spoke to Gerry.

Gerry inhaled sharply and leaned in to examine the brooch more carefully. 'Well, I never,' she said softly. 'Aren't we just a pair of old hoarders,' she said after she released the brooch and took a step back. Elise dabbed her face lightly with the hankie, hopeful that her long-life make-up would live up to its promise of staying put.

'Right then,' Gerry said, clapping her hands together in the same way she did at uni when there was a decision to be made or a plan to be devised. Back then, she had been a natural-born leader, who attracted people to follow her with her confidence and charisma. It seemed little had changed.

'We've got a few options. Number one: we can stay here playing show and tell all night; it could be fun, but we'll probably get hungry. Number two: we can head to a little French place around the corner, which has sensational food and authentically arrogant waitstaff. Or, number three: we can head back to my place, where I can cook for you.'

'You? Cook?' Elise asked incredulously. The English rose she knew in university had spent her formative years being served by a household of staff and had struggled to boil water in the college common room.

Gerry nodded enthusiastically.

'You should see me now,' she said, her eyes wide with the same enthusiasm Elise recognised from the vivacious, vital young woman she'd fallen in love with. 'I'm a whiz in the kitchen.'

Elise chuckled. 'This I have to see.'

'Good,' she replied, with a ceremonial nod of her head. 'My place is a short walk from here. If you're up to it, of course.' She surveyed Elise's legs for signs of functionality.

'A walk sounds lovely,' Elise said, extending and retracting her right foot and then her left, as though performing the hokey-pokey. 'They've got a few miles left in them still, I think. Besides, if I remember correctly, you're more than capable of piggybacking me if I get into a bind.'

Gerry tilted her head, as if searching for the reference, and then smiled broadly. She remembered too.

It had been a hot summer's day when they took a bus from the city to a national park to tour its cave system, which promised cooler temperatures than above ground. The water that oozed through the cave ceiling funnelled down long pointed stalactites, or fell to the tops of knobbly, waxy-looking stalagmites. Each drop contributed to a dynamic gallery of shapes and forms. And each drop contributed to the ground being extremely slippery. About 30 metres into the cave, Elise slipped and badly twisted her knee. Gerry rushed to her aid but slipped in the same spot. Unhurt, but covered in mud, Gerry had piggybacked Elise out of the cave and back to the bus. They had laughed the entire way there.

'I'm afraid my days of rescuing people out of ancient subterranean karst systems are well and truly behind me,' Gerry said. 'But I can whistle a taxi like a champion, if need be.'

'My God, Gerry,' Elise said, taking in her features, her gestures and her mannerisms. 'You haven't changed a bloody bit.'

'Neither have you,' she said, linking her arm in Elise's. 'And I'm so glad.'

~

Elise and Gerry walked arm in arm through the streets of Kensington, which served as much as a gesture of affection as it did a way of safely navigating London's uneven pavement. They arrived at a small street opposite Kensington Gardens and stopped in front of another charming white London terrace.

'Here we are,' Gerry announced.

'It's lovely, Gerry. It would be such a shame to burn it down with your cooking. Are you sure you don't want to eat out?'

She tutted. 'Come now.'

Gerry welcomed Elise into a lovely foyer decorated with a large chandelier and black-and-white marble chequered floor tiles.

Elise caught her reflection in the large, ornate Venetian mirror hanging on the wall. Even without her glasses, she could make out large, dark smudges under her eyes.

'Bloody hell,' she shrieked, wiping her eyes self-consciously. 'Why didn't you tell me I looked like a panda?'

'You look beautiful,' Gerry said earnestly, her eyes tracing the features of Elise's face. 'Just like the day I met you.'

'Jesus, Gerry,' Elise guffawed. 'I hope not! That doesn't say a lot about how I looked back then.'

'No, you dill,' she chuckled. 'I just meant—'

'I know, I know,' Elise said, taking Gerry's extended hand. She was comforted that Gerry's hands were as lined and gnarly as her own. She wasn't the only one who had changed. 'I was so nervous about what you'd think of the way I look now.'

Gerry tutted again.

'I mean, women our age get used to being invisible; it comes with the territory. Actually, I've come to like being able to manoeuvre through life without anyone paying any attention to me. And nor should they; youth is much more interesting. So it's been a bit confronting to imagine what you'd think of me now. But, after all these years, even with our wrinkly casing, we're still the same people at heart, aren't we? Even if part of me has been dormant for the past six decades.'

Gerry smiled.

'To be honest,' Elise continued, 'I wasn't sure the person you knew all those years ago still existed until a few weeks back.'

'Well, come on then,' Gerry said warmly. 'Let's make the most of getting to know her again.'

~

Elise was genuinely impressed by Gerry's bacon, egg and beans fry-up and told her so.

'I know,' Gerry replied, dabbing her mouth with a crisp white napkin and placing it delicately on the beautifully polished timber table. 'It's a gift.'

Gerry sat at the end of the table, and Elise was to her right. They were on high-backed velvet chairs opposite two long, thickly draped windows that overlooked the street. A magnificent portrait of a brunette woman with rosy cheeks wearing an ornate necklace and holding a fan hung over the mantle. The painting shimmered with accents of gold leaf. It reminded Elise of a Gustav Klimt painting, and she knew better than to assume it wasn't; Gerry's family were lovers of fine art and certainly had the means to acquire it.

Gerry rose from her seat. 'Fancy some tea?' she asked, gathering up the dishes from the table.

'Please,' Elise said, nodding. While she waited for Gerry to return, she looked at the photos on Gerry's sideboard and baulked at the snap of Gerry smiling alongside Princess Margaret on a tennis court, and the one where her arm was draped over a young Billy Connelly's shoulder. Elise imagined Paul McCartney telling Gerry and his wife Linda to say 'cheese' when she landed on a photo of them smiling up at the camera from their deck chairs on a beach.

As she scanned the collection of pictures, Elise felt a sting of sadness for all the years she had missed with her. Although she knew it was irrational, she felt jealous of the men and women in the photos who were captured celebrating special occasions or sharing a happy time with Gerry. She was particularly jealous of Princess Margaret; Elise had always admired her collection of sunglasses.

Gerry reappeared from the kitchen, set the cups of tea down and sidled up to Elise.

'Remember this one?' She lifted up a black-and-white photo in a slightly tarnished silver frame and held it for Elise to see.

Elise recognised it immediately. The photo had sat on Gerry's bedside table at college, but was often placed face down or turned around when one of them – usually Elise – became uncomfortable with an audience to their lovemaking.

The photo depicted Gerry and her sister standing behind their seated parents. As per the style of the time, their expressions were serious, sombre even, but there was a sparkle in Gerry's eye that transcended the picture's monochromatic tones and hinted at her warmth and sense of humour. It was like she was sharing a private joke with the viewer.

'Feels like a million years ago now,' Gerry said, placing it back on the sideboard. Elise wasn't sure if she was referring to the time since the photo was taken, or since when Elise would have last seen it.

'Come on,' Gerry said, gesturing through the door to the loungeroom and picking up the cups of tea. 'Let's sit.'

They sat side by side on a large plush cream sofa decorated with plump pale-blue cushions. The cushions had a gold detailing that matched two resplendent gold club chairs to their right. Gerry cupped Elise's hands in her own.

'I'm so glad you're here,' she said, her eyes locked on their united hands. 'But ...' Her voice trailed off.

Elise held her breath in anticipation of what might come next.

'I know it was a long time ago,' Gerry said, 'but I'll kick myself later if I don't address the elephant in the room.'

The wings of the butterflies that had been lying quietly in Elise's stomach since they'd left the hotel began rousing.

'Why didn't you write?' Gerry asked finally. Firmly.

Elise instinctively let go of her hand. 'Why didn't *I* write? I did! I wrote every second day for weeks, and then every week for months. Until I finally gave up.'

Gerry stared at Elise, her eyes wide.

'It was *you* who didn't write,' Elise continued. Her tone was a little more shrill than she intended.

'Elise,' Gerry said in a low, slow tone that Elise recognised from the few occasions they had exchanged cross words in college. 'That is simply not true. I wrote to you even before I left the country. I wrote you a letter and gave it to Miss What's-her-name, the house mistress, to give to you after I left. Then I wrote week in and week out, but you never replied. I assumed you'd received them; they were never returned to me.' Her words began to speed up, tumbling out of her. 'I thought you'd had a change of heart; that you couldn't see a future with me. Then, when I read in the university alumni magazine that you'd got married, I assumed you'd chosen a path for your life that could never involve me.'

Gerry shifted ever so slightly away from Elise, who immediately felt like a chasm had opened between them. If Gerry had written, why hadn't she received her letters?

'I even phoned you a couple of times.' Gerry's voice was high and breathless. 'But the house mistress told me you were out. I didn't know if you were, or whether that was what you'd told her to say.'

Elise sat with her mouth agape. Why hadn't she known that Gerry had called? Rapidly, the pieces of the puzzle fell into place.

'Miss Turniss,' Elise said finally, with a hiss. 'The house mistress's name was Miss Turniss. But we called her Miss Too-Priss because she was a stuck-up old cow. Remember? And she didn't give me anything from you.'

'But, I ... But, she ...' Gerry started. As she sat back against the sofa, Elise saw her expression change. The penny had dropped for her too.

'That bitch,' Gerry said viciously. 'She promised she would give you the letter after I left. But she didn't. And then, what? She must have intercepted my letters and lied to me about you being out when I called.

'But that doesn't explain why I didn't get any letters from you,' she continued.

'Of course it does,' Elise replied. A wave of anger rose within her like

147

volcanic lava. 'How do you think I posted them?'

Gerry closed her eyes. 'You put them in the tray outside her office to be sent.'

Elise nodded.

They sat motionless, processing the gravity of what they had learned. 'Do you think she knew about us?' Gerry asked, wringing her hands.

'I guess she must have. Why else would she have done that?'

Elise felt dread in the pit of her stomach as she imagined Miss Too-Priss reading her letters. It was the same feeling that had perverted her feelings for Gerry all those years ago – an ugly mixture of shame, embarrassment and guilt. She had spelled out her innermost feelings across the pages of those letters, which she had decorated with doodles of flowers and birds. Miss Too-Priss was such a nauseatingly pious woman; she must have been outraged to discover the true nature of their relationship.

'That fucking bitch,' Gerry said, her shoulders slumping. 'All these years, I thought ...' Gerry's sorrow-filled words melded into a deep sigh.

'I know,' Elise replied, taking Gerry's hand again. 'Me too.'

Gerry's face contorted as her brow furrowed and her eyes squinted and filled with tears.

'I'm sorry,' she blurted, tears spilling down her face. 'I'm just so angry, and sad, and relieved and—'

She stood up abruptly, disappearing into the other room, and reappeared a moment later with a box of tissues encased in a decoupage box that she placed on the coffee table in front of them.

'The thing is ...' Her voice cracked and she paused before continuing. 'You were my first love. Our relationship shaped all the ones I've had since. Before I met you, I knew I was a lesbian; I knew I wasn't attracted to men. This terrified me because I didn't know what it meant for my life; for my future.' She blew her nose and continued. 'When we met, I found that I could be happy. It mightn't have looked like what I was told it should be – marriage to a man and a gaggle of children. But I knew happiness with you.' She dabbed at her eyes. 'After I left Australia and I didn't hear from you, I didn't think I'd ever be that happy again.'

'Oh, Gerry,' Elise muttered through the apple-sized lump in her throat.

'At the time, I thought that my love was unrequited,' Gerry continued, 'or that I was being punished for my ungodly attractions. I held onto that feeling for years. I spent ages not being able to fully give myself over to love, in fear that it would be taken away from me again.'

Elise searched for something to say. 'I'm sorry, Gerry,' she offered in lieu of anything more poignant. 'I'm so sorry.'

'I mean, I have loved,' Gerry said, her tone lightening a touch. 'Just not with the gay abandon that I had when I handed my heart over to you.'

They both chuckled at her pun. Gerry's expression softened again.

'Lord, when I think of the number of times I asked Miss Too-Priss whether there was any mail for me ...' Elise started. 'And all the while, she was keeping it from me. Keeping *you* from me.' Elise felt a fresh flush of fury rise inside her. 'Who did she think she was?' she spat, allowing her anger a voice.

'You know, one thing I've learned over the years is that when people think they've got "right" on their side,' Gerry said, making air quotes with her fingers, 'they're capable of doing just about anything.'

Silence settled between them.

'Honestly, I didn't know what was right or wrong after you left,' Elise said finally. 'I was so certain about my feelings for you. I loved you wholly. Completely.'

Gerry reached for her hand again.

'But it wasn't because you were a woman, or even in spite of you being a woman. It was because you were you. Does that make sense?'

Gerry nodded.

'After you left, I felt like part of me had died. It *did* die. And then I met John, which confused me even more. I didn't know at the time about bisexuality. I grew to love him, and I enjoyed being with him. He was kind and generous, and was always looking for ways to make our lives better. He was completely supportive of my career, and championed me to keep working where other husbands might have wanted to pigeonhole me as a housewife. And he was a wonderful, kind father and doting grandfather ...'

Elise trailed off, becoming self-conscious talking about John with such affection, but Gerry was nodding supportively.

'I just don't want you to think I chose the "easy" route by marrying John.'

Gerry smiled warmly. 'I would never assume anything.'

'We had a good life,' Elise continued. 'But that doesn't detract from what I felt ... what I feel for you.'

'Of course, it doesn't. I know what we had. I was there too, remember. You don't have to convince me of anything.' She smiled nostalgically.

'I used to dream of you, you know?' Elise said. Gerry's eyebrows slid up her forehead. 'Yep. On and off for years. Sometimes you'd come back and tell me through sobs and kisses that there had been a big misunderstanding. We would exchange promises that we'd never be apart again, and run off into the sunset like in the movies. Other nights, you would taunt and tease me, and tell me that you'd never loved me at all.'

'I'm sorry Dream Me was such a bitch,' Gerry joked. 'If it makes you feel any better, a couple of times I thought I saw you.'

'Really?' Elise asked.

'One time I was so convinced it was you that I followed someone two blocks before I caught up with her. It wasn't, of course. But I hoped.'

They both sat back on the sofa as silence hung between them. It felt right to spend a few moments allowing some of the dust to settle.

'That Too-Priss cow,' Gerry said, shaking her head slowly. 'I know we can't dwell on what might have been ... but it would have saved a lot of heartache knowing what had actually happened.'

The clock on the mantle chimed to indicate the hour.

'Will you stay?' Gerry asked as she placed her hand on the side of Elise's face.

Before Elise knew it, their lips were touching and the tingle along her spine had returned.

Chapter 22

Beth

'What do you make of all of this?' Nick asked, before taking a sip of his pint. 'Your gran and Aunt Gerry, I mean,' he added by way of unnecessary clarification.

'Well,' I started, piling the beer coasters into a satisfyingly neat stack in front of me. 'It's a lot, I guess.'

We were sitting at a small wooden table by the window of a tiny pub on the street corner near the hotel. The floor, tables, chairs, bar and roof beams were dark timber, and the smell of furniture polish was valiantly competing with the smell of beer and stale cigarettes, the latter despite the 'No Smoking' signs dotted everywhere. A portrait of a jowly boxer dog dressed in full military regalia hung in a gilded frame over a fireplace with a crackling fire.

'I had always thought my grandparents were happily married. It shouldn't have come as a shock that they had relationships before they met each other, I suppose. But it was a bit of a surprise to learn that Gran's first love – Gerry – was a Geraldine and not a Gerald.'

'I'll bet,' Nick said with a soft chuckle.

He was using his middle finger to trace the patterns of the wooden table top. They were nice hands – strong yet elegant. His long fingers were tipped with admirably tidy nails.

'Also, I feel sad they had to hide their relationship from the world, and that Gran suffered her heartbreak alone,' I continued.

'I think women like your gran and Gerry got pretty good at holding their secrets close to their chest,' he replied.

A series of high-pitched squeals pierced the air like an alarm. A twenty-something woman wearing a short black dress and impossibly tall high heels toddled through the doorway and towards two similarly clad women standing at the bar.

'So, tell me more about yourself,' Nick said, seemingly oblivious to the commotion. He didn't even flinch when the barman tripped and smashed a glass in his haste to serve the women. 'What do you do when you're not helping your gran rediscover romances of yesteryear, or working to save possums?'

'Well,' I began, scrambling for anything that would be interesting enough to share. I doubted he would be impressed by my fastidious domestic regimen or my impressive discipline for regular dental check-ups and timely tax returns.

'I run. I read. I enjoy hiking. And I volunteer with Gran on her flora translocation projects whenever I can. I spend as much time as I can in the bush, really.'

'I would love to visit Australia one day,' Nick said. 'I've travelled quite a bit, but my ex-girlfriend never wanted to go. She was terrified of snakes and was convinced the place was overrun with them. But I've always wanted to see the outback and spend time exploring the coasts,' he continued wistfully. 'As a kid I had a guidebook of Australia's "big" attractions. I loved that book, and used to spend hours looking at pictures of the Big Pineapple, the Big Prawn and the Big Merino, planning a fantasy road trip to visit them all. From memory, there was even a Giant Earthworm that you could visit.'

I didn't have the heart to tell him that the Giant Earthworm had closed down.

'I guess I liked the idea of a place that was naturally good-looking but with a sense of humour. A bit like the Australians who live there.'

I assumed he meant Margot Robbie or the Hemsworth brothers but the corner of his mouth slid up to create a decidedly endearing lopsided grin, which made me think he meant something else.

'Hopefully I'll get there one day, and maybe you can show me around.'

'I'd love to,' I said, instantly regretting using a phrase that made me sound like a Disney princess accepting an offer from a prince to dance. I cleared my throat awkwardly. 'I mean, yes. No worries. Of course I will. There's loads to do. We have normal-sized things to see as well.'

He smiled eagerly. 'I'd love to take a selfie with one of those friendly looking fellows that I see all over Instagram too ... a quacka?'

'A quokka,' I corrected.

'Ah, of course!' he said, slapping his palm to his head like a character in an old slapstick movie. He drained the rest of his beer. 'What about travel, Beth?' he asked. 'Apart from this trip, do you have travel plans in your future?'

'Well, actually,' I began, 'I do. But let me get another round first.'

Nick had bought the first round, and I was determined to buy the second, even though my glass was still half full, or half empty, depending on your perspective. It was nice enough of him to take me out; I didn't want him to feel like he was burdened by the bill too. And, while I wasn't planning on spending with reckless abandon, thanks to my lotto win, buying a beer or two didn't require me to recalibrate my entire holiday budget.

'Thanks,' Nick said, as I returned to the table and placed the drink in front of him. 'So. Travel. Any exotic destinations on the cards?'

'Well. Maybe,' I started pensively. 'I've had some ... unexpected changes to my circumstances recently.'

His right eyebrow raised slightly as his body inched towards me. 'Go on,' he encouraged.

I thought about the brochure that Amarita the lotto win concierge had given me that warned against telling people about my lotto win. It was true that I couldn't be sure Nick wouldn't use this information to rip me off. But Gran had told me Nick and his family had 'come from money', so it seemed unlikely he had a habit of befriending Australian tourists in the hopes they had recently struck gold. Also, I wasn't sure if it was the jetlag, or the beer, but I felt a keenness to share the news with him. Apart from Gran, I hadn't told a soul.

Nick listened intently as I told him about the lotto win, how I'd asked Gran if she wished she'd seen or done anything, and that I'd googled Gerry's name.

'I see,' he said, rubbing his hand over his cleanly shaven chin. 'I wondered what had made Elise search for Aunt Gerry after all these years. I thought she might have been fulfilling a dying wish or ticking off her bucket list. So what else have you got planned for your winnings, then? Are you going to use it to solve other mysteries? I think they're still trying to work out who Jack the Ripper was. And I don't think they've found the Hanging Gardens of Babylon yet. Maybe you could hunt down Tupac, if he's still alive, and insist he make another album?'

'I don't think so,' I laughed. 'So far I've bought a new car and a new pair of shoes.'

I didn't feel it was necessary to share the details of my new underwear with him.

'They sound like good, solid investments,' he said with mock seriousness. 'Good for you.'

'I'll give some to charity, but I'm keen to do some more research when I get home to help inform who I'll support. And I plan to give some to my family too. I just haven't settled on the amount yet.' I drank from my beer. 'They don't actually know about the win yet.'

Hearing myself say it out loud made me feel self-conscious that I was telling a near-stranger about the biggest thing to happen to me before I'd told my family, even though they'd made it impossible.

'Really?' he asked, his eyebrows raised.

'It's a bit of a long story.' I said, hoping that would be enough to allow me to change the topic.

He raised his eyebrows further as if encouraging me to go on.

'I wanted to make it a surprise,' I said in a feeble attempt to provide a response that would satisfy any need for further discussion.

He nodded and smiled again. 'But aren't you going to spend it on something *you've* always wanted to do? It seems like you've done a good job fulfilling your gran's lifelong dream of connecting with Aunt Gerry; have you given any thought to what yours might be?'

He made a gesture with his hands like a game show host presenting a cache of prizes and gave me a grin. 'The world is your oyster, Beth.'

'Not "oyster",' I said. 'I didn't win that much. More like a slightly less glamorous member of the mollusc family. A snail, perhaps?'

He laughed. 'Let me guess – you're the type of person who goes with the flow and just lets fate determine where you're headed?' he asked.

I tried to resist the urge to roll my eyes. But muscle memory, combined with jetlag, and the beer, meant a little roll slipped in anyway.

'What? You don't believe in fate?' Nick asked with a smirk. 'But how else do you explain your lotto win? Of all the numbers you could have had, of all the balls that could have been drawn, you picked the winners.'

'Urgh,' I groaned, 'you sound like my sister, Jarrah.'

'I take it that's not necessarily a good thing,' he replied.

'She's ...' I searched for a succinct way to describe Jarrah and all her foibles, 'a lot. We're very, very different. Are you close with your sister?' I remembered that he mentioned her in the car and was keen to steer the conversation away from my own family.

'I am,' he replied. 'Although I don't see as much of her as I'd like. She's married with a couple of kids, and they live up north.'

The pub filled and then emptied around us as we ate dinner; talked about our respective jobs; disclosed our tastes in music, books and movies; and compared our mutual dislike for karaoke.

'Last drinks, folks.'

The bartender's announcement was met with booing from a rowdy group of soccer fans. They were analysing a game playing on a TV mounted to the left of the dog portrait with the conviction and assumed expertise that comes with drinking several pints in quick succession.

'What time is it?' I thought out loud; I had completely lost track of time. A slight slur laboured my words as fatigue weighed on my entire body and, despite my best attempt to stifle it, a yawn bubbled up from deep within me.

'Goodness. Sorry.' Nick seemed genuinely apologetic. 'I've kept you out far too late. It's probably tomorrow's yesterday where you've come from.'

I had no capacity to tell what time my body clock thought it was, or to refute his unnecessary sense of responsibility, so I resorted to bobbing my head around unintelligibly.

We stood in unison and gathered our belongings. As I fumbled with my bag and phone, my scarf slipped from my hand. Nick bent down quickly to pick it up. He placed one end of the scarf on my left shoulder and then gently circled my head with the other end before resting it on my opposite shoulder. He performed this entire motion without breaking eye contact; his blue eyes looked more grey in the low light.

'There you are,' he said, smiling warmly and giving my arm a gentle squeeze.

As we stepped onto the street, the crisp night air slapped my cheeks. Groups of revellers in various stages of inebriation emerged from the surrounding pubs and walked off into the night, leaving behind echoes of their chatter and laughter.

'I wonder where Gerry and Gran ended up?' I asked rhetorically as I side-stepped a collection of half-filled bottles and glasses on the footpath, which implied a celebration had ended abruptly.

'They're probably at a nightclub doing shots and dancing on the tables,' Nick replied jovially.

I laughed. Before last month I wouldn't have dreamed Gran would find herself in a nightclub doing shots. But, recently, I had become much less trusting of the reliability of the status quo.

Nick smiled. 'I just hope they had a good night, wherever they ended up.'

I was impressed at how genuinely invested Nick seemed in Gerry and Gran's reunion being a success. I wasn't sure whether his thoughtfulness and good manners were a feature of his aristocratic lineage, or whether it was just that he was a really nice person.

By the time we had arrived at the door of the hotel, the cool night air that had at first felt refreshing had chilled me to the core.

'Thanks so much for tonight,' I said, clenching my jaw to stop it from chattering. I hoped he felt my sincerity; during an argument, Jarrah once told me my attempts at sentiment were easily mistaken for sarcasm. 'I really appreciate you taking me out. I'm sure being saddled with your great-aunt's ex-girlfriend's granddaughter is probably not how you wanted to spend your evening.'

'Don't be silly,' he said warmly. 'I had a great time. And I plan to hold you to your promise to return the favour in Australia one day. In the meantime, I'll check in with Aunt Gerry to see what she's got planned for the next few days.'

Nick held out his outstretched arms and took a step towards me.

Usually, I avoided unnecessary physical contact with others. My family had worn me down over the years and, of course, it played a necessary role during sex and medical examinations, but I just wasn't much of a fan. However, I was not repelled by the prospect of Nick's embrace in the way I would have been if it was anyone else's. In fact, I felt an unfamiliar compulsion to step towards him.

I extended my one free arm; the other was laden with my bag.

He stared at my hand and then awkwardly thrust his own out as if to meet mine in a handshake. I startled and retracted mine backwards. We then engaged in a mortifying push-pull of jolting and thrusting our arms at one another over several cringeworthy moments.

'Sorry,' I said finally, stepping backwards to disengage. 'I thought you were ... I mean, I thought we were going to ...'

'No. No. I'm sorry,' he said, a hint of red colouring his cheeks. 'I shouldn't have assumed.'

'It's fine, really,' I said, feeling my own cheeks warming and a prickle of disappointment.

He held up his hand for a high five. We both laughed as I lifted my hand to connect with his. The moment of awkwardness dissipated into the cool air.

'Well, thanks again,' I said, stepping towards the hotel door.

'I look forward to seeing you again,' he said with a tiny wink.

Once upstairs, I listened at the room door for any indication Gran might be in there with company. After a few moments of silence, save for the muffled television coming from the room next door, I unlocked and opened the door. The room was dark.

I turned on the lamp, fished around inside my bag for my phone and wrote a quick message to Gran.

Hi Gran. Hope you've had a terrific night. I'm back at the hotel, but let me know if you'd like me to come and get you to bring you back.

I sat on the edge of the bed and opened a browser to search the internet for information about things to do in London. I was keen to make an itinerary for the coming days. Usually I would have made one well before I arrived, but time had not allowed for it.

A message popped up from Gran.

Thanks, pet. It's been great. I'll stay at Gerry's tonight. ;) No need to come and get me. Love you, Gran xxx

I read the message again and wondered if a sleepover and winky face meant the same thing for an eighty-two-year-old woman as it did for someone my age. I shuddered involuntarily. I was happy for Gran, but I definitely didn't need to think of her engaging in a night of passion. Not to mention, it was sobering to realise she was getting more action than I was.

Chapter 23

Beth

I got to the end of the paragraph of my book and realised it was the third time I had read it. I was trying to concentrate on the novel I had perched on my thighs – a fascinating and insightful book about feminism in modern Australia – but my mind constantly wandered to thoughts of Gran.

The last I'd heard from her was the text she'd sent the previous night to say she was staying at Gerry's house. I couldn't get through by calling her, and she hadn't responded to any of the messages I'd sent this morning, which I assumed meant her phone was dead.

It wasn't like Gran had a curfew; she was a grown woman capable of making her own decisions. But I wondered how long I should wait until I alerted the Scotland Yard – or whichever authority dealt with missing Australian grannies – that she'd set off last night to reunite with a long-lost lover and I hadn't seen her since. I couldn't ignore that it was beginning to sound like the makings of a true crime podcast.

My phone started to ring. I eagerly grabbed at it to see if it was the Australian embassy calling to tell me she'd been caught up in a known international granny-trafficking operation – or Gran herself.

'Hi Mum,' I said, answering the call. I knew I couldn't tell her I'd lost Gran until I knew all the details; there was a very real risk she'd be on the first flight out if she thought Gran was in danger. She'd been keen to come even when she didn't think that.

'Hi, Bethie. I'm just checking in to see how it's all going,' she began generically.

'It's great. I forgot how much I love London. It's such an incredible city.'

'It sure is,' she replied.

'I mean, what's not to love about a place where entire streets are made up of house facades that are exactly the same as the one before it, and the one after it,' I continued. 'It's like each street is a satisfying architectural repeating pattern. It's—'

'Yes, it's great,' she said quickly. 'And Gran, she's having a good time so far too?' Her tone was thick with innuendo.

'She is,' I said, cautious not to say anything that would reveal that I hadn't seen her since she set off for her reunion last night.

'And Gerry ...' she paused, as if waiting for me to provide an answer to the question she hadn't yet formed.

At dinner on the night before we left, Gran had told the family about Gerry and their planned reunion. I was grateful – it was one less secret I had to keep. She casually dropped it into conversation in the way people do when they want to share something significant without making a big deal of it. But my family was the wrong audience for understated announcements. They made a massive fuss, which, admittedly, she seemed to enjoy. Even Jarrah's nattering about 'true love' and 'soulmates' was somewhat tolerable when it was directed at someone else.

'I haven't met her yet, but she sounds amazing. She's so accomplished and well respected,' I said, as much to placate her concerns as my own.

'Yes, I'm sure she's wonderful.'

162

I heard the click of the room key in the lock. 'Sorry Mum, I have to go. I'll chat to you later,' I said, hanging up the call and abruptly springing from my bed.

'Hi,' I said, a little more shrilly than I'd intended as Gran appeared through the opening door. 'How are you? How is she? How was it?'

Gran laughed as she struggled over the threshold, partly because the door was heavy and partly because I was unintentionally obstructing it.

'Let me in, darling, and I'll tell you all about it.'

'Sorry,' I said, shuffling out of the way. 'I've just been so excited to hear ...'

She moved inside and extended her hand to cup one side of my face, and then calmly walked towards the table where she placed her bag.

'It was wonderful,' she beamed. 'She's just as I remembered: elegant, sophisticated and worldly, and with just as much charm as she always had.'

Gran described their dinner and how they'd talked into the night. But she hurried over the details, as Gerry would be arriving shortly to collect us for brunch, and for a wander through Portobello Road Markets.

'You didn't need to come back here,' I said as she rummaged through her suitcase. 'I could have met you there.'

'What? And have me walk around in these all day?' she gestured to her new clothes. 'It was bad enough doing the ... what's that expression you young ones use?' She paused, searching for the term, and then clicked her fingers. 'The *walk of shame*,' she whispered.

Gran saying that she'd done a walk of shame was definitely not on my 'things Gran would say' bingo card.

Gran hummed as she made her selection of clothes to change into and ran the shower. Even through the closed bathroom door and over the running water, I recognised Etta James's 'At Last' as soon as I heard the first two notes, before she manoeuvred through various trills and scales.

She emerged from the bathroom a few minutes later. I noticed that

163

she'd reapplied some, but not all, of the make-up she'd used the night before and was wearing another top that I didn't recognise.

'You ready?' she asked with a bounce in her voice as she checked her watch. 'We'll wait downstairs.'

Gran shooed me out the door with an urgency I hadn't experienced since school mornings when Mum overslept and would hustle us off to school with a piece of plain toast for breakfast, a handful of coins for a lunch order and instructions to use our fingers to comb our hair.

Once downstairs, Gran paced the lobby, checking her watch every few minutes.

'Why don't you sit down, Gran?' I encouraged. I was worried all this frenetic energy would cause her blood pressure to rise.

'No, darling, I'm fine. Being up is good for the circulation. Move it, or lose it. That's what they say.'

After a few more minutes of Gran pacing and checking her watch, and me imploring her to sit down, the door of the hotel opened. A woman who I immediately knew to be Gerry entered.

Gran was right about Gerry being graceful; she had an air of poise and refinement. The way she carried her head, atop her long, elegant neck, reminded me of how people stood in deportment school when they had a book balanced on their heads. Gerry seemed to personify what people meant when they described someone as being of 'good breeding'.

Gerry and Gran walked towards each other and hugged without exchanging a word. They lingered in each other's arms for longer than what you'd expect of two platonic old friends.

They parted from their embrace, but locked hands.

'Here,' Gran said, motioning towards me finally. 'Come and meet Beth.'

'Oh, Beth!' Gerry let go of Gran's hand as she moved towards me with open arms. 'It's so good to meet you.' She hugged me tightly before leaning back to study my face. 'She looks like you,' she said, turning to Gran, her voice animated by surprise. 'I mean, not exactly the same. But there is definitely a resemblance.' She turned back to study me again. 'Lucky you.' She smiled at me in a way that made me feel a bit more special than I had in the moments beforehand; like I should be proud of something. I just wasn't sure what.

The hotel door opened again, and Nick appeared.

His eyes darted quickly around the foyer, searching eagerly. They stopped when they met mine.

'Good morning, Beth,' he said, a broad smile transforming his face. I felt my cheeks warm. I realised I was glad to see him; Gran hadn't mentioned he would be coming along too.

'And good morning to you,' he said, turning to address Gran, which I hoped meant he didn't spot me blushing. 'Ready for the markets?'

~

After what turned out to be a lovely walk, with a pitstop for brunch, we rounded the corner into Portobello Road Markets where the pastel hues of the terraced buildings set the tone for the colour and character of the street.

I turned to ask Gran what she wanted to see first and discovered she was no longer nearby. I scanned the area around me and spotted her and Gerry standing together at a stall that sold candles in all different shapes, colours and sizes.

Gran held a candle to her nose and inhaled deeply, before holding it out for Gerry to sample. Gerry cupped her hands around Gran's, drank in the scent and then leaned in and whispered something. Gran smiled and shook her head gently.

While their movements were slight, and their words hushed, their casual intimacy spoke volumes. It was obvious just by looking at them that their connection was as deep as the history they shared.

'They seem to be having an awful time together,' Nick said sarcastically as he sidled up next to me.

'I'll say,' I responded, unable to take my eyes off them as they laughed and whispered as if they were alone in the universe, despite standing in a heaving crowd of market-goers.

'Why don't we set a place to meet up later on?' he suggested. 'That way they can do their thing, and we can do ours.'

'Good idea,' I replied, impressed again at Nick's thoughtfulness.

As we approached Gran and Gerry, Nick made a loud, fake coughing sound to break them from their moment.

'We were thinking,' Nick started, 'that we should agree on a place to meet later on. Aunt Gerry has dragged me through enough antique stalls to last a lifetime. It's your turn now, Elise. I am happy to hand over the baton.'

Gerry rolled her eyes in defeated agreement as Nick bowed deeply in faux submission.

'Besides, there's a stall down there where an old hippy sells antique bongs, which I know Beth is going to go crazy for. And I'm keen to see if I can add to my collection of wigs.'

He winked at me, and I laughed. We agreed to meet for lunch at a pub at the end of the road, and Nick and I set off, leaving Gerry and Gran to debate whether patchouli had any business being in a scented candle. Definitely not, according to Gerry.

We meandered through the stalls that sold everything from second-hand clothes and jewellery to records and prints to antique silverware and signs to vintage boxing gloves. The stall owners were as diverse as the wares they were selling.

A few shops in from the start of the road, a woman in her seventies (give or take a decade or two adjusted for hard living) spun large bundles of hot pink fairy floss the same colour as her long dreadlocks. A few stalls along, a man with an impressive Dali-esque moustache sold a compass to a couple of pretentious-looking hipsters, who appeared to be pleased with themselves for embracing vintage tools while googling how to use them on their smartphones. Further along again, a crowd had gathered around a shop that sold antique clocks, where a street performer dressed as the White Rabbit jokingly berated the shopkeeper that every clock was on a different time.

Nick and I made fun of the Instagrammers we spotted, who were insisting their friend/boyfriend/girlfriend/mother/father/sister/brother/significant other take photo after photo as they perfected their best unposed pose. And we stopped to watch an Elvis impersonator who was belting out 'Blue Suede Shoes' while being completely and delightfully upstaged by a little girl who was dancing along with him.

'Ever been on a blind date?' Nick asked as we stopped outside a bookshop. 'With a book, I mean.'

Nick pointed to a table of brown paper-wrapped book-shaped parcels. A sign advertised: 'Let the universe decide your next literary adventure'. There was an asterisk at the end of the line that corresponded to a clause of small print that warned: 'Just like in life, refunds and exchanges will not be provided. Any purchase is final'.

'Oh, that's right,' Nick said, giving me a gentle nudge on the arm. 'You don't believe in fate.'

'But what if I hate the book?' I said, picking up one of the parcels. 'It would be a complete waste of money.' I set the book down again.

'But what if you don't?' he asked, picking up the parcel and handing it back to me. One side of his mouth inched up to create a lopsided grin that rendered me completely incapable of forming a counterargument.

'I mean, look what happened when you bought a lotto ticket on a whim,' he continued. 'It led you here.'

He had a point.

'Fine, then,' I said with mock surrender. 'Let's see what the universe has in store for my next literary adventure.'

We each picked up a brown parcel and handed over two pounds to the shopkeeper.

'After you,' Nick said, gesturing for me to open my book.

I tore open the brown paper wrapping to reveal a slightly tattered copy of *Falling for the Highlander* – a spectacularly cheesy-looking romance novel.

'You've got to be kidding me.' I performed an exaggerated eye roll as I turned the book around so Nick had an unobstructed view of the cover. It depicted a topless man wearing a kilt, who was gazing seductively over his shoulder towards the viewer, his muscly back glistening in the moonlight.

'I wonder how many pages the author dedicates to discussing the size of his sporran,' I said, feigning seriousness.

Nick laughed loudly. 'Well, if I'd known the universe wanted you to enjoy some romance with a Scott, I would have worn my kilt,' he said eagerly. 'I've got Scottish heritage, you know. We've even got a family tartan.'

I replayed his words in my head to ensure I had interpreted them correctly. Was Nick flirting with me?

'Your turn,' I said, unable to ignore the fact that my heart rate had quickened at the prospect he was.

He gently removed each piece of sellotape in an attempt to build suspense.

'Oh goodie,' he said, turning the book to face me. 'I've been looking for a new hobby.'

'*Toilet Paper Origami: a step-by-step, DIY guide to perfecting fancy folds*,' I read aloud through laughter. 'What the hell is the universe trying to tell you with that book? When your life turns to shit, make sure you fashion your three-ply into a flower?'

'What I want to know,' Nick said, 'is what you're meant to do if you are a scruncher?'

We continued laughing as we stowed our books in my bag and set off to meet Gerry and Gran for lunch.

~

We arrived at the pub and ordered a couple of beers while we waited for Gran and Gerry to arrive.

'There they are,' Nick announced when they appeared though the door.

He stood as they arrived at the table, in what I assumed was an unconscious show of good manners.

'I was worried you'd been mistaken for an antique in one of the shops and snapped up by a collector,' he said jovially to Gerry as they sat down.

'Ohhhh,' she groaned, clutching her heart in mock offence.

Nick hugged her warmly.

'Did you find anything interesting, Elise?' Nick asked.

'A couple of bits and pieces,' she said coyly. 'Just doing my bit for the local economy. Service to King and Country, and all that.'

'I'm sure whatever you bought here can't be as weird as your most recent purchase at home,' I said.

Gran scoffed.

'Dare I ask?' Gerry asked cautiously.

'It's a jackalope,' Gran responded enthusiastically. 'His name is Herrick, and I love him.'

'Ohhhh,' exclaimed Gerry. 'I've always been fascinated by jackalopes. I saw one mounted in a hotel in North America, and the locals had me convinced for a whole week that it was a real animal. I even went for a hike through the mountains looking for one.'

'Well,' Gran said, raising her eyebrow at me, while addressing Gerry. 'You're in luck. I had planned to leave the jackalope to Beth in my will as my most prized possession. But since you're the only one who will appreciate him, he's all yours.'

Over the next couple of hours, we enjoyed a hearty English-style pub lunch with gentle banter and robust discussions about books, arts, travel, sociology, natural history and coriander.

'So, what's on for the rest of the day?' Nick asked as we were settling the bill and gathering our things.

'Well,' I began, trying to gauge whether he was implying his own involvement in the afternoon's agenda or just making polite conversation, 'I was thinking I might head to Leicester Square to see if I can get tickets for something tonight.'

'I'm keen,' Nick said eagerly. 'I mean, if you don't mind me tagging along.'

'Not at all. You're welcome. Gran? Gerry? You in too?'

'I don't mind what we do,' Gerry directed to Gran. 'I am completely at your disposal. Today that is; tomorrow you're all mine. I have a surprise for you.'

'Really? What sort of surprise?'

'You'll see. We'll set off at 10.30.'

'Do you know anything about this?' Gran asked Nick.

He shrugged his shoulders.

'You?' she asked me.

I shook my head.

'I suppose I'll have to trust you, then,' she said, gently pinching Gerry's arm in jest. 'But you'd better look after me. I'm a lot older than the last time we went traipsing around the countryside together.'

As I watched Gran and Gerry laugh together, I marvelled at how much had happened in a month. Before I won the lotto, Gran and I had been going about our business like normal. And now Gran was having a surprise rendezvous in London, and I was making plans to spend the afternoon with Nick.

~

After a light dinner and a spectacular performance of *Matilda*, we all walked back to the hotel through the crisp London evening.

'Beth, darling,' Gran called from five or so metres behind me, the distance she and Gerry had maintained between us the whole way home. 'I'm just going to grab some things from the room, and then I'll head back with Gerry.'

'What? Tonight?' It caught me off guard that she and Gerry would be spending another night together. I wondered if we should have bothered with a double room at all.

'I can run the two of you home, then,' Nick offered. 'I'll just go and get the car and bring it around.'

'Thanks, Nick,' Gerry said. 'That would be wonderful.'

'I'll say goodnight to you here, Beth,' Nick said. 'Do you have anything planned for tomorrow?'

For the second time that day, I wondered if he was asking about my intended itinerary because he was making small talk, or if he was interested in participating in it.

'With Gerry keeping Elise busy with the surprise,' he continued, 'I wondered if you wanted to … or, um … maybe we could … I mean, only if you …'

He was fidgeting with the zip on his jacket. I had felt an easy energy between us for the whole day, but now he almost seemed nervous.

'It's just I'm going away the day after tomorrow,' he declared.

I felt my stomach lurch.

'It's a four-day conference on meteorology in Copenhagen. I'm presenting on some exciting research we've been doing, so I can't miss it, I'm afraid. And then I'm staying on so I can go to a friend's wedding. At the time I booked it, it seemed like a coincidence too good to be true that they're a week apart in the same place. But now …' His voice trailed off.

I searched for a rationalisation to make sense of what I was feeling. But the only emotion I could readily identify was disappointment, which, of course, was ridiculous. I knew what it meant to be asked to present at an international conference, and he certainly wasn't under any obligation to hang around London for me.

'I get back the day before you leave town, if I'm not mistaken. And I'd really like to see you again before I go. If that's okay with you, of course.'

I nodded feebly.

'That's good news that you get to see each other again before you go, and you've got tomorrow too,' Gran said. 'With us tied up, you'll be free to spend the whole day together.'

I was grateful; it wasn't the first time she'd jumped in to compensate for my social awkwardness.

I nodded.

'Perfect,' he replied enthusiastically. 'It's a date.'

But was it?

~

'That was nice of Nick to offer to do something again tomorrow,' Gran said, as the lift doors shut to take her, Gerry and me up to our floor.

'Yes. It was. He's been very *friend*-ly.' I emphasised the first syllable of the last word to shut down any inference she was making.

Gerry smiled, her right eyebrow raised a fraction.

'He's such a lovely young man,' Gran continued. 'And he's very easy on the eye.'

'Okay. That's enough of that, thanks,' I commanded.

'What?' she asked with feigned innocence. 'I'm not doing anything at all.'

It was my turn to raise an eyebrow.

'I was only saying ...'

'You don't need to say anything at all. He's going away. Remember?'

'But you've got tomorrow,' Gran said as she reached for Gerry's hand. 'And, trust me, you need to make the most of every moment. Life is too short for missed opportunities.'

Chapter 24

Elise

'Gerry Burnsby ... if you don't tell me what we're doing here right now ... I'll ...'

Elise gently poked at Gerry's torso as the two women arrived at the entrance to Kensal Green Cemetery.

A car honked urgently as a pedestrian with his face bowed to the illuminated screen in his hand walked straight out into traffic near the cemetery entrance, causing at least two cars to swerve.

'PISS OFF,' the pedestrian shouted maniacally, saluting the drivers with his middle finger.

'Seriously,' Elise said, strengthening her grip on Gerry's arm. 'What are we doing here?'

'You'll see,' she said in a singsong voice, seemingly oblivious to the pedestrian who was now chasing a car down the road, yelling and shaking his fist.

At the entrance to the cemetery was a large arch with a thriving population of weeds growing at the top. The white paint on the arch was peeling and dirty, and litter had collected in the black wrought-iron fence that framed four unkept garden beds.

Once inside the cemetery, Elise and Gerry followed a maze of crushed gravel paths, past graves, monuments and little chapels. Shiny new headstones adorned with recent dates and photos of their occupants sat alongside concrete tombs in various states of disrepair where time and the elements had stolen the details of who they honoured.

A crow cawed at the same time that a squirrel rustled in a nearby bush. Elise startled. 'I don't usually make a habit of hanging out in cemeteries, you know,' she said, nervously looking over her shoulder to ensure they hadn't roused any ghouls.

'They're this way, I think,' Gerry chirped as they reached a fork in the path and she tapped at a map on her phone.

'Who?' Elise insisted.

'Two great lovers,' Gerry replied.

After a few more steps, Gerry pointed to a group of graves to the left of the path.

'They were separated for decades, before being finally reunited here, at their final resting place.'

The plain-looking grave, situated in a crowded cluster of others, was about six feet long and was adorned with a cross that stretched its length. The corners of the concrete were crumbled and broken away, and lichen mottled much of its surface area.

Gerry bent down to move some of the long grass that was growing up the side of the grave, revealing some faint letters etched into the side.

'John Henry Gould', she said as she traced the characters of his name with her fingers, 'and, of course, his one great love, Elizabeth. Apparently, when it was created, it also said *Here lies John Gould, "The Bird Man"*, but you can't make out much of anything anymore.'

A pigeon cooed softly from its vantage point on a nearby grave.

'My goodness, Gerry,' Elise exclaimed, 'this is amazing.'

'I haven't been here for years. They've even got some new neighbours.

Good for them,' Gerry said, scanning their surrounds. 'I came here a few times after I got back from Australia. I think I even sat right there and wrote one of the letters you never received.' She pointed to a spot of overgrown grass at the foot of the grave. 'I enjoyed the idea that I was sitting alongside such a capable, proficient natural historian. Even if the rest of the world didn't yet know how incredible Elizabeth Gould was.'

The two women stood silently as they paid their respects to a woman who had brought so much to natural history, with so little acknowledgement, and who had bonded the two of them in their own love for natural history.

'It seems like such a plain monument, for someone who captured the colour of the natural world so richly,' Elise said, using her hand to clear away some leaves that had settled on the grave. The pigeon startled and flew off into the nearby trees.

Gerry reached into her bag and produced a parcel wrapped in a tea towel and tied with some kitchen twine.

'What have you got there?' Elise asked curiously.

Gerry peeled back the layers of the fabric wrapping to reveal two piccolos of champagne.

'Gerry!' Elise exclaimed, looking around guiltily for witnesses. 'It's eleven in the morning.'

'I know,' she said cheekily, as she handed Eli a bottle. 'But I thought we owed it to her to have a toast in her honour.'

They each found a space on the grass surrounding the grave and sat down, which for Gerry meant leaning her weight on the grave as she lowered herself to a kneeling and then seating position. For Elise, it involved bending as low as she could before dropping the rest of the way and hoping for the best.

They cracked the twist-top seals on the small bottles in unison.

'To Elizabeth Gould,' Gerry said, bringing the neck of her bottle to Elise's.

'And women of science everywhere,' Elise replied.

They sipped the slightly warm champagne through the metal straws Gerry had produced from her bag and welcomed the sun as it poked out from behind the clouds.

After only a few sips, Elise felt the muscles at the base of her neck soften. She didn't know if it was the champagne, the sun on her skin or being there with Gerry, but she felt an overwhelming sense of peace. It was as though a deep wound, which had resulted in a thick, unsightly keloid scar, was healing.

'Nice day for it.' A man bearing an uncanny resemblance to Freddie Mercury shouted to them over the Queen anthem 'We Are the Champions', which was blasting from the phone in his pocket.

Elise looked to Gerry in bewilderment.

'Freddie Mercury is buried here too,' Gerry whispered by way of clarification. 'But he's not wrong. It's a perfect day for it.'

They soaked in the sun and finished their drinks.

Getting up off the ground was a little more involved than getting down. Gerry hoisted herself up to kneeling and then stood with relative ease. Elise's manoeuvre would be familiar to anyone who had seen a baby giraffe attempting to stand.

'Rightio,' Gerry said, clapping her hands together after they'd both risen. 'We'd best be going. Part two of our adventure awaits.'

'There's more?'

'Ooo, yes, mi amor. This journey is far from over.'

~

Gerry and Elise caught the bus from the cemetery to the stop outside London's Natural History Museum. The spectacular gothic building dwarfed the people gathered at the entrance.

'Impressive, isn't it?' Gerry said as they admired the intricate sculptures that adorned the facade, and the patterns created by different coloured bricks in the building's many arches. Elise paid particular attention to the gargoyles – each with its own unique expression.

'The architect designed it as a "cathedral to nature", Gerry said.

'I think he nailed his brief,' Elise said as they walked towards the impressive front entrance.

Once inside and away from the hum of the London streets, the women were enveloped by Hintze Hall. The treasures housed in the nooks – each a giant in its own right – offered a reference to the scale of the hall's gigantic proportions. An American mastodon, with its long protruding tusks; a taxidermied giraffe standing alongside a tall giraffe skeleton; and a giant swordfish in a tank all looked comparatively small in that vast chamber.

Elise stood underneath a giant blue whale skeleton that was suspended from the ceiling. But it was the magnificent tapestry of botanical artworks from around the world behind it that caught her attention.

Gerry made her way to the information booth. After a short exchange with a man behind the desk who gave her directions, she beckoned Elise to follow her.

They walked to the end of the hall and then along a corridor to the right. They reached the door of the Reading Room and Gerry pressed a doorbell. While they waited to be let in, they watched on as a woman gave a captivated audience an animated account of cordyceps – a fungus that turns ants into zombies.

The chatter and laughter of tourists and other visitors bounced off every hard surface, and the piercing squeals of toddlers protesting at being strapped into their prams accented the cacophony. Groups of excited school children, being corralled by weary-looking teachers, dodged and darted around, clipboards in hand. But within moments of walking through the heavy glass door to the library, Elise felt like she'd escaped to another world. The library was quiet and calm.

'Now, behave yourself while you're here,' Gerry whispered to Elise with mock seriousness as they made their way down a short corridor to a reception desk. 'I won't have you getting me thrown out of here.'

Elise smiled as she recalled the hours she and Gerry had spent in the university library. They'd pick one of the less popular sections – usually an obscure ancient history, or a dead language – and shelter in the privacy of the aisles. One afternoon they were ejected from the library after they caught an incurable case of the giggles. Elise couldn't remember what they'd found so funny, only that the librarian did not share their amusement. But they had an assignment due the following day, for which they needed access to a number of books, so they had returned, and, while Elise had weathered the brunt of the librarian's whispered shouts, Gerry snuck in and concealed the books they needed up her jumper.

A young man at the reception desk looked up and smiled.

'Hello,' Gerry began, 'we're here to see Daphne Carmichael. I'm Gerry Burnsby.'

'Ah, yes,' he replied. 'She's expecting you. Just take a seat over here.' He pointed to one of several tables in the centre of the room. 'I'll get you to clean your hands while you wait, if you don't mind.' He gestured to a box of wet wipes on the table before returning to his desk.

Elise looked to Gerry for context.

'You'll see,' she said coyly.

As Elise dragged the wipe across her hands, she took in the room. The library walls were lined with dark timber bookshelves that reached more than five metres in the air. Tightly spiralled staircases led to a balcony that traversed the inside of the room, providing access to the books on the upper shelves.

A couple of metres from their table, a life-sized statue of Charles Darwin, crafted in a bright white stone, sat on an antique chair with one leg crossed over the other. He was engrossed in the book he was holding, which was decorated with flowers.

'I wonder what he'd make of all this,' Elise said, gesturing around the room, but implying the world.

'God only knows,' Gerry replied. 'And he was basically an atheist.'

A handful of people sat at the tables around them, hunched over books or tapping away at keyboards. A cohort of librarians busied themselves at the shelves and desks around the room.

'Gerry!'

A woman with long, blonde hair, a soft wispy fringe and elfin features approached them. She was carrying an enormous book and what looked to be some kind of foam bricks.

She reached the table, set down her load and pulled Gerry in for a long hug.

'It's so good to see you, Gerry,' she said as she exited the embrace. 'I'm so glad you got in touch. It's been too long.'

'I know,' Gerry replied warmly. 'It certainly has. I'm so grateful you made time for this.'

'Of course! Anything for you, you know that.'

Gerry gestured to Elise.

'Daphne, this is Elise Simpson. Sorry, it's Elise Evans. Force of habit.'

'It's so lovely to meet you, Elise,' Daphne said, extending her hand for Elise to shake. 'I've heard so much about you.'

Elise felt a tickle of pride that Gerry – who had a catalogue of fascinating things to discuss and people to talk about – had chosen to talk to Daphne about her.

An older man at one of the nearby desks glared at the trio – theirs were the only voices in the library, and Elise assumed he heralded from a time when libraries were places for *shh*!

Daphne turned her back on him and surreptitiously rolled her eyes.

'You must be so excited about seeing this,' she whispered to Elise as she gestured to the items on the desk.

'I'm afraid Gerry hasn't told me what I'm here to see,' she whispered back. 'Today is full of surprises.'

'We're on a treasure hunt of sorts,' Gerry offered.

'Well, that makes it even more exciting,' Daphne replied as she placed two big black foam wedges in front of Elise and then carefully lifted the oversized book onto them.

'I understand you have an interest in John and Elizabeth Gould,' she continued, 'so Gerry thought you might enjoy seeing this ...'

Elise looked down at the dark green leather-bound book. The leather around the edges of the book was slightly scuffed, and the spine was coming away from the cover at the top and bottom. The cover was decorated with an intricate gold pattern that bordered the edges, but offered no clues about the book's contents. Elise, however, having been fascinated by Elizabeth Gould's work for most of her life, knew exactly what it was.

She gasped.

'This is the original *The Birds of Australia* by John Gould, which contains illustrations by the one and only Elizabeth Gould,' Daphne confirmed.

Gerry nodded, smiling broadly.

'Go ahead,' Daphne said, gesturing to the book.

Elise beamed at Gerry as she carefully opened the cover.

The thick parchment inside the book was the colour of milky tea and was freckled with tiny brown splodges. It reminded Elise of when she'd helped Beth 'age' some paper using black tea for a history project. Every other page was marked with a small red stamp: 'British Museum Natural History: ZD'. ZD stood for Zoological Department.

'I'm going to leave you ladies to it,' Daphne said, standing. 'But I'll be hovering around if you need me.'

'Thanks so much, Daph,' Gerry said warmly.

'Yes, this is incredible, thank you very much,' Elise gushed.

Elise slowly and tenderly turned the pages of the precious tome. She pored over the illustrations by John Gould and Henry Richter – the artist who worked on the series after Elizabeth passed away – and delighted in John Gould's descriptions of the birds he encountered while in Australia.

Where the illustrations were particularly bold, they had transferred to the opposite page of text, creating a ghosting effect that looked like a watermark.

After a few minutes, Elise reached the illustration of a lyrebird – the first that carried the credit 'J&E Gould'.

'Oh! Here she is,' she exclaimed, again attracting the glare of the older man.

'It's incredible to think Elizabeth Gould coloured *this* very work more than ...' she paused to calculate the book's age, '170 years ago.'

Like so many species in the natural world, the male lyrebird's plumage was resplendent compared to its female mate's comparatively drab appearance. Elizabeth Gould's tiny brushstrokes meticulously depicted its long tail feathers and captured the imperfections of the feathers.

Elise felt compelled to use her fingers to smooth where the feather barbs had split into sections. She chuckled as she read aloud Gould's account of the lengths to which he went to collect a specimen.

While among the brushes I have been surrounded by these birds, pouring forth their loud and liquid calls, for days together, without being able to get a sight of them; and it was only by the most determined perseverance and extreme caution that I was enabled to effect this desirable object, which was rendered all the more difficult by their often frequenting the almost inaccessible and precipitous sides of gullies and ravines, covered with tangled masses of creepers and umbrageous trees.

'Poor bugger,' Elise whispered to Gerry. 'Sounds like those lyrebirds made him really work for it.'

Another successful mode of procuring specimens, is by wearing a tail of a full-plumaged male in the hat, keeping constantly in motion and concealing the person among the bushes.

Elise chuckled. 'Imagine someone crawling around in the bush with a hat full of lyrebird feathers.'

As she moved through the pages, she was able to distinguish Elizabeth Gould's illustrations from Richter's without needing to look at the credit.

'Look at the way her strokes are finer,' Elise said. 'And the detail she's applied to the background. It's no wonder John Gould grieved her death so deeply. He didn't just lose his wife, and the mother of his children, he lost a bloody good professional collaborator too.'

The birds were grouped in species, and when Elise reached the illustration of the first of the finches she smiled. She knew there was a reason she was looking through the third of seven volumes.

Page after page, beautiful little finches were depicted perched upon plants or feeding their young. Elise admired them all, but with every page she turned, she felt the suspense build for what she knew was coming.

Eventually, she turned the page to find the original version of the painting that had hung on her wall since Gerry left. The painting of the *Amadina gouldiae*, known commonly as the Gouldian finch.

'Look how vibrant the colours are,' she marvelled. 'My version has certainly faded over the years.'

'Haven't we all,' Gerry said with a smirk.

Elise swatted away her self-deprecation and began reading the text aloud.

It is in fact beyond the power of my pen to describe or my pencil to portray anything like the splendour of the changeable hues of the lilac band which crosses the breast of this little gem, or the scarcely less beautiful green of the neck and golden-yellow of the breast.

It is therefore with feelings of no ordinary nature that I have ventured to dedicate this new and lovely little bird to the memory of her, who in addition to being a most affectionate wife, for a number of years laboured so hard and so zealously assisted me with her pencil in my various works, but who, after having made a circuit of the globe with me, and braved many dangers with a courage only equalled by her virtues, and while cheerfully engaged in illustrating the present work, was by the Divine will of her Maker suddenly called from this to a brighter and better world; and I feel assured that in dedicating this bird to the memory of Mrs Gould, I shall have the full sanction of all who were personally acquainted with her, as well as of those who only knew her by her delicate works as an artist.

The tears that had gathered in Elise's eyes breached her lower lids and tumbled down her cheeks.

She fished around inside her sleeve to find a tissue; she would have been mortified to spill tears all over the invaluable tome.

'It's not often that scientific reference books contain touching love stories,' Gerry said, handing her a tissue from her bag. 'And who said the English couldn't be romantic?'

'Do you mean you, or John Gould? Because today ... all of this ...' Elise gestured at the book, 'has been wonderful.'

Gerry smiled warmly.

'I think you've got corny in your old age,' Elise joshed.

'Maybe you just bring it out in me,' Gerry replied.

Before Elise knew what she was doing, she took Gerry's hands in hers and brought them to her face and kissed them. Sixty years ago, she would have recoiled from such a public display of affection, and she would never have dared initiate it, especially with Charles Darwin's ghost and a grumpy old codger next to them watching on.

'I don't want to leave you,' she said urgently, and a little too loudly. 'I don't want to look back on this second chance at happiness with you and regret not taking full advantage of it.' The older man looked up again. Elise felt her ears redden but she was compelled to go on.

'When we were growing up, there were so many expectations about who we'd be and how we'd live,' she continued, her voice hushed. 'For the most part, I followed those conventions to the letter. I got married. I had a family. I had a happy life, a loving marriage and I adore Rosie and the kids. I felt I never had any right to complain about my life.

'Somewhere along the line,' she continued, 'the conventions I measured myself against stopped being set in stone, and the people who enforced them were no longer around. I watched as other people felt free to live how they wanted to live, and love who they wanted to love. But I didn't feel like that applied to me. I suppose I felt like I was touring this whole new world with a set of old visa conditions. Until now. Until this trip. I'm not ready to give this ... to give you ... up again.

'But all of this depends on what you want too, of course,' she added hurriedly.

'Well ... about that.' Gerry leaned in. 'What about if I travel back with you to Australia?'

'Really?' Elise replied excitedly, not caring who heard her.

'Yes,' Gerry answered enthusiastically. 'I've got a few bits and pieces on the go here, but nothing I can't defer for a little while. The university is always nagging me to take some annual leave. And I haven't been to Australia for so long; it will be lovely to spend some time there again.'

'Oh, Gerry,' Elise exhaled. 'That would be bloody marvellous.'

Chapter 25

Beth

'If we're going to spend the day together today, there's something you need to know about me,' I announced to Nick when he arrived at the hotel.

His eyes narrowed as he studied me intently. 'Go on,' he urged suspiciously.

'I love all of the ceremony, history and tradition of the royal family,' I said boldly. 'I know The Firm represents an antiquated system. I know the institution represents colonisation and oppression across the Commonwealth, and especially for the First Nations people of Australia. And I think it's ridiculous that we still award power to people based on their progeny. But there's something about it all that I find ...'

I searched for a word to summarise the admiration I felt for an institution governed by centuries-old rules and regulations and the envy I had for those born into aristocracy; I wished my family had been more structured and predictable.

'... reassuring,' I said finally.

'Phew,' he exhaled deeply. 'You had me worried then. That's fine. Me too.'

'Really? You do?'

'Well, yes, in principle,' Nick replied. 'I mean, there are many things that could use a shake-up. But I've lived my life against the backdrop of the royal family. It's hard not to have a soft spot for them.'

I was glad to hear this, as most of the activities I had planned for the day included paying homage to the family that had dominated my history books, appeared on my currency and consumed my imagination for as long as I could remember.

I detailed my plans to visit the Tower of London and Kensington Palace.

'But first,' I said, producing two tickets I had purchased through the hotel, 'the London Eye.'

Nick's left eye twitched, in what was definitely not a wink.

'I hope that's okay,' I asked rhetorically. I had scheduled the entire day around our London Eye session time and based on the most efficient way of navigating the city by public transport. And I'd purchased non-refundable tickets; changing the plan now was completely out of the question.

'Sure. Yes. Great,' he said, a little too enthusiastically. 'This will be great. I've never been on the London Eye. So ... great.' He smiled broadly as he fiddled vigorously with the arms of the sunglasses he was holding. 'Great,' he repeated. 'Let's get going then.'

A bus and tube trip later, we stood in line with the hordes of other tourists at the base of the London Eye.

Nick had been quieter than normal en route to the attraction, except to disclose that he 'wasn't great with heights'. He insisted that he was keen to join me on the wheel, but his constant fidgeting, furrowed brow and the fact he'd been to the bathroom twice since we'd arrived at the attraction suggested otherwise.

'Are you sure you want to do this?' I asked after I noticed a film of sweat had formed on his top lip. 'You don't have to come up with me. I can see if I can sell your ticket to someone in the queue, and we can meet up after I finish.'

'It's fine,' he said unconvincingly. I'm fine. It will be—'

'Fine?' I offered.

He smiled sheepishly.

As we were called to board the pod, Nick grabbed my hand and exhaled deeply before he made his way to the centre of the vessel and sat on the surfboard-shaped bench. We had joined an older couple whom we later discovered were German; a mother, father and two surly looking teens; and a couple with thick Mancunian accents, who announced to everyone that they were on their honeymoon, although they needn't have bothered – their public display of intimacy made this an easy guess.

'Have a good trip, folks,' the attendant said as he closed the pod door and fastened it shut.

Nick's breathing quickened.

'We'll be fine,' I said. 'Besides, whatever happens is fate, right?'

He rolled his eyes and then shut them tightly.

'You're not going to keep your eyes closed the entire time, are you?' I asked after a few moments.

He opened one slightly into a comical reverse-wink.

'There's no way I want to see any of this. It's bad enough imagining how high off the ground I am. There's no way I want to have that validated.'

'But the view is the whole point,' I pleaded. 'Why did you come on board if you weren't going to enjoy it?'

'I never said I would enjoy it, but I came on board because you—' He paused as the pod stopped moving forward and swayed slightly on the spot. 'What's happening?' he asked urgently, grabbing for my hand. 'Why are we swaying?'

'I think we're just taking on more passengers, mate,' said the newly married groom. 'Nothing to worry about.'

188

Nick opened one of his eyes again for just long enough to see who'd spoken to him.

'Yes, good. Thanks,' he muttered, before slamming his eye shut again.

'You not a fan of heights, mate?' the groom asked, leaning in and waving his hand in front of Nick's face to check how tightly closed his eyes were. Nick's lack of reaction indicated they were ironclad.

'No. No, not really,' he replied through a tightly clenched jaw.

After a few more minutes, Nick's firm grip on my hand had become uncomfortably strong. I exchanged one hand for the other and gave my freed one a shake to resume blood flow to my fingers. The view across the city was spectacular. The sky was mostly clear with a smattering of large, white cumulus clouds and thin white lines – the legacy of planes flying to and from the city. The views stretched to the hazy horizon. I was struck by how flat the city was and, despite its population, how green it looked. It was a testament to the forward thinking of city planners, and good soil.

We climbed towards the maximum height, which the brochure that Nick had shredded to pieces told us was 130 metres.

'We're halfway,' I whispered.

Nick swallowed audibly.

'The view is amazing, if you want to take a peek,' I encouraged.

He shook his head defiantly.

'I still don't know why you came if you're so terrified of heights,' I said, as much to him, as to myself. It made me uncomfortable to see him distressed. I felt I had given him ample opportunities to change his mind about coming, and I didn't like the idea he had committed to something he didn't want to do because of me.

'Do you want me to describe what I can see?' I offered. 'I'll be your eyes.'

He nodded timidly.

I described all the iconic landmarks that I could identify: the sprawling flag atop Buckingham Palace that indicated the King was in

189

town; the iconic London Bridge and The Shard, which rose boldly above the rest of the city's skyline.

I noticed his rate of hand wringing had slowed since I'd started talking, and his breathing seemed to be calmer. So I carried on.

I told him about the parade of boats that chugged along the sullied waters of the River Thames. And I described the London Eye itself – the steel spokes and cables stretched out from a central point like a giant bicycle wheel.

The muscles around his closed eyes had relaxed slightly and the fine lines that radiated from the corner of his eyes, which usually gathered when he smiled, had softened. With his eyes still closed, I took the opportunity to study his face.

He had a slight bulge on the bridge of his nose, which I assumed was the result of a break. His lightly stubbled jaw contained an array of colour; some strands were quite strawberry, while others were light blond. With the sunlight streaming through the pod behind him, some strands looked golden, framing his lips perfectly.

He opened his eyes the tiniest bit, and caught me staring.

'Can I help you?' he said, but not unkindly. I felt my cheeks flush. Thankfully, he lifted his gaze over my shoulder.

We were approaching the bottom of our rotation and were in line with the top of the nearby buildings. Seeing the spectacular sprawling Palace of Westminster was made all the more special when Big Ben started to chime.

'So this is what I've been missing?' he asked.

'See. I told you it was an amazing view.'

'At least I can say I've done it now,' he said. 'That should shut up my mates. They've been trying to get me on it for ages.'

'Have you always hated heights?' I didn't have any phobias, so I found it curious when otherwise rational people had irrational responses towards things. Of course, I exercised caution where needed and avoided unnecessary risk where possible, but I found that I could overcome most concerns with a rigorous risk analysis, some statistical research of likely outcomes and a robust strategy for making sure things went to plan.

'Sort of.' He started wringing the brochure again, so I chose not to push it.

'Well, lunch is on me to celebrate,' I insisted. 'It's the least I can do since you came on this with me.'

'Sounds good,' he said, smiling. 'Although I'd probably have preferred to pay for lunch if it meant I got out of coming on this death trap.'

'It will be worth it,' I said. 'I've booked a window table at the restaurant at the top of The Shard.'

His smile dropped.

'I'm joking,' I said, standing up as the pod neared the base of the attraction.

'Ha! Bloody hilarious,' he said dryly. He wrapped his arm around my shoulder as we stepped out onto the platform and onto solid ground.

Chapter 26

Beth

By the time we'd made it off the London Eye, the sun had disappeared behind the clouds and the temperature had dropped. I was glad I had my jacket, which conveniently tucked away into a small bag that fitted easily into my backpack.

'It's getting chilly,' Nick said, looking to the sky as if searching for answers about what it had planned for the rest of the day. 'I should have brought a jacket. You'd think as a meteorologist who's lived in London their whole life I'd know better.'

I had learned the hard way that Australia's autumn and spring temperatures were not the same as those in London. My first trip to London was in an April, when I wrongly assumed light sweaters, T-shirts and jeans would suffice. After enduring the freezing elements for days, I finally relented and bought a woollen jumper, thick tights, a scarf and gloves to protect me from the elements.

'My place isn't far from Kensington Palace. Do you mind if we duck in quickly so I can grab my jacket?' Nick asked, crossing his arms for warmth.

'Of course not,' I replied, happy to have an opportunity for a nosy at where he lived. 'I can hang back, if you need to rush ahead to stash any dead bodies you've got lying around.'

'No need,' he replied with a coy grin. 'The trash went out this morning.'

We took the tube, which offered some welcome respite from the plummeting air temperature, and then emerged from the underground station as big heavy raindrops started to tumble.

'This way,' Nick said dashing off up the street. 'It's not far.'

We arrived at his front door a few minutes later, both puffing but only slightly wet. Nick led me through a lovely light foyer and up the stars to his flat. We stepped into a large, light room, with a modern white marble kitchen on one side and a tastefully decorated lounge area on the other. The dark timber parquetry floor was stunning.

'Sorry about the mess,' he said, rushing to put a plate, which carried a scattering of toast crumbs, and an empty coffee cup in the dish drawer under the island bench. The rest of the room was immaculate. But it wasn't just that it was tidy; there was a sense of precision and order that reminded me of my house. The few items stuck to the front of his fridge were arranged neatly and evenly spaced; it certainly wasn't the haphazard jumble of mismatched fridge magnets and old electricity bills that my parents had. And I was impressed to see a whiteboard meal planner set his culinary intentions for the week. I tried not to smile when I saw 'fried rice' had been crossed off and replaced by a big circled star on the night we met at the pub.

'I was in a hurry to get out the door this morning to come and see you, so I didn't quite get to putting my breakfast dishes away.'

'Are you kidding? I grew up in a house that could have been in an episode of *Hoarders*,' I said. 'This place is amazing.'

Apart from a large television mounted opposite a plush cream couch, the walls of the rooms were bare. A thriving fiddle-leaf fig occupied one corner of the room, while a bookshelf ran the length of the opposite wall. I moved towards it for a closer look; I have always thought you could tell everything you needed to know about a person by the books they kept.

The top two-thirds housed all the usual suspects: biographies of noted world leaders and sporting heroes, a couple of the classics, a number of *New York Times* bestsellers and an impressive collection of travel guides. The books were interspersed with a few framed photos and a selection of small ornaments. The bottom two rows were a block of sunflower yellow, created by what I immediately recognised as the spines of *National Geographic* magazines.

'Have you lived here long?' I asked.

'Sort of,' he replied, making his way through the lounge to one of two closed doors. 'I've lived here for about five years. But it's been in my family for a while. My family ...' He paused as if carefully selecting his words. '... has a few properties around the place.'

From what Gran had told me, it didn't surprise me that his family would hold an extensive real estate portfolio. While he needn't have downplayed his family's wealth on my account, I appreciated he didn't flash it around. In my experience, this spoke to how much they had.

Nick entered the room off the lounge, leaving the door open just enough for me to spot a bed with a light grey linen cover, which had been roughly pulled up over the mattress, and a stack of books on one of the bedside tables.

He appeared a few moments later with a jacket in hand and three scarves – one black, one grey and one blue-and-maroon striped.

'Do you think you'll want a scarf?' he offered, holding out the selection of scarves for me to choose one.

I was touched by his thoughtfulness. I thanked him, took the black one and wrapped it around my neck. It was incredibly soft – a quick check of the label told me it was cashmere – and it carried the subtle spiced notes of his aftershave. I inhaled deeply. He draped the grey scarf across his shoulders.

'Is that your soccer team?' I asked, pointing to the blue-and-maroon scarf he'd placed on the arm of the couch with the amount of care that might be afforded to a sleeping baby or an unexploded ordnance.

'Soccer? You mean football,' he said with a smirk. 'Yes. I've been a mad Aston Villa fan since … forever. I live for their games, actually.'

I nodded noncommittally. I knew nothing about soccer, but being Australian, I understood the hold that sports teams have on people.

'Do you mind if I use your bathroom before we go?'

He directed me to the guest bathroom, which was as tastefully decorated as the rest of the apartment. His home was distinctly masculine. But unlike the shared houses I had experienced through Jarrah over the years, where 'masculine' was an adjective used to describe a space where giant pyramids were constructed out of beer cans, bongs doubled as vases, and milk crates were used for everything from coffee tables to bed bases, this apartment was the epitome of masculine sophistication.

As I entered the bathroom, I noticed his copy of *Toilet Paper Origami* was perched on the edge of the vanity. I immediately looked to the current toilet paper roll and saw the next few sheets had been folded several times to create an impressive origami swan. Despite it being a waterbird, it seemed such a shame to send it down the waterways, so I reached for one of the spare rolls in the basket next to the toilet instead.

'Impressive swan,' I said as I emerged from the bathroom. 'It's great to see the universe's plan for you to become a renowned toilet paper artist is really working out.'

'Oh yes, thanks,' he replied coyly. 'I'm glad you appreciate it. I went thought half a roll perfecting that.'

As we emerged from his building we found the rain has stopped, but it felt like the temperature had taken another dive. We continued towards Kensington Palace, hands in our pockets, and chatted about everything from Meghan Markle to his attempt at the London Marathon (which robbed him of eight of his toenails and the ability to walk up or down stairs for a fortnight). I had become accustomed to people searching the room for someone more interesting with whom to speak, or becoming distracted by other things, but he seemed genuinely interested in what I had to say.

Apart from the thirty minutes he'd spent with his eyes clenched shut on the London Eye, Nick looked at me when I spoke. Directly at me. Even if it meant craning his neck, or turning backwards. I enjoyed the feeling of being seen and heard.

A trio of men, all wearing broad grins and duplicates of the blue-and-maroon scarf Nick had left at his apartment, were making their way towards us.

'Hello mate,' said one of the men.

I looked to Nick, who was shaking his head and smiling in warm recognition. 'Hello, lads. Fancy seeing you here.'

Nick extended his hand to the man who'd first greeted us. They joined hands and pulled each other into a quick man-style hug. He repeated the ritual with the other two.

I felt an all-too-familiar itch of self-consciousness and instinctively held back. I assumed Nick wouldn't want to introduce me to his friends or, if he did, it would only be to make it clear that I was just the granddaughter of his great-aunt's lover and nothing else.

'Beth,' Nick said motioning towards me instead. 'Come and meet these three renegades. This is Chris, Simon and Anil. We went to school together, and they've been making my life a nightmare ever since.'

'Mate! You don't know how good you've got it,' Simon said, giving Nick a wry smile and moving towards me with his hand out.

'You alright?' he said, shaking my hand. 'I've heard lots about you.'

I looked to Nick for clarification, assuming he was mistaking me for someone else.

'Yes, it's nice to meet you, Beth,' Anil said, reaching in to shake my hand. 'He's filled our group chat with details about what you've been up to since you arrived.'

'He has?' I said, flummoxed that Nick had been talking to his friends about me.

'I hope he's been a gracious tour guide,' Chris said, taking his turn to shake my hand. 'It sounds like you might be returning the favour before too long, if Nick gets his way. I think he's already started to pack his bags.'

Nick glared at him theatrically to indicate it was in good humour. 'Yeah, well, I do hope to get to Australia someday. But let's not get ahead of ourselves.'

I couldn't be sure, but I thought I spotted a tinge of warmth to his cheeks. Could he have been blushing?

'What are you two doing today that meant you couldn't come and watch the game with us?' Anil asked, flapping his blue-and-maroon scarf provocatively.

'This would be the first game you've missed in ... how long?' asked Simon.

Nick laughed awkwardly. 'I'll catch the replay later. Beth has a soft spot for the royal family, so we're headed to Kensington Palace for a tour around the gardens.'

'Nice one,' Anil said. 'Well, meet up with us for a drink afterwards, if you're keen. You too, Beth. We'd love a chance to get to know the person who has captured the attention of this one for the past few days.'

He elbowed Nick's arm.

'Sod off, you lot,' Nick said playfully.

'If we don't see you later, Beth, it was really nice to meet you,' Anil said. 'I hope you enjoy the rest of your stay.'

'Sorry about all that,' Nick said after we'd said goodbye. 'They can be a bit much sometimes.'

'They seemed really nice,' I said. 'You're lucky to have such good friends.'

He nodded in agreement.

'I hope I'm not keeping you from watching the game. Please don't feel like you've got to hang out with me if you've got other things to do,' I continued, a sense of self-consciousness prickling at me that he might see me as a burden.

'Don't be silly,' he said quickly. 'I'm enjoying spending time with you.'

'Yes, but ...' I started, unable to recall a time when anyone had said that to me.

Nick grabbed my hand and stopped walking. It was the second time that day he had held my hand, but this time felt tender, not like on the London Eye when he had been hanging on as though his life depended on it.

'I've really enjoyed getting to know you, Beth,' he said, looking directly into my eyes. 'It's true that Aunt Gerry asked me to take you out that first night to show you around. But I assure you, the other times have been because I enjoy your company.'

'Well, as long as you're sure,' I said, comforted by his unwavering gaze. 'I'm enjoying spending time with you too.'

We resumed our walk towards Kensington Palace, our hands still clasped. I wondered if he'd forgotten that they were, while I could think of nothing else.

Chapter 27

Beth

After we walked through the gardens of Kensington Palace, Nick happily agreed to accompany me to the Tower of London. The sky was as grey as the bluestone bricks of the ancient building and, partway through our visit, the heavens opened.

As tourists retreated inside to seek refuge from the weather, their wet footprints made the tiny spiral staircases and narrow corridors slippery underfoot.

'I think I'm done here,' I said after we'd filed past the Crown Jewels, thoroughly examining them for evidence of their authenticity, and I had tired of the jostling and vying of the other visitors.

Heading into the inclement weather was a welcome reprieve; the comparatively empty London streets provided respite from the crowds.

'You're welcome to go and meet up with your friends,' I said as we sheltered under the eaves of a tube entrance where generations of pigeons had made their homes in the rafters and coloured the facade white with their guano. 'I'll be fine to do some exploring by myself. Honestly.'

Despite his reassurances, I had been feeling guilty that he was missing the game ever since we'd bumped into his friends.

'I can catch up with them any time,' he said sincerely. 'Besides, the game's over now anyway.'

He checked his watch.

'But ...' he said slowly with an eager smile. 'If you were interested in watching the replay and getting out of this weather, we could head back to my flat, order takeaway and watch it on the telly.'

Something about the way he smiled caused a flutter in my stomach. He wanted to spend more time with me? At his flat? I wondered if he intended for me to interpret his invitation as a suggestion of something more than just takeaway and soccer re-runs.

I couldn't ignore that getting out of the cold that was burrowing into my bones wasn't the only reason the idea seemed appealing, but then thoughts of my unruly bikini line and unshaven legs populated my consciousness. I wracked my brain to remember what underwear I was wearing and then cringed when I recalled I was wearing the pair of knickers that promised an invisible panty line, but looked like something I'd found in Gran's suitcase.

We hailed a cab, opting for the quickest, driest route, and arrived at his house a few minutes later. Normally, I would have resisted paying for transport when a walk would suffice, but this seemed like a good time to make an exception.

Once inside, Nick brought up the game on the television and produced two bottles of beer from the fridge.

I had thoughtlessly perched myself in the middle of the three-seater sofa, which meant, when he sat down, we were positioned unintentionally close to each other. I would usually have scurried away to the furthest corner of the couch, but I felt anchored to the spot with an unshakable reluctance to increase the distance between us.

Nick asked me about AFL and explained the nuances of his version of football. In between animated shouts and jeers at the television, he told me that much of the limited time his father had spent with him as a child was focused on playing or watching the game.

'We really only spoke when we were kicking a ball between us, or watching others do it on telly,' he explained. 'But I guess that's the thing about sport; it's a universal uniter of people, even if they don't connect in other ways.'

'Do you get along now?' I asked, immediately regretting the question and worrying that he might think I was prying; I hated when people asked about my family.

'There's no animosity at all,' he answered matter-of-factly. 'We're just not very close, I suppose.'

Over my second beer, and in spite of myself, I told Nick about Jarrah's willowy beauty and Elijah's perpetual coolness, and how I had always felt 'vanilla', while my siblings were chocolate and strawberry covered in sprinkles with a cherry on top.

'You know, for what it's worth, my favourite flavour is vanilla,' he said earnestly.

I felt my cheeks flush. I had never enjoyed receiving compliments. They made me so uncomfortable, and something about hearing it from him made me doubly bashful.

'Besides, you're far from boring,' he continued. 'I find you fascinating and funny.'

I looked at him incredulously, having never been described by anyone as fascinating or funny, let alone both, and certainly not by a man. But no one had ever made me feel at ease like Nick did either. I felt comfortable being myself.

I became aware of the silence around me. I looked at the TV; the game was still playing, but there was no volume.

'What happened to the TV?' I asked.

'I muted it,' he said casually. 'You were talking.'

'So, you're saying you find me funny and fascinating, and you actually listen to what I have to say,' I guffawed. 'Where have you been all my life?'

Nick grinned at me, and my breath caught as I took in how attractive he was.

The moment was interrupted by the abrupt chime of his doorbell.

'Ahh, dinner's here,' he announced.

We sat and ate what he promised was the best pizza in the area.

'So, I have to ask,' I said, as I marvelled at him eating his pizza with a knife and fork (I was the only other person I knew who did that), 'your fear of heights – does that extend to flying?'

After his friends had confirmed his keenness to visit Australia, I wanted to know if there were any barriers that might prevent it from happening.

'Well,' he started, rising to get another beer from the fridge, 'in order to answer that, I need to clarify I am not afraid of heights, per se.'

'But today at the London Eye, you were terrified.'

He handed me a drink. 'I'm not afraid of heights, I'm afraid that I will get stuck twenty metres in the air and need to be rescued.'

He took a long sip of his beer as if steeling himself.

'A couple of years ago, I was planning to propose to my girlfriend of six years. I wanted the proposal to be perfect, so I bought the ring, consulted her parents and organised for a private hot air balloon ride. I packed a picnic brunch, with champagne and all her favourite foods, and drove us just out of London to where the hot air balloons depart from. I'd even arranged for the pilot to push play on our favourite song and film the whole thing. I waited for what I thought was the perfect moment and then dropped to one knee, which wasn't as easy as it sounds in a wicker basket, suspended from a balloon powered by a flame. They're quite wobbly.'

'Wow, that sounds very ...' I trailed off. I knew the appropriate phrase for a scenario of this ilk was 'romantic', but grand gestures of affection had never appealed to me; they seemed showy and unnecessarily ostentatious. (Not that I had a lot of experience being on the receiving end of them.) Nevertheless, I couldn't dismiss the thought that being the subject of Nick's attention must have been nice.

'I know,' he said, 'it was a bit over the top. True to his word, the pilot managed to capture the entire proposal, where I professed my love to her and told her I wanted to spend the rest of our lives together. He also captured the bit where she told me she'd fallen out of love with me, and wanted to travel to America to work as a summer camp counsellor.'

'Oh dear,' I said.

'Yep. And he was so committed to filming my humiliation that he failed to realise we were veering off course and into a tree.'

I tried to stifle a laugh, but failed.

'We dangled up in that tree for two hours while we waited to be rescued. Every thirty minutes or so another branch would break under our weight, bringing us closer to injury and increasing my panic. While I've got over her, I suppose I've never got over the trauma of the event itself.'

He shuddered as if the memory still haunted him.

'It must have been terrifying,' I offered, in my best attempt at empathy, 'and very awkward.'

'It was both of those things,' he continued. 'But it doesn't end there. The video uploaded to a shared album and I found out later she had sent it to some of her friends, who forwarded it on to some of *their* friends. Before too long, it went viral.'

'Oh God,' I offered feebly in solidarity.

'I still get people tagging me in social media posts where she says no to my proposal and I can be heard squealing as we hit the tree. I think someone even put some of the words to music and made a song out of it. So, I made a promise to myself that I would never again risk being suspended in the air and needing to be rescued, and especially not when

I'm just trying to impress a girl. But today I made an exception.'

'So you *did* only go on it for me?' I asked, shamelessly hoping he'd expand on his feelings for me.

He smiled coyly. I felt compelled to hug him or to tell him the girl was a fool and she didn't know what she was missing, or possibly both. But I too had built up security measures to ensure I didn't get hurt by other people.

'Anyway,' he continued, 'to get back to your original question, no, I'm not afraid of flying. I figure at least if I'm in a plane crash there's a good chance that I'll plummet to my death, so I won't have to deal with the fallout of any misread romantic cues or viral videos.'

The distance between us shortened, although I couldn't be sure if it was him moving towards me, or me to him. My heart rate quickened.

'But I hope I've got better at reading signals since then,' he said.

By the time he'd placed his hands on either side of my face, I realised he was going to kiss me.

'Is this okay?' he whispered.

I nodded and inched my face towards his.

As our lips met my stomach flipped.

'I've been wanting to do that since I met you,' he said after a few moments, his mouth only a fraction away from mine.

I couldn't believe that Nick – a handsome, clever, funny, kind, sensitive and thoughtful man, with soft lips, a nice smell, well-kept fingernails and a genuine interest in me – would want to kiss me. This wasn't like the time at Sophie Arbunkle's birthday when Tim Alloy's friends told me he wanted to kiss me by the swing set, only to leave me standing there for half the night. Or when I succumbed to the advances of Dave – a guy from my geospatial science tutorial who I'd had a crush on for most of the year – who kissed me at an end-of-semester party and then confessed he'd thought I was someone else. Nick wanted to kiss *me*.

Nick pressed his lips against mine again. But this time the tenderness of his kiss had transformed into something more urgent. More passionate. I was sure he could feel my heart thumping as I pushed my chest against his. A warmth coursed through my body; it was how I imagined lizards felt on the first sunny day after winter.

I tried to focus my thoughts on the sensations of my body: the feeling of his hands that he'd moved from my face to my lower back; the smell of his skin; and the rise and fall of my diaphragm as my breath became deeper. But an intrusive voice in my head kept asking the question about what this all meant for two people who lived on opposite sides of the world.

I was comfortable with this being a one-off holiday event; I was not a prude and had no sense of pious obligation for sex to be part of anything long-term or monogamous. But I wondered how being with Nick would shape my future, when every exchange with a man from this day forward would be compared to this perfect moment. And that was even with the intrusive thoughts about him seeing my unkept bikini line and granny knickers.

I defiantly pushed all that noise from my mind and surprised myself with my own boldness as I sat up and swivelled my body to straddle him in his seated position on the couch.

Nick moaned.

'Oh, God. Sorry. Are you okay?' I asked hurriedly. 'Did I hurt you?'

He lifted his eyes to meet my gaze.

'Quite the opposite,' he said with a grin. 'I'm very glad you're here.'

I wasn't sure if he meant in London, in his apartment or on his lap, but I enjoyed being the object of his desire.

We pulled and tugged breathlessly at each other's clothes, our hands and mouths exploring each other.

'Wait there,' he said suddenly, lifting me to one side and springing off the couch. 'I'll be right back.'

He took off into his bedroom.

His abrupt departure slapped me back into reality and I was wracked with disappointment. Was it something I'd done? Was he not attracted to me? Had I misread the situation?

But when he returned holding a small, foil condom packet, which he wordlessly announced with a wink, I allowed myself to relax again.

He lay down on the couch and pulled me towards him.

'Should we move to your bedroom?' I asked. 'What if we mess up the couch?'

The throw cushions that had been tastefully arranged were becoming strewn all over the place.

'Fuck the couch,' he replied with a wry smile.

'Fuck the couch,' I agreed as I lowered myself onto him.

Our bodies fit together like smooth-edged puzzle pieces, and we moved together in perfect unison – slowly at first.

'You are magnificent,' he whispered, which provided an alternate track to the soft nagging voice in my head that made me self-conscious about the silvery stretch marks on my breasts.

At first, I fought to stifle the groans that formed from deep within me. I'd always thought it was an exaggerated cliché in sex scenes on TV and in movies when people screamed in ecstasy. Eventually, I gave into them, and found that they freed some of the energy that was building inside me, like releasing a pressure valve.

I became aware I was gripping the pillow behind his head so tightly that my knuckles were white; it felt like it was the only thing anchoring me to Earth.

As I breathed more deeply, I sensed the smell around me had changed. The sophisticated notes of his spiced cologne had mixed with something earthier, something more organic. Sweat and skin; the smell of sex. It made me even hungrier for him.

'Oh, Beth,' he murmured as our movements quickened, and the sensations consuming my body intensified. I'd never heard my name said with such desire.

Eventually, I surrendered to the pleasure.

'I'd like to do that as many times as possible before I go away tomorrow and you leave London, if that's okay with you,' he said, as we lay on the couch, our legs entwined, our respiration rates returning to normal.

Previously, I'd had little interest in post-coital canoodling, but I was enjoying lying with him.

'So, why didn't you suggest we do that days ago, if you'd wanted to?' I asked.

He issued a little huff. 'To be honest, I wasn't sure how you'd react. I'm not sure if you know this, Beth, but you can be a little tricky to read. You don't give much away.'

I lifted myself onto one elbow and feigned surprise. 'Me? I've never been told that in my life,' I said sarcastically.

'I'm sorry I didn't, though,' he said, pulling me back into his embrace. 'That was fun. Also, it might have distracted you from wanting to go on the London Eye.'

'At least I know that every time you see it, you'll think of me,' I speculated.

It felt like a cloud had just passed over the sun when I realised that this perfect night might live only in our memory, prompted by the sight of a large, bicycle-wheel-shaped landmark.

He traced the length of my arm with his fingers, sending a fresh wave of goosebumps down my spine.

'Will you stay?' he asked, pulling me closer.

'I should really check what Gran is up to,' I replied, not able to silence the voice that reminded me that if she was staying with Gerry and I was staying with Nick then our hotel room would be sitting vacant. It was a complete waste of money.

I untangled myself from his embrace and reached for a cushion to cover my breasts. As I pried myself away from this blissful oasis, I felt like someone had turned on the lights in a dimly lit bar and it was only a matter of time before the patrons noticed the worn carpet and torn pleather furniture.

I reached for my phone on the dining table and saw I had a message from Gran.

Hi darling. I'll stay at Gerry's tonight. Hope you've had a good day. X

Nick stood naked in the middle of the lounge room. I took in his slim, toned physique with a sense of renewed yearning.

'Fancy spending the night at the hotel?' I asked coyly. 'Gran is staying at Gerry's.'

'I'll grab my stuff,' he said with a mocked urgency that made me giggle.

As he walked towards his bedroom, he left me with a glimpse of what I concluded was his most endearing angle.

Chapter 28

Beth

The first thing I saw when I opened my eyes the next morning was Elise the Kangaroo bobbing along the hotel room floor. The large foil balloon Nick had brought with him to the airport had started to wrinkle and deflate, which had hollowed its face and transformed its smile into a downward frown.

The second thing I saw was his note.

I didn't want to wake you. You looked so peaceful. Thanks again for last night. I can't wait to see you when I get back from Copenhagen. Nick x

I felt as glum as Elise the Kangaroo looked. I couldn't shake the sense of self-pity I felt that I had finally found someone who I connected with, and who seemed to like me too (if his enthusiasm during the last 12 hours was anything to go by), but a scheduling conflict had taken him away – for now, at least. That he would be back for my last night in London was some consolation.

I opened the blinds on a beautiful, sunny morning. There was no point in moping around, I thought. I was in London.

I went for a run through Kensington Palace Gardens and then met Gran and Gerry for brunch. The three of us then made a trip to the Royal Observatory at Greenwich. We arrived in time to watch the large red Time Ball rise to the top of its mast and then drop again, which it had done every day at 1pm since 1833. Now a novel tourist attraction, it was once a critical instrument for mariners and Londoners.

The Royal Observatory was the home of the prime meridian – a geographical reference line from the North Pole to the South Pole that divides the Eastern and Western Hemispheres. A brass strip about the width of my foot, which was laid in the ground, indicated Longitude 0°. This was used as a reference point for all astronomical observations, and became the centre of all world time.

The prime meridian was a completely arbitrary human construct. Its location was chosen in the late nineteenth century by a panel of delegates from around the world. Greenwich was chosen as the site for convenience – it was close to a large telescope – and to reflect Britain's widespread colonisation. Unlike the equator, which is determined by the Earth's axis of rotation, it could have been anywhere and done the same job. And yet, for eighty-eight years, it was the point at which the world's time was determined.

I enjoyed reading about the scientists who had sought universality and order, and so developed systems and processes that united the world and impacted everything from trade to passenger rail travel. But my mind kept wandering back to Nick. It was infuriatingly distracting.

'How are you going, darling?' Gran asked, as she walked the prime meridian line with her arms held out for balance as though she was walking the plank on a pirate ship, or taking a sobriety test in America.

'I'm good,' I replied. The line was marked along its length with the names of capital cities and their longitudinal degree. I tried to ignore how long it took for Gran to walk the distance between Greenwich (Nick) and Australia's cities (me). The physical depiction of the space between our two coordinates was a stark reminder of the distance between our two worlds.

'Did you have a good time with Nick last night?' she asked, her eyebrow raised insinuatingly.

The sound of his name made me grin. I imagined I looked idiotic but was literally unable to wipe it from my face.

'Beth Dwyer. Look at you,' she gently pinched my arm. 'You're smitten!'

Usually, I would get defensive at such an allegation. I had always thought that being 'smitten' – relinquishing one's affection to another in such a naive and childlike way – was frivolous and would end in heartache. I'd seen it happen countless times to Jarrah. But today I didn't feel defensive.

I diverted my eyes and pretended to busy myself looking at the place names on the ground.

'Well, what about you?' I asked, hoping to deflect any further questions. Gerry had wandered off to find a bathroom so I took the opportunity to check in while it was just me and Gran. 'Has this been everything you hoped it would be? Is she everything you remembered? I feel like we haven't really had a chance to chat.'

'Oh, darling. It has been so wonderful,' Gran gushed. 'It's funny, you know, over the years I've never forgotten how I *felt* about Gerry. But it's been so good to be reminded of *why* I felt that way. She really is terrific. Honestly, I feel like a missing chapter of my life has been found in a dusty book on a hidden shelf in an old library and read anew.'

Now it was her turn to look smitten.

'In fact,' she said with a slight hesitation, 'it's gone so well that she's planning on travelling back with us.'

'Really?' I said loudly, startling two small children who were jumping

211

from Chicago in one hemisphere to Rome in the other. 'That's huge.'

'I know,' she replied excitedly. 'I mean, we haven't worked out all the details, but we've agreed in theory that we're not ready for our time together to end. What do you think?'

'It's not about what I think, Gran,' I said definitively. Usually, I would happily provide my frank and fearless opinion or carry out an analysis of the situation, whether it was solicited or not. But after everything she and Gerry had been through, this seemed like a good time to forgo such a process. 'This is all about you, and what you want.'

'I know, I know.'

'For what it's worth, I can see how happy you are,' I offered.

She grinned broadly. 'Do you know,' she started, 'on the night before I got married, my mother told me that you get three great loves: your first love, the one you have a family with, and the one you grow old with. How lucky am I that Gerry and your grandpa are mine.'

After we finished at the observatory, I went back to the hotel and Gran returned to Gerry's house. While I was more than happy to spend the night alone to catch up on sleep, my thoughts again returned to Nick and how nice it had been to spend time with him. Was it possible to miss someone you'd only just met?

As I walked through the lobby, the receptionist called to me.

'Ms Dwyer, I have a message for you.'

I had just left Gran, so it wouldn't have been from her. And my family would have sent me a message on WhatsApp.

'I've been asked to give you this,' the receptionist continued. She handed me an envelope. I tore it open to find a note written on a hotel 'with compliments' slip.

I thought you, Aunt Gerry and Elise would enjoy getting high with some special plants this evening. A car will collect you from the hotel at 6.30pm. Enjoy! Nick x

'What the hell?' I muttered out loud, attracting the curiosity of the receptionist. Judging by the amount of weed I had smelled wafting around the city, I assumed that marijuana was now legal in the UK. Or at least decriminalised. But surely he didn't mean 'getting high' in the literal sense, did he? *Did* he?

I messaged Gran with all the information I had.

A surprise! How wonderful. She replied, with a winky face.

She was being sarcastic; Gran knew I hated surprises. Every day of my childhood was filled with 'surprises' – a term my parents used for chaotic or unplanned situations. I'd had enough surprises to last me a lifetime. My instinct was to hand the envelope back to the receptionist and send Nick a polite, yet assertive, 'thanks, but no thanks' text. But something about the fact that *he* had arranged this surprise made me less uncomfortable than if it had been anyone else. In fact, I felt an uncharacteristic flutter of excitement to see what he had in store.

~

At 6.30pm sharp, Gran, Gerry and I piled into a car, which drove us along the edge of Hyde Park, down Constitution Hill, past Buckingham Palace, along the River Thames for a while and past the monument to the Great Fire of London. I was relieved when we pulled up in front of a soaring tower, and not a crack den.

We filed past an enormous living green wall (such a thing wouldn't survive one summer in Australia) and a sign for 'Sky Garden'.

'How lovely,' Gerry said. 'I've been meaning to come here for ages. I wonder how he managed this?' she mused. 'It's usually booked out for weeks.'

A message chimed on my phone:

Sorry I couldn't be there with you tonight. (Not sorry to miss the

height, though.) Dinner is in thirty minutes at the top. Just give your
name at reception. I hope you have a great time. x

As we rode in the lift to the top of the building, I googled our destination and learned it was London's highest public garden.

We arrived at a surprisingly dense and lush sky-high park, greeted by spectacular 360-degree vistas across London. A warm yellow glow from the setting sun bathed the entire space, which smelled earthy and felt slightly humid.

As an environmental scientist working in a metropolitan area where multiple users vie for open space, the concept of building a public park at the top of one of the tallest buildings in London fascinated me.

We walked the periphery of the structure and pointed out key landmarks. I smiled as I looked to the London Eye which, at its highest point of 135 metres, was 15 metres shorter than where I stood. No wonder Nick wasn't keen to come up here.

We followed the steps and paths that traversed the garden beds and explored the impressively rich collection of plants, which included ferns, cycads and birds of paradise. Then we enjoyed a delicious dinner.

I was so touched. No one had ever planned anything like this for me. And it didn't feel trite; it felt like a genuine and thoughtful gesture of affection. From the choice of venue, to picking up the dinner tab, to having a bottle of champagne delivered to our table when we arrived, Nick had surprised me – in the best way.

~

I spent the next ten days deepening my affection for London and its surrounds.

Gran, Gerry and I travelled to Sussex to visit the Kew Gardens Millennium Seed Bank. The underground storage facility for more than

2.4 billion seeds represented 16 per cent of the world's species, including a number Gran had personally collected.

'Some of my babies are in there,' she announced to a bemused tourist who seemed not to understand Gran's particular affiliation with each species she'd worked on or, alas, English. Nonetheless, it was impressive to think that seed from the warty swan orchid that she had been working to conserve in the nature reserve adjoining her childhood home had been collected, prepared, catalogued and stored there for perpetuity.

On the days Gran and Gerry spent together, I happily wandered through the National Portrait, Tate and Saatchi galleries and the British Museum alone. I baulked at the wealth at Harrods, and took a trip out to Hampton Court Palace. Each morning, I ran through London's magnificent parks, and I joined the thousands of other tourists to watch the changing of the guard. On two non-consecutive days, when I didn't have anything planned, I challenged myself to simply wander around the city without agenda or expectation. I thought I would feel bored, or untethered, but I stopped to eat when I felt like it, spent time in parks when the sun shone and ducked into shops and other buildings to escape the cold and rain. On those days, I caught the performance a talented fire twirler entertaining a crowd outside a tube entrance, spotted a Banksy work in Mayfair, and sat and watched while a great spotted woodpecker made its nest. I could now also say I'd had a drink in London's narrowest pub. None of these things were on my agenda, but I enjoyed them all.

A highlight was a visit to Warner Bros. Studio Tour for a behind-the-scenes look at the making of the Harry Potter movies. I had been eight when I first read Harry Potter and I'd fallen in love with it from the first page. As I wandered through the Great Hall set, which was furnished with long tables piled with food props and lit by floating candles, I recalled how devastated I was when I hadn't received a letter when I was eleven to say I'd been accepted to Hogwarts. I'd yearned to have a reason to leave my family for a life of magic and adventure. And I had been sure Hermione Granger and I would have been the best of friends. Like me, she was assertive, academically minded and an unapologetic perfectionist. As a Muggle-born witch, she knew what it felt like to be different from her family too.

As I was sitting outside 4 Privet Drive, enjoying a mug of butterbeer, my thoughts turned to my own family. With everything that had been going on with my lotto win, Gran and Nick, I had contributed even less to the family chat than usual.

I lifted the mug of butterbeer up to my face and extended my arm to take a photo of myself with it. I posted it to the family chat with the caption 'Sampling the local brew'. Within a few moments, Jarrah liked my picture.

Hope you're having the best time, Bethie. I know how much you love the world of Harry Potter. Did you have to take the train from Platform 9³/⁴ to get there? x

I decided it wasn't necessary to advise her that Platform 9³/⁴ was at King's Cross Station, which was not on the same line as the one that I travelled on to Watford, where the studio was located. Instead, I decided to just accept her well wishes; I didn't think she was paying attention when I was immersed in the world of Hogwarts.

I opened my message thread with Nick and uploaded the photo there too. He had been in my thoughts constantly (infuriatingly so; it was like a cerebral earworm). But I was mindful that he was away for work, and then spending time with friends, so I didn't want to bother him with inane chatter or self-indulgent selfies. However, he had initiated most of the message chats we'd had since he'd left and when I'd told him visiting Harry Potter's world was on my to-do list, he'd told me he was a fan too. I hit send.

I had tried hard not to wish away my holiday. I absolutely loved London, and had enjoyed exploring it without having to rush or adhere to a restrictive budget. And, even with my lotto win, it was expensive to get here and I had to be conscious about how I used my annual leave; it seemed unlikely that I would return any time soon. But as each day passed, and Elise the Kangaroo balloon became more flaccid, my anticipation grew for my last night in London – when Nick returned.

And I wasn't disappointed.

Our flight back to Australia was scheduled for the following morning, so Nick and I agreed I would meet him at his flat and we would have dinner together. We didn't discuss our plans for afterwards, but I found a beautician to take care of my personal grooming, and I splurged on yet another set of underwear that I was not self-conscious to be seen in, to prepare for any eventuality.

Nick opened his door to his flat and pulled me in by the waist. He kissed me before we'd even exchanged a word.

'Hi,' he said finally through the lopsided grin I had been thinking about since I last saw him. His arms were still around me.

'Hi,' I replied dumbly.

He was more attractive than I remembered, if that was even possible.

'I took the liberty of making a reservation for dinner at a great place just around the corner,' he said. 'But it's not for forty-five minutes. So we could go somewhere for a drink. Or ...'

He bit the bottom of his lip, which inspired a variety of thoughts for how we could spend the next forty-five minutes.

We didn't make it to dinner. Indeed we didn't make it far through the doorway into his flat for a good thirty minutes. But the evening was perfect. And so was he.

~

Very early the next morning, Nick made coffee as I showered. As the warm water cascaded over me, I ran through the list of reasons I was glad to be going home. I was looking forward to getting stuck into the next phase of my possum project, I was keen to salvage my indoor plants that I was sure Mum would have forgotten to water, and it would soon be jacaranda season – my favourite time of the year, when the city was awash with purple. I repeated the list several times; it was all I could do to convince myself that leaving London was the right thing to do.

Chapter 29

Elise

Despite a few close calls, Elise and Beth managed to board the plane with all their luggage, and their passports. But Elise was also boarding with a plus-one, and she sensed that Beth was boarding with regret that she had to leave hers behind.

As the plane hurtled down the runaway and launched into the air, Gerry reached over the divide of the adjoining business class pods and squeezed Elise's hand.

'Who would have thought?' Gerry said.

'Who indeed?' Elise chortled.

Elise allowed herself to reflect on the significance of the past two weeks. She had touched down in London with a menagerie of winged insects flapping around her insides. She'd had no idea how her reunion with Gerry was going to go, or whether she should even have visited in the first place. She certainly never imagined it would go as well as it did.

Nor had she expected Beth to open her heart to love on the trip. Elise had surreptitiously watched on as Beth had farewelled Nick at the terminal with an uncharacteristically long embrace. The whispered exchanges and stolen kisses they shared when they thought no one was looking spoke volumes about their affections for each other. But Elise knew Beth well enough to know there was no point in probing for details. She would share them if she wanted and, if not, she would guard them like a state secret.

'I don't ask this to apply any kind of pressure,' Gerry started, somewhere over south-eastern Europe. 'But have you given much thought to how you will introduce me to people?'

Elise had been thinking about it. A lot.

'You mentioned your immediate family was supportive, but what about the other people in your life? Will they be as accepting? I hope you understand that I won't lie about myself. And I won't be shoved back in the closet.'

'Of course not,' Elise replied earnestly. 'I would never ask you to do that.'

'I know you mean that,' Gerry responded. 'But I assume I'll be sleeping in a bed with you. What happens when visitors come over? Will we be dragging my pyjamas between rooms to make it seem like we're just two old friends enjoying a platonic sleepover?'

'I don't think *that* will be necessary,' Elise replied, understanding its pertinence. 'Perhaps we'll just forgo pyjamas altogether and save ourselves the hassle.'

Gerry smiled meekly.

'I was actually planning on asking how you wanted to handle it too, Gran,' Beth said, leaning forward out of her pod. 'You know what I'm like, and between our field trips and mutual colleagues I'm worried I'll say something I'm not meant to, to someone I'm not meant to tell.' She looked to Gerry. 'I have a rich and mortifying history of putting my foot in my mouth – socks, shoes and all. I am a watertight secret-keeper, but I'm a terrible liar.'

'I'm not going to lie to anyone,' Elise confirmed quickly. 'I just don't think I need to make a song and dance about it. There are people I'm looking forward to telling because I want them to know how happy I am. But everyone else can draw their own conclusions and ask me about it if they feel they need to.'

'It must make you so happy to see how different things are for people now,' Beth directed to Gerry, 'after everything I'm sure you must have gone through in your lifetime.'

Gerry nodded.

'Yes. I see now that when you came out all those years ago,' Elise said, 'it wasn't just your sexuality you were defining.'

'*Allll* those years ago?' Gerry drew out the 'L' for emphasis. 'You're making me sound old.'

Elise didn't take her bait.

'You declared your sense of self-worth to the world, despite all the hostility and judgement you faced. You claimed your right to be yourself, even if it didn't fit with other people's expectations of what that should look like. That was so courageous. I'm not sure I would have been that brave. It's taken me sixty years—'

'It wasn't exactly that simple, Elise,' Gerry said firmly but not unkindly. 'It's true that I've enjoyed a lot of love and friendship that I wouldn't have found if I hadn't been true to myself, but I've lost people too. And there are people – people dear to me, including my parents – who never knew all of me.' She paused as if still burdened by the weight of it. 'Back then, it wasn't so much about "coming out", but letting people in. And, I didn't just come out once and that was that,' she continued. 'I "come out" every day.' She used her fingers to insert the phrase into quote marks. 'Each time I meet someone new, I have to make a decision about whether to correct their assumptions, and carry out a risk assessment about how that might go. I've been doing it for decades, and it's fucking exhausting. To be honest, sometimes it's just not worth it. Who cares if a shop assistant I'll never see again, who is selling me a pint of milk, views me through their heteronormative lens and assumes I've got a husband at home to make tea for?' Gerry let out an exasperated sigh, as though the fatigue of having to declare her sexuality for the past fifty-odd years had finally caught up with her.

'But that should never deter one from shouting who they are from the rooftops – if they want to.' She directed this to Elise with a smile that indicated that, while she was tired, she still had a lot more fight left in her to ensure people could celebrate their sexuality.

'Or from grabbing a second chance with someone you love with both hands,' Elise added, after a moment's pause and a lifetime of contemplation.

~

After a stopover in the Middle East – where the old conventions of not shouting one's sexuality from the rooftops felt like a safer bet – the trio arrived at Perth airport in the middle of the night.

Elise spent much of the drive home trying to remember what state she'd left the house in. She wasn't self-conscious that her home wasn't as fancy as Gerry's; she loved her house and Gerry was not a snob. But she was worried she'd forgotten to take the bin out before she left, which might have attracted a plague of mice, and regretted it had been a fortnight since she'd washed the sheets, and possibly decades since she'd got new ones.

'Beth, I honestly don't know how to thank you,' Gerry said after the three women had arrived at Elise's front gate, surrounded by suitcases. 'It sounds so cliché, but what you've done for us has been life-changing.'

'I didn't do anything,' Beth responded modestly. 'I just googled your name and helped with the logistics.'

'That's not true at all,' Gerry rebuffed. 'I dare say your gran probably needed a bit of encouragement to reach out to me after all this time, let alone board a plane and travel halfway around the world to see me.'

'Oh no, there was no way I was going to miss out on flying business class before I die,' Elise joked.

Gerry opened her arms to Beth, who stepped into her embrace.

'I mean it,' she said as they parted again. 'Thank you. And I hope you can see that opening your heart to love can lead to wonderful things.'

'Trust me. You'll never convince Beth of anything using sentimentality,' Elise said, stepping in to hug Beth. 'But Gerry's absolutely right.' Elise squeezed Beth tightly. When she let go, Beth was smiling. 'Now, get out of here, for God's sake, and give us some privacy.'

Beth laughed. She turned and picked up her suitcase, loaded it into her car parked in the driveway, and then backed out onto the road, waved to them, and drove into the night.

'Your garden is absolutely stunning, Elise,' Gerry said as they turned to walk up the path.

The water in the birdbath shimmered in the night, and the air was crisp and still. Elise paused to soak in the sense of relief one gets when one arrives home after being away, even if it's been a marvellous trip.

'Oh look,' Gerry exclaimed in a whispered shout as she pointed to the electrical wire that led from the street to Elise's roof. 'Is this the welcoming committee?'

The two round yellow eyes of a southern boobook owl stared out from the darkness. Jack had told Elise the species went by several names, including mopoke.

'His name is Liber,' Elise whispered, relieved to see the neighbourhood owl didn't appear to have gained weight from feasting on a plague of mice that had overrun the house.

The two women quietly edged their way up the path in an attempt not to frighten Liber, but the squeaking of the suitcase wheels startled it, and it took off silently into the night.

'Welcome,' Elise said, turning on the hallway light once they'd made it inside.

Elise paused to remember the moment John had carried her over the threshold when they'd moved into the house as newlyweds. He had been so proud.

Elise gestured to the first door on the right off the hallway. Her bedroom. John's bedroom. Their bedroom. The room she would now share with Gerry, for a while at least.

'We'll put your case in here, for now,' Elise said, noticing Gerry's gaze land on a large framed photo of John, taken on his seventieth birthday. Elise had had the photo enlarged shortly after he died to keep next to her bed during a period of insomnia. It had helped her sleep when she felt like he was watching over her.

'I can move that,' Elise said, gesturing hurriedly towards the frame.

'It's fine,' Gerry replied, putting her hand up to stop her.

'Are you happy to unpack later?' Elise asked, suddenly eager to move out of the bedroom. 'I'll pop the kettle on. Are you hungry?'

As the two women moved down the hallway, past Herrick hanging in the loungeroom and towards the kitchen, Elise saw her house through a new lens – Gerry's lens – and became conscious that John was everywhere. His printed labels were still stuck on the doors, the gadgets he purchased from mail order catalogues filled the cupboards, and fifty-five years of memories were woven into every piece of fabric, painted into every wall and sealed into every surface. Being with Gerry in London, Elise had felt free of some of the strings that connected her to her marriage with John. He was never completely absent from her thoughts, but he certainly wasn't staring at them from a framed picture on the mantle. Elise felt like her two worlds were hurtling towards each other, destined for a clumsy collision. She braced herself for the fallout.

'Tea would be lovely, thanks,' Gerry said, resting her hand on Elise's arm and giving her a smile. 'Your home is lovely, Elise,' she said as she looked around the kitchen. 'I can see it's been a wonderful home and is full of cherished memories. It must feel a little odd to have me in it. I hope you feel okay with me being here. I realise it must be ... a lot.'

Elise nodded. It was a lot, and the long-haul flight wasn't helping her to process it.

'I can always stay in a hotel if you'd prefer. There's no pressure for me to stay here. This was all very spur-of-the-moment.'

'No,' Elise said urgently. 'Absolutely not. I'm happy to have you here. I *want* you here. It's just that you've been tucked away in my heart, and in a trinket box I stored in a cupboard, for a long time. And now here you are, standing in my kitchen.' Elise's words crackled.

'Of course,' Gerry said calmly, taking the box of tea that Elise had been holding in one hand and the teapot she'd been clutching in the other for the past few moments. 'I understand.'

She spooned the loose-leaf tea into the teapot, poured in the water from the kettle and set it on the table.

'I'm just going to use your bathroom,' Gerry said.

Elise explained where it was and then flopped down into one of the dining chairs. She felt lightheaded again.

'Seems I *have* been here in this house all along,' Gerry said, grinning as she returned from the bathroom.

Elise looked to her for clarification.

'The Gouldian finch painting at the end of the hallway,' she said.

'You're absolutely right. You most certainly have been.'

~

Elise and Gerry spent the next two days enveloped in their own private cocoon of nostalgia; Elise wasn't ready to share Gerry with anyone just yet. A trip up to a national park and a tour of the caves had them giggling like young girls again. Walks around the river and through the university

225

brought back memories of the time they'd spent together. Gerry wanted to take a dip in the Indian Ocean again, but neither of them made it past their ankles; the years had stripped them of their immunity to the cold.

Seeing Gerry again made Elise feel like time operated on a spiral coil rather than a linear plane. On the one hand, it felt like a million years had passed since her days at university, while on the other, it felt like the last sixty years had been nixed altogether. Elise could hardly believe that after all this time of keeping Gerry and their relationship a secret, she was preparing to introduce her, as one of her two great loves, to the world, starting with her family.

Chapter 30

Beth

'Yia sou,' my father bellowed from the front door as Gerry, Gran and I made our way towards it. I hadn't warned Gerry about my family's penchant for themed events, which tonight appeared to be Greek in nature.

I could feel a familiar sense of embarrassment rising from the pit of my stomach; the same one I had felt when I brought my school friends home. I was usually diligent in providing newcomers with a disclaimer about what they might be exposed to and, as I glanced up at my dad standing in the doorway with his hands outstretched, wearing a white linen shirt and shorts, with a wreath fashioned from olive leaves atop his head, it seemed like an oversight of monumental proportions. Gerry was probably used to formal English dinners, with dress codes and silver cutlery. What would she make of this circus? And, worse, what would Nick think, if he were here?

'Yia sou,' Gran replied warmly, kissing my dad on both cheeks.

'Yia sou, Gerry!' my dad exclaimed as he reached for her and brought her in for an all-encompassing bear hug – another thing I should have warned her about. But Gerry did not seem phased. In fact, she seemed amused, and she leaned her whole body in to reciprocate. Perhaps Gran had warned her, I thought.

'It's so good to have you here, Gerry,' my dad said with the familiarity that you might expect of someone who was welcoming a long-lost friend back into the fold.

'Thanks, Thorn. It's great to meet you. I've heard so much about you. To be honest I'm dying to know if you live up to the hype.'

Dad smiled broadly. 'I like her already, Elise.' He ushered Gran and Gerry inside and then turned to me. 'Bethie.' He drew me in for a hug. 'It's good to have you back.'

Mum appeared, embraced Gerry warmly, and then held both her hands as she told her she was glad she and Gran had reconnected. Jarrah and Elijah appeared and greeted us with hugs.

I was happy my family didn't know about Nick and what had happened between us. Being chronic oversharers themselves, they would have wanted to know every single detail. I was pleased the Spanish Inquisition had been directed at and about Gran.

Since leaving London I'd had an irksome twinge in my gut that I struggled to name. Sadness? Disappointment? Regret? *Longing*?

My phone had chimed with a WhatsApp message from Nick as soon as I switched it from aeroplane mode when we landed.

Hope you had a good flight. Say hi to a quokka for me if you see one.

We had exchanged messages about a range of things ever since, including the weather, how Gerry was enjoying her visit so far and our favourite sexual manoeuvre the other had performed on the last night I was in London.

Our exchange of banter flowed even more freely by text than it had in person. We enjoyed a funny, witty repartee and, in spite of myself, I felt a rush when I heard the chime of my phone to say I'd received a new message. Dopamine and serotonin had a lot to answer for.

But even if Nick was here, I wouldn't have wanted to bring him *here*. It would be mortifying to subject him to my family's antics. On the one hand, there was the risk he would find them ridiculous, which might make him question my character since I was genetically linked to them. But, considerably more concerning was the danger he would be captivated by the Dwyer charm and find me boring and uninteresting by comparison.

'Right,' Dad said, once Gerry had been introduced to everyone, and we'd settled into the loungeroom. 'Who's for a shot of ouzo?'

'Opa!' Gerry replied enthusiastically.

Gran and Gerry sat next to each other on the couch. There was a casual intimacy about how they were sitting that I had observed the whole time I'd seen them together. It was the type of ease you see in couples where an invitation to be in each other's space is implied. They both had their knees pointed towards each other, and their bodies were as close as possible to one another without actually touching. I had to admit that I had missed Gran in the days since we'd got back. We'd spoken so regularly in the weeks before we left and I'd barely seen or heard from her since we'd landed. But it was so good to see her so happy.

Gerry was indulgently answering my dad's questions about her time at university in Australia and entertaining his playful attempts to extract incriminating stories about Gran. I felt like, after the revelations about their relationship, any tales about having one drink too many or coming in past curfew would be benign in comparison to a same-sex affair. But she played along anyway.

'So what else have you got planned while you're here, Gerry?' Mum asked.

'I don't know what else we've got planned,' Gerry replied, looking to Gran in the way couples do when answering questions about one's plans is a job for two.

'Actually,' Gran said, turning her body further towards Gerry and placing her hand on Gerry's knee. 'We do have something planned for

Monday. We've got to go and check on my little orchid babies.'

During our visit to the Millennium Seed Bank, Gran had told Gerry all about the project to reintroduce the warty swan orchid at the bush reserve next to Woodside Ridge in the hopes it would attract the wasp.

'Oh, how wonderful,' Gerry replied. 'It will be lovely to head out there again after all these years.'

'I think it's meant to be a warm one on Monday,' Dad said.

'Yes, I saw that,' Gran said before turning back to Gerry. 'I hope you haven't lost your chops for a hot Australian day.'

The conversation over our Greek-themed dinner of slow-cooked lamb and fried cheese was as lively and as animated as ever.

Gerry managed to cut through my family's competition to occupy centre stage and entertained us with amusing anecdotes and captivating tales of her adventures. Everyone seemed completely taken by her.

'Gerry seems great,' Mum said as she washed and I dried the dishes in the kitchen after dinner.

'I think I even saw Mum giggle,' she said as though it was as implausible as having seen her cartwheel. 'I mean, I've seen her laugh, of course. But *giggle*? That's definitely a new one. I didn't even know she made that sound.'

'They definitely get along well,' I offered.

Mum absentmindedly soaped a plate that was well and truly void of food remnants until I took it from her hand and broke her daydream.

'You know,' she said, 'one of the hardest things about losing one of your parents is worrying how the other one will cope and whether they'll be lonely.' Her voice was hushed, as if speaking the thoughts out loud made it more likely the notion would come true. 'Mum is more than capable of looking after herself, obviously. But when you lose a spouse, you also lose your companion.

'I'm not sure how it will all work,' she continued, 'with Gerry living in London and Mum living here. But I'm glad she's got someone. And

I'm sure they'll work it out if it's meant to be.'

She handed me a washed cup.

'What about you, Bethie?' she said, her voice bouncing again. 'What did you get up to? Did you have a good time in London?'

An image of Nick involuntarily flashed in my mind's eye. I felt my cheeks flush.

'Beth Dwyer,' she said mockingly. 'Are you blushing?'

'Who's blushing?' Jarrah said as she appeared in the doorway, her impeccable timing adding to my mortification.

I diverted my eyes and busied myself putting the stack of dried plates I had created on the bench away in the cupboard.

'Ohhhh,' Jarrah exclaimed. 'Bethie. Did something happen in London that you'd like to share with us?'

'No,' I responded curtly. 'I have no intention of sharing anything with you about what happened in London.'

'So something *did* happen, though?' she narrowed her eyes in contemplation.

I scoffed, aware that the once light blush on my cheeks had transformed into a prickly, angry heat that spread across my chest, neck and face.

'Is this about Nick?' Gran asked innocently as she walked into the kitchen carrying empty glasses.

I glared at her.

'Nick! Who's *Nick*?' Jarrah squealed, clapping her hands like she'd won a prize.

'Nick is Gerry's great-nephew,' I said, my head halfway into the saucepan cupboard, trying to hide my mortification. 'He was nice enough to hang out with me for a few days.'

'From what I saw, it was a bit more than that,' Gerry said, arriving with the salt and pepper shakers from the table. 'I think he was *quite* taken with you.'

'Urgh. Where are you all coming from?' I moaned, feeling overwhelmed that the attention of everyone in the room was on me.

'We had a good time together,' I said, directing my words to Gerry. 'And I was grateful he was happy to hang out.'

Four pairs of wide eyes stared at me from under raised eyebrows.

'And that's all I'm going to say about that.'

'Oh come on, Bethie,' Jarrah said with an irritating whine as she stroked my arm patronisingly. 'Give us *something*.'

'Fine, then. I'll just tell you this one thing,' I said, leaning in towards her as if preparing to share a juicy tidbit. 'It's none of your business,' I whispered.

'Argh. You're no fun,' she cried. 'No matter. I'll get it out of Gran.'

She winked at Gran who replied by making a zipping action across her lips and throwing an imaginary key over her shoulder. As always, Gran had my back. What on earth would I do without her?

Chapter 31

Elise

'It's okay, I suppose. If you like this sort of thing,' Gerry said, smiling, as she scanned the nature reserve next to Woodside Ridge. It was as magnificent as ever.

The field trip to monitor the orchids was scheduled early to avoid the heat of the day, but the air already felt dry and warm. The insects called loudly into the morning.

'Here,' Elise said, taking her phone from her pocket. 'Let's send a pickie to Beth. After all, we've got her to thank for you being here.'

The two women huddled together and snapped a shot. When Elise looked at the photo, she saw it had captured her looking at Gerry in profile. It reminded her of the photo she'd kept in the box from all those years ago.

She held up her hand to catch a signal and sent it to Beth.

Gerry walked towards one of the grass trees and cupped a handful of its long green spines, which exploded out of its ancient charred black trunk like prickly fireworks.

'You won't want to spend too much time touching that,' Elise said, nodding towards Gerry's hand. 'Ticks.'

Gerry recoiled sharply.

'Oh, God! That's right,' she said, inspecting her hands. 'I forgot everything in Australia is trying to kill me.'

'Not everything,' Elise said with the blasé casualness of an Australian who has spent their life navigating venomous snakes, spiders and jellyfish, and dodging sharks. 'But you probably should watch out for snakes on a day like this.'

Gerry did an impressively vigorous dance for a woman of her age, lifting her knees on the spot like an Irish dancer. It was the same manoeuvre she'd done sixty years ago when she, Elise and a group of friends had ridden their bikes to a lake a few kilometres from the city. The wetland was a haven for waterbirds – black swans glided across the water's surface, swamphens stalked around the grass looking for invertebrates, and regal white egrets picked amongst the reeds. Tiger snakes thrived there too.

The group had set up a picnic on the grass under a weeping willow when Gerry spotted a juvenile tiger snake sunning itself about 10 metres away. She jumped around as though the ground was on fire, screaming 'get it away from me' before hopping on her bike and cycling off. It took Elise about ten minutes to catch up with her and flag her down, and a further thirty to convince her to come back and enjoy the picnic. She returned, but insisted on eating her sandwich from the safety of one of the middle branches of the weeping willow tree and leaving as soon as the last mouthful was finished.

'They won't bother you ...' Elise started, smiling at the memory.

'I know, I know, "unless you bother them",' Gerry finished the well-known mantra. 'Then we shouldn't have any trouble ...' she shouted into the bush, wagging her finger wildly, 'if we both stay out of each other's way.'

As the insects fell silent, Elise heard a rustle coming from a small scrubby bush to her right. She hoped the snakes had taken heed.

A short-beaked echidna waddled into sight. Its stocky legs and inwards-angled feet made easy work of moving across the leaf-littered ground. The tip of its pointed nose was covered in dirt, suggesting that it had been digging for food before it was startled by an old English lady shouting into the bush.

The two women watched with their mouths agape as it passed between them and into nearby bushes to their left.

'Well, I never,' Elise exclaimed, having never seen one in the area before.

As she bent down for a better look, a stunning single deep-red orchid rising out of the ground caught her eye. Its petals were similar in colour to another species found commonly in the area – the blood red orchid – but they weren't quite as long, were slightly more stout and curved upward, more like the ubiquitous fringed mantis orchid. The centre of the flower – the labellum – was bright green with touches of the rich, deep red. Roughly the size of a marble, the labellum had comb-like teeth along its edges, which were longer than Elise had seen before in any other species.

'What have you found there?' Gerry asked, coming in for a look.

'I honestly don't know,' Elise replied. 'I don't think I've ever seen this species before. I'll get Emily to have a squiz when she arrives. If anyone knows what it is, it's her.'

The two women searched the area and found one other plant a few metres away. It had two flowers. Emily and Jack arrived as Elise was crouching awkwardly, trying to take photos of the flowers with Gerry's phone so they could compare them with species registered on the online database. She'd only managed to take three pictures up her nose and one of her thumb.

'Welcome back!' Jack boomed as he exited the car and then strode towards Elise for a big hug.

'Thanks, Jack. It's good to see you. This …' Elise stammered, momentarily forgetting how she'd planned to introduce Gerry to people, 'is my Gerry.'

'It's beaut to meet you, Elise's Gerry,' Jack said warmly, shaking her hand. 'Fantastic you could come along today.'

'Hi Gerry, I'm Emily Lim,' Emily said efficiently as she emerged from behind the car.

'Emily, darling. Come and have a look at this, will you?' Elise called, gesturing towards the orchid.

The group crowded around the orchid, almost knocking their heads together.

'Ever seen this before?' Elise asked.

Emily knelt down to examine the plant more closely. After a few moments, she sat back on her heels and looked up at Elise.

'You know, I don't think I have.'

Elise, Gerry and Jack hooted and whooped at the prospect they'd discovered a new species as Emily disappeared back to the car. She reappeared with a plastic folder, which contained everything needed to collect a specimen.

'You do the honours,' she said, handing Elise the equipment.

'Thank you, darling,' Elise said, appreciating the significance of the gesture. It would have been well within Emily's remit as the officer in charge of the project to collect the specimen, but gathering the sample made Elise the undisputed discoverer of the species, if it was indeed new to science.

Elise used the secateurs to carefully remove one of the flowers from the double-headed plant. She gently lowered it into a clear plastic bag and added some water to keep it moist. Emily assisted as she measured the plants, and recorded notes about their habitat, composition, colour and plant neighbours.

The group searched the area again for more of the plants but, as the morning warmed, they agreed they'd focus on the warty swan orchids and return to survey for the new plant once they'd checked it against reference material at the herbarium.

The heat, combined with too much time spent leaning down and the excitement of her discovery, had given Elise a low-grade headache and made her feel lightheaded. As she made her way to a nearby tree to steady herself, she tried to recall if she'd remembered to take her blood pressure medication. The sun was breaking through the crown of the trees and soaking the bush in warm golden hues. Elise smiled as she watched Gerry help Jack and Emily unload the equipment they needed from the vehicle. She felt like there had been a divine merging of her worlds, like her life had come full circle in the most perfect, poignant way.

Her thoughts turned to John. She would always love him and be grateful for the life they'd shared. And Rosie and her babies had brought her so much joy, and she knew that if she hadn't lost contact with Gerry all these those years ago, she would never have had them in her life.

But now she had Gerry again. Beautiful Gerry.

The warmth of the light seemed to intensify, and wisps of purple, magenta, teal and green danced around the edge of her peripheral vision. The vibrancy of the colours reminded Elise of the feathers of a Gouldian finch.

Elise heard Gerry calling her name, but her voice seemed distant and muffled, as if being transmitted through an old radio. The colours swirling in her periphery intensified and her field of vision narrowed. She tried to blink the colours away but, as each moment passed, she could see less and less of her surroundings. Unable to see, she felt disorientated. But she wasn't afraid; she felt completely calm.

Elise could hear Gerry saying her name over and over. She remembered that, as a twenty-year-old, Gerry's refined diction when saying her name – *Elise* – had made her sound more important than she felt. Elise hadn't thought she would ever hear her name spoken that way again.

She felt Gerry's lips kiss her forehead. She wanted to reach up and hold her, but her arms wouldn't move. The hues of the colours in her mind's eye began to lighten, and the brightness intensified. She felt a radiant heat, which warmed every cell in her body. She imagined it was how cats felt when they lay next to a window on a sunny winter's day soaking in the warmth. Her body felt weightless, and she sensed she was floating towards the all-encompassing glow.

She closed her eyes.

Chapter 32

Beth

I reached into my back pocket to retrieve my ringing phone.

I had spent the morning with Alannah doing a site visit of the area where the possum bridge was being installed. Usually, I wouldn't dream of using my phone while on a site visit, but Nick and I had been exchanging messages all morning and I was powerless to resist the urge to read and respond to them immediately.

Part of me was infuriated at myself; I was carrying on like a lovesick puppy with someone I had only just met. The other part of me had never felt more hopeful at a chance of a relationship with someone, even if he did live on the opposite side of the world.

'Mum mobile' flashed across the illuminated display.

I rejected the call and pushed the 'send message' option.

I'm on site for work. I'll give you a buzz from the car in an hour or so.

I had received a photo from Gran and Gerry at Woodside Ridge earlier, which I would reply to at the same time.

I returned my phone to my back pocket where it sat for less than a second before it rang again. 'Mum mobile' it announced again.

It wasn't unusual for my family to lack respect for my boundaries. When I was a kid, them knocking on my bedroom door was part of the process of opening it, rather than a request for permission to enter. And they frequently turned up unannounced to my house with little regard for whether I was busy or didn't fancy company.

But something in the pit of my stomach implored me to answer it.

'Hi Mum,' I said warily. 'Is everything okay?'

Mum sniffed audibly down the phone. 'It's Gran, Bethie.' She inhaled sharply. 'She died.'

I replayed the words in my head, desperately hoping that I could derive an alternative meaning from what I knew they meant.

I felt my breath quicken. Every cell in my body felt like it was vibrating and the only thing keeping me from disintegrating right there on the spot was the skin that was holding it all together.

'What happened?' I managed to ask finally.

'She was out on a field trip with Gerry,' Mum replied, now through guttural sobs. 'And she collapsed. By the time the ambulance got to her, she'd gone. They think it was a stroke.'

I realised I was now sitting on the ground, but didn't remember lowering myself down. Alannah had arrived by my side and was mouthing 'Are you okay?', their brow furrowed with concern.

I wanted to ask Mum a million questions: what was she doing beforehand? Did anyone give her CPR? Had she been carrying heavy equipment? Who was with her when she died? Where was she now? Where was Gerry? Upon reflection, some, which I was no less compelled to ask, seemed absurd: what night does her bin go out? Had anyone thought about cancelling her library card? Who would clean out her fridge?

But all that came out of me was a noise that sounded like a wounded animal.

'I'm coming now,' I said finally, suddenly feeling a compulsion to move. Somewhere. Anywhere. 'I'll be there soon. Where are you? Where is she? Where should I go?'

'Come to the house, Bethie. Gerry's here, and they've already taken Mum aw—' She didn't even finish the word before she started sobbing again. 'Oh Bethie, what are we going to do without her?' Mum wailed between large wet sniffs.

'I have absolutely no idea,' I replied, feeling like my heart was actually breaking in my chest.

I lowered my head into my hands and allowed the tears I had been stoically trying to hold to cascade down my face.

'We'll see you soon, Bethie. Drive carefully. Is there someone that can bring you?'

I turned to Alannah, who was holding out a crumpled tissue that looked like it may have been used. I took it anyway and dabbed at my face, although it felt a little like trying to mop up a large-scale flood event with a face washer.

'Yes, Alannah's with me; we'll work something out.'

Alannah nodded fervently. 'Anything you need,' they whispered, extending their hand to my arm and giving it a gentle squeeze.

'I'll be there soon,' I said and then hung up on what I knew was probably the most significant phone call of my life.

~

As we rounded the corner into my parents' street, I thanked Alannah for driving me and for their assurances that they would tell Geoff what had happened and see to the handful of urgent work items that needed to be completed over the next couple of days.

I exited the car and walked up the path towards the front door as I had done a million times before. It struck me that so much was the same, but everything was different. *I* was different now. Before today I was a person who, despite feeling like I didn't fit in anywhere, had Gran. She knew me. She understood me. She was the one person on the planet who loved me because of the person I was, not in spite of it.

I knew that from this day on, my life would be divided into two parts: with Gran and without her.

My head seared with an intense headache and I felt like I was going to throw up. Dad opened the door, and I fell into his arms and sobbed into his shoulder. He cooed my name as he stroked my hair, and then guided me into the kitchen where Mum and Gerry were sitting at the table.

Mum stood up and wrapped me in a hug, her usually athletic frame seeming smaller somehow. She pulled back to look at me.

'How are you doing, kiddo?' she asked. Her eyes were red and brimming with tears, and her nose was shiny and swollen. A drip of clear snot dangled from the tip.

I shook my head solemnly, unable to articulate the magnitude of emotions that seemed to come in waves like an unrelenting tsunami.

I looked to Gerry. Somehow, she still looked elegant sitting there in Mum's kitchen wearing a polo shirt I recognised as Gran's and a pair of hiking trousers. But she looked vulnerable, as if someone had chipped away a strong clear lacquer, revealing a delicate layer beneath.

I noticed she had a smear of dirt up one of her arms and across her left cheek. It must have been horrific for her, to be out in the bush with Gran having collapsed, in a country she'd only landed in a few days beforehand.

'I'm so sorry, Gerry,' I spluttered.

'Oh, Beth,' she replied, standing and making her way towards me. 'I'm the one who's sorry. I know how much your gran meant to you.'

We hugged.

'What happened?' I asked, bracing myself for Gerry's recount of how it had come to be that I woke up this morning happy and full of optimism, and now I was grieving the loss of the most important person in my life.

Dad handed me a glass of ice-water. I sat down at the kitchen table, took a large sip and discovered it was, in fact, a very stiff gin and tonic. I coughed and then took another big gulp.

'Thatta girl,' Dad said, giving me a wink.

Gerry described that they had been at the nature reserve next to Woodside Ridge, where they had just seen an echidna and a curious-looking orchid.

'I'd noticed that she was a little breathless as we were walking to the car to get the equipment,' she said. 'But it was a warm morning, so I just figured she was a bit puffed.

'When I looked back ...' she paused as her voice cracked, 'she was just standing there, leaning against a tree, looking towards the sunlight. She looked ashen, but not sick. Just vacant, as though she was somewhere else entirely. I called out to her, but she didn't seem to hear me.' Tears were streaming down her face. 'I rushed over, but by the time I reached her, she'd just slid down the tree, and landed in a crumpled heap, like someone had let go of the strings on a marionette doll.'

She blew her nose loudly; it reminded me of the sound Gran made.

'We rolled her over and Emily – the trip leader – started doing CPR.'

Emily was efficient and competent, exactly the sort of person you'd want conducting CPR if you needed it.

'She tried and tried,' Gerry continued, her voice strained. 'But we couldn't save her.'

Mum and I sobbed in unison.

'I should have known she'd go and do something like this,' she continued with a sad irony-ladened chuckle. 'Lure me to the furthest corner of the world in the promise of making up for a lifetime of lost moments, and then go and die on me.'

Mum, Dad and I laughed, grateful for the brief moment of release that macabre humour brings to grief-stricken people.

My phone chimed in my bag. I reached in and saw a message from Nick.

I must know. Do Australians wear thongs as underwear or footwear? I'm researching cultural differences in case I ever make my way out there. I'd hate to get it wrong. Although I suspect you'd look great in both.

I slipped my phone back into my bag without replying. I wasn't ready to announce Gran's death to anyone – even him. An irrational part of me felt that doing so would somehow make it more real, and remove any last glimmer of hope for negotiation.

'I can let him know, if you like,' Gerry said quietly, intuitively knowing it was a message from Nick.

'That's okay, I can do it. Just as soon as I find the words. Unless you want to,' I added hurriedly, aware that Gerry might want to reach out to her family about Gran herself. She would need support from her people too.

'Whatever you want, Beth,' she said kindly. 'But not before you're ready.'

I smiled gratefully and blinked away the fresh tears that had gathered in my eyes.

'Gerry, are you comfortable, or would you like a shower and a change of clothes?' Mum asked. 'I can lend you some, or we can run you back to Mum's.'

A vision of Gerry in one of Mum's flowing boho dresses popped into my head, and I worked hard to suppress the urge to laugh.

'Thanks, Rosie,' she said, lifting one of her arms slightly and sniffing in the direction of her armpit. 'I hope I'm not unpleasant to be around.'

'No, no,' Mum exclaimed, 'not at all.'

'I'm just not sure I'm ready to wash the morning off my body just yet.' Gerry's words tumbled out of her and at the completion of the sentence, she burst into tears. 'I'm sorry,' she sobbed. 'It's silly. But I just hate the thought of washing her touch off me.'

My heart ached for Gerry. How cruel that their long-awaited reunion had been so short-lived. And I couldn't shake a twinge of guilt that if I'd left well enough alone, Gerry would be living her life in London, instead of sobbing at Mum and Dad's kitchen table on the other side of the world. I hoped that the time she'd spent with Gran, and the sense of resolution they'd both received, would make up for the loss she felt now.

I took another big gulp of my drink.

'Where are the others?' I asked Dad.

'Jarrah will be home shortly, she just had to wait for someone to relieve her at work. And Elijah's on his way home now,' he explained.

'Jarrah's at work?' I asked curiously.

'Yes, she got a temp job at a not-for-profit that supports homeless young people. It's just for a couple of months, while someone's on leave, but she's enjoying it, apparently.'

'That's terrific,' I said sincerely.

The next few hours were spent crying, laughing and drinking around the table. It could have been awkward to have Gerry spend this day with us, given we'd only just met her, but it was really nice to hear stories about Gran that we hadn't either lived or heard a thousand times. Gerry told us that when she and Gran were living in the college, she'd baked a batch of cinnamon twists because she knew Gran missed her mum's baking. But, instead of using a teaspoon of cinnamon she'd used a whole tablespoon. Gran was so touched by the gesture, and she didn't want Gerry feeling bad, so ate the entire batch before Gerry could try them and discover what she'd done. As Gerry recounted the story, I remembered all the times Gran had made cinnamon twists for us and told us they were flavoured with love.

I couldn't believe I'd never taste her cooking again.

Chapter 33

Beth

As the sun set on the day, my phone chimed again. It was another message from Nick.

It's okay, I googled the answer about thongs. Unfortunately, I did it at work, so may get sacked for looking at pictures of women in their underwear. Hope you're having a good day. x

I moved into my parents' lounge room so I could type my reply away from my family's chatter, which had grown louder with every passed hour and each consumed drink.

I placed my cursor in the message field.

Gran died today.

I paused to wipe away the fresh deluge of tears that cascaded down my cheeks.

She was on a field trip with Gerry when she collapsed. They think she had a stroke. I'm just so shocked. And so very, very sad. I think Gerry feels much the same, but we're taking good care of her. X

I pushed send on the message without re-reading it; I didn't want to have to read those three hideous words – Gran died today – again.

A few moments later a dancing ellipsis appeared on the screen indicating he was replying. It disappeared again, and my phone rang in my hand.

'Oh, Beth. I'm so sorry,' Nick said when I answered.

I tried to say something, but all that emerged from my mouth was a giant, wet sob. A few moments passed before he spoke again, but the silence wasn't strained or awkward; it felt more like an acknowledgement that conversation wasn't necessary to communicate the gravity of the situation.

'I suppose there's no point in asking how you are?' he said finally.

I managed a tiny ironic huff. I appreciated him saying that, as I've always found it deeply irritating when people ask it of bereft people, as though it wasn't completely obvious. After a few deep breaths, I told him as much as I knew about what had happened and the preliminary funeral plans that had been discussed over the course of the afternoon.

'Is there anything I can do? Can I ...' his voice trailed off as though he was running through a list of ways he could help from across the other side of the world.

'Would you like me to come over?' he asked after a few moments.

'Don't be silly,' I said instinctively. 'That would be crazy.'

'I know, I know. But I wish I could be there for you. And Aunt Gerry.'

Of course, it would be ridiculous; we'd only just met each other and, if he came out, he would inevitably have to meet my family, which would be a palaver at the best of times, let alone this one. But I wanted him here anyway. I longed for him to swat away my insincere protests and tell me he'd be on the next plane out.

He didn't, and I felt annoyed at myself for being disappointed. My ability to form rational thoughts about him had been further impaired now I'd added grief and several gin and tonics to the serotonin and dopamine that were already corrupting my judgement.

I massaged my forehead with my spare hand, trying to alleviate my throbbing headache.

'You probably want to get back to your family,' Nick said after a few more moments of silence.

'Not really,' I laughed. 'But I probably should. When I left them, they were discussing whether they should have her ashes shot from a cannon, or turned into tattoo ink so we could all get matching portraits of her etched into our bodies. I should probably get back to keep them on the straight and narrow.'

'Tattooed portraits?' Nick repeated.

'Actually, I think that was Gerry's idea.'

He laughed.

I couldn't think of anything else to say. I felt like my mind was operating in slow motion, and my body had been sucked dry of all its energy.

'I'm really sorry, Beth,' he said tenderly. 'She was terrific, and I'm really glad I got to meet her. I just wish I could do more to be there for you.'

Staunchly independent, I had never needed anything from anyone, much less from a partner. I learned young that it was better not to rely on Mum or Dad for anything, and I had been single for so long that even if I couldn't do something, I would learn how to, or pay someone who could.

But Nick's words comforted me; I liked the idea that someone wanted to be there for me, not because they thought I needed it, but because they wanted to be.

'Thanks, Nick. It means a lot. I'll be okay, eventually.'

'If you need anything, just call. Any time,' he said. 'Promise?'

'Promise.'

I hung up and walked back into the kitchen to find my family debating whether Gran's barley soup or meat pies were her superior dish. Neither, I insisted, came close to her rice pudding. I remembered the night we contacted Gerry was the last night she'd made it for me.

'Where is Gerry?' I asked Mum quietly, while the others carried on the discussion.

'I think she popped to the loo,' she responded. 'But that was a little while ago. I should check on her.'

'It's okay,' I said, already standing again. 'I'll go.'

I arrived to find the toilet light was off and the door was open, but I noticed the door to the garden was ajar.

I poked my head outside and spotted her. She was slumped in one of the many white plastic outdoor chairs that littered my parents' garden. The number of these chairs had multiplied each time my parents hosted a party. By my calculations, they had enough to seat the crowd of a Boxing Day Test.

Gerry was staring up at the night sky, her tear-stained cheeks glistening in the moonlight.

'They're a lot, aren't they?' I asked rhetorically, selecting the cleanest-looking chair to sit in. 'My family, I mean.'

'Oh, they're great,' she replied. 'I just needed some fresh air. I think the day, and the gin, have caught up with me.'

I nodded in solidarity.

'Nick rang, so I've let him know,' I said, after a few moments. 'I'm sure he'll be in touch with you soon.'

She gave me a wry smile. 'It's good to see you two are still getting on well, despite the oceans of distance between you.'

Not for the first time, I wished that the great minds of the world would stop messing about with space travel and focus on perfecting teleportation across Earth, so I could see him again, even if just for an hour. Hearing Gerry talk about the distance between us reminded me again of the challenge we faced. And I couldn't ignore that if things didn't work out between us, it would add extra heartbreak to the devastation of losing Gran. *Was it better to have loved and lost?* I pondered. Maybe it would be best to just let it go as a holiday romance, before anyone (me) got really hurt.

'I can't help but wonder how this is all going to work,' I said eventually.

'You know, my dear, take it from me.' Gerry's words were slightly clumsy, providing irrefutable evidence that the day, and the gin, had indeed caught up with her. 'Don't let your head get in the way of your heart. Elise and I both saw the way you two were together. It was lovely. She said she couldn't remember seeing you like that before.'

I felt my cheeks flush again at the mention of Nick, and then a fresh pang of sadness that Gran wouldn't be around anymore to observe me doing anything again.

'I've known him since he was born, and I could tell he was smitten too. Who knows ...' she continued, boisterously gesticulating with her glass in a way that seemed contrary to her usual refinement, 'maybe you and Nick were the reason Elise and I reconnected after all these years. Perhaps our love story was just the prelude to yours. Our affair sixty years ago had to happen, so you two would meet today. Maybe it was written in the stars.'

She arced her arm above her head to highlight the twinkling night sky above. The ice in her glass clinked as though providing a sound effect for the sentiment.

'I suppose that makes Elise and me star-crossed lovers,' she said, her voice quivering as she slumped further into her chair.

'You don't really believe all that, do you, Gerry?' I asked, curious that a science brain as brilliant as hers would entertain supernatural theories. Of course, there were plenty of esteemed scientists who believed in gods, in their various forms. But surely astrology stretched the notion of faith too far for most.

'We have to believe in something to make sense of all this,' she said wistfully. 'Besides, astrology *was* science once upon a time. Astrologers were highly respected scholars, and astrology was thought to influence everything from the weather and crop health, to personalities and human medicine. In fact, astrology was still used in medicine until the end of the seventeenth century. Did you know that?'

I nodded. 'And of course, Australian First Nations peoples have turned to the stars for stories about creation for millennia.'

I didn't know whether it was the lotto win, finding out about Gran and Gerry, meeting Nick, the gin, the fact that someone other than Jarrah was pointing to the stars for meaning, or just the overwhelming yearning I had to make sense of it all, but I was a lot less sure it was all nonsense than I had been a month ago.

I looked up, willing the stars for a sign that Gran was out there somewhere looking down on me. I realised it was the first time in more than eighty-two years that night had fallen on a world without her in it.

'Have you thought about where you might like to stay tonight?' I asked, trying to distract myself with other thoughts before I dissolved into a puddle of salty tears to be absorbed into the weedy grass of my parents' backyard.

She looked befuddled.

'I mean, where you'd be most comfortable. Obviously, you're welcome to stay at Gran's for as long as you'd like. But if you're not keen to stay there alone, there's a bunch of spare beds here, if you can handle *them*.' I gestured towards the house, and my family in it, with a nod of my head. 'Or you're welcome to stay at my house. It's nothing fancy, but I do have a sofa bed. I could sleep on that, and you could take my bed. Or I could come and stay with you at Gran's ... if you'd like some company there.'

I hadn't given it a lot of thought before now, but in offering to stay at Gran's, I realised I was desperate to spend time in her space. I wanted to smell it before her scent had dissipated and surround myself with the memories that were housed within the walls.

'Thanks, Beth. That would be grand. I'd love some company tonight. It would be nice to stay at your gran's together.'

'You let me know when you're ready to leave, then,' I said, rising to go back inside. 'It's been a massive day; I'm ready whenever you are.'

'I'll be in shortly. I'll just polish this off and make a wish on one or two of them.' She lifted her quart-filled gin and tonic in a wobbly salute to the stars twinkling above.

Chapter 34

Beth

By 9am the day after Gran died – when I finally dragged myself out of the spare bed at her place – word of her passing had well and truly spread. I had accompanied Gran on many of her volunteer trips, so several of her friends and acquaintances I knew from the herbarium had reached out with messages of condolences. There was also one each from Alannah and Geoff from work.

The texts contained variations on the same themes: shock of hearing the news, admiration for Gran, and thinking of our family 'at this sad time'.

One of the more irksome statements that appeared verbatim in at least a couple of the messages was that 'we must be glad she died doing what she loved'. There was, I supposed, a comfort in knowing she had died in the bush near her childhood home on the country that coursed through her veins, doing what she enjoyed, with someone whom she loved. But the suggestion that any of this made me 'glad' was preposterous.

What did make me glad was seeing that there was also a message from Nick.

I hope you managed to get some sleep. I'm thinking of you. x

I put my cursor in the reply box.

Thanks. I slept a bit. The hard part was waking up and realising that it wasn't all just a bad dream. We've got a day of funeral planning ahead of us, so that should add a new layer of heartache. I imagine it will be like a bad group assignment, but with my family, who have less decorum or reliability than uni students.

It was the middle of the night in London, so I knew he wouldn't reply right away.

I heard a commotion at the front door and knew my family had arrived. When Gerry and I had left Mum and Dad's place in an Uber (my car was still at work, since I hadn't made it back to the office from our site visit yesterday), we agreed they'd come around to Gran's to plan the funeral.

I pulled on yesterday's pants, and fastened my bra under the T-shirt I'd slept in. I opened the spare bedroom door quietly, so I could sneak to the bathroom to brush my teeth and splash some water on my face before I saw anyone. As I crept down the hallway, I passed Herrick and noticed that a spider had added a web to the beads that hung from his antlers. How dare it just assume permission to make its home on Gran's beloved jackalope, I thought irrationally. Then, as I reached the bathroom, I heard Mum say that someone had sent her a link to a company that did open-air cremations – like a big bonfire. I felt myself bristle; it would be a testing day.

Once in the bathroom, I hunched to look at my reflection in the mirror. The lids of my eyes were puffy and I could feel the beginnings of a stye coming up. The skin around my nose was red from my attempts to manage the snot and tears that had flowed with a staggering persistence since I'd taken Mum's call.

I slid the mirrored bathroom cabinet open and leaned in to look for one of the spare toothbrushes Gran kept for if we stayed over. Like the packets of tampons and pads she kept in a basket next to the toilet, despite it being several decades since she'd been through menopause, she stocked the spare toothbrushes so we would have everything we'd need to feel at home.

I inhaled sharply at the sight of her own toothbrush. Yesterday, this was just Gran's toothbrush – an unremarkable utensil for removing plaque from her teeth. But now it was *Gran's toothbrush* – an artefact of her life that seemed irreplaceably valuable.

The toothbrush was standing, handle down, in a water cup, with a tube of toothpaste that had at least two rolls at its base (one must roll, not squeeze, according to her). The toothbrush's bristles were dry – a testament to them having missed their pre-bed and post-breakfast call-up.

On the left of the water glass was the tube of BB cream, eyeshadow compact, mascara and lipstick she'd bought and worn for her reunion with Gerry. I blinked away the tears that gathered in my eyes at the thought of how happy she had seemed the night she had worn them in London.

Next to the make-up was the hairbrush that she'd had for as long as I could remember. Her delicate white hairs were coiled around the bristles – a messy tangle of her DNA; a nuclear link to her life. I resisted the urge to pull a strand to keep. What on earth would I do with it?

Unable to look at the contents anymore, I closed the cupboard door quickly. My teeth would have to wait until later.

I opened the bathroom door to find Mum loitering in the hallway.

'Oh, Bethie.' She pulled me into a hug. 'How are you doing?'

Mum was wearing a long flowing green dress with a sheer green overlay adorned with large gold embroidered butterflies. She had a chunky gold necklace around her neck, which pushed uncomfortably into my collarbone.

'I'm okay,' I replied, exiting her embrace when I felt enough time had passed to satisfy her need to hug me.

'How was it, staying here last night?' she asked, looking at me intently. I could tell she was searching my face and body language for clues about my current state; she often did this when she was dissatisfied with the comprehensiveness of my verbal replies.

It had felt strange to stay in Gran's house without her there to make sure I'd had enough to eat, was warm enough and had a glass of water beside my bed in case I woke up thirsty during the night.

I had heard Gerry get up at midnight and use the bathroom. Her footsteps were slightly heavier than Gran's and she didn't know which of the creaky floorboards needed to be avoided to stealthily navigate the hallway.

At about 2am, it was my turn and, as I padded down the hall, I noticed an illuminated arc on the carpet outside Gran's door; the lamp on Gran's bedside table was on. It seemed that grief-induced insomnia, combined with the tail-end of jet lag, was a cruel adversary for us both.

But I was glad I had stayed. I knew Gran would have wanted us to watch out for Gerry, and it comforted me to be in her house.

'It was fine,' I responded casually.

'When you're ready, come into the kitchen,' she said, turning to walk back down the hallway. 'I've got the kettle on.'

I noticed her stride seemed slightly tentative; it lacked its usual buoyancy. It struck me for the first time that *she* was the older generation now Gran was gone.

I entered the kitchen as Dad, Elijah, Jarrah and Gerry, who were seated around the table, all erupted into laughter.

'Hey, Bethie,' Dad said when he spotted me. 'How are you?' His voice was deeper than usual, and his face contorted into an exaggerated frown. It was a look I came to expect from everyone I encountered over the following days.

'I was just telling Gerry about the time we gave your gran a ride on a

Harley-Davidson for her eightieth birthday,' he said as I sat down at the table.

Gran had always wanted a ride on a motorcycle, so we recruited the services of Daz – an entrepreneurial biker – and his Harley-Davidson to take her for a spin. Daz's Harley had a sidecar, which we'd assumed she would find more comfortable than riding two-up. But she insisted on sitting on the sliver of seat left behind him once he had positioned his enormous body on it.

'If Queen Elizabeth could ride a horse at ninety, I can throw a leg either side of a motorcycle at eighty,' she announced defiantly. Daz roared with laughter. The rest of us worried that we might have caused the birth and death dates on her headstone to match.

Gran loved the ride but told us afterwards that, as they had hurtled down the freeway at 100 kilometres per hour, the wind had caused Daz's beard, which hung down to his belly button, to split at his chin, wrap around either side of his head and tickle her face like two hairy tentacles.

'Maybe we can have a Harley pull her casket along on a trailer?' Jarrah offered enthusiastically.

'Nice idea, Jarrah,' Dad said kindly as I was about to snap a retort, 'but I think those types of traditions are reserved for bikies and people who have ridden all their lives.'

I felt tension creep into my shoulders. I had prepared myself for the fact that my family would approach organising Gran's funeral in much the same way they threw together most of the events in their lives – with complete disregard for methodical processes.

'Did Gran ever specify what she wanted for her funeral?' I probed, opening the notes app in my phone to retrieve some thoughts I'd jotted down during one of the hours I lay awake the night before.

'Not that I remember.' Mum leaned her chin on her hand as she searched for memories.

I realised I was in the denial stage of grief, and probably a little hungover, when I nearly suggested we ask Gran. The abrupt realisation this was impossible smacked me a new blow.

'Well, why don't we take our cues from what she wanted for Grandpa's funeral?' I suggested, blinking away a fresh flow of tears. 'I can't remember all the details, but the funeral director must have them on file or something. I mean, we know where she held the service, and I remember she once insisted on a plain and inexpensive casket. We can assume that what she chose for his funeral were the things she'd like for hers.'

My family nodded their heads in unison. Gerry dabbed her nose with a tissue.

'You're right, Bethie,' Mum said. 'Good thinking. The funeral director is due at 10.30. We'll ask then.'

'But before we get to that, we need to register her death,' I continued. The word 'death' caught in my throat. 'I researched the process last night, and there's paperwork that needs to be filled out and certificates that need to be obtained. Mum, do you know where her birth certificate is? And we'll need the date of her marriage, and the birth dates and occupations of her parents.

'And we should let her friends know,' I continued. 'Word has already spread through her volunteer networks, but we need to tell her family friends, and any relatives out there. Perhaps this afternoon, when we've got the details of the funeral, we can go through the contact list in her phone and her rolodex and divvy up the calls.

'Then, at some stage, we'll need to advise the tax office, social services and Medicare; get in touch with her accountant and bank; and think about what services we disconnect from the house.' I ran through the checklist I'd made on my phone.

'My goodness, Bethie,' Mum said, having obviously given none of this any thought at all. 'We're so lucky to have you around to think of all these things.'

She reached out and squeezed my hand, and Dad gave me a side hug. I couldn't recall a time they had praised my organisation skills. For a moment, I felt appreciated.

~

Nora, the funeral director, was a portly middle-aged woman who arrived wearing a sympathetic smile, a white suit and a navy blue broad-brimmed hat. She removed her hat as she crossed the threshold and then greeted us one by one with an unexpectedly firm, gloved handshake. She irritated me immediately.

Mum welcomed Nora into Gran's kitchen, and we shuffled around the table to accommodate an extra chair.

'I always enjoy the opportunity to meet with a deceased person's family in their home,' she announced. 'It helps me to get a sense of who they were. And I can see by looking around that Eliza was a very special lady.'

'*Elise*,' I said, more curtly than I'd intended but not more than she deserved. 'Her name was *Elise*.'

'Oh my goodness,' Nora replied, rifling through her papers as if looking for evidence of a clerical error of someone else's doing. 'I'm so very sorry. El*ise*.'

Having not uncovered anything that would exonerate her from her faux pas, she uncapped her pen and poised it officiously above the lined pad she'd produced from her navy briefcase.

'Now,' she began, scanning each of our faces. 'Have you thought about when you might like to have the funeral?'

'We were thinking this Friday,' Mum replied.

'Right,' Nora said and then moistened her index finger with what I thought was an unnecessary amount of licking, before thumbing through a large diary that she had also produced from her briefcase.

'The thirteenth. Good. Good. Yes, that will work nicely.'

It peeved me that Nora found it necessary to assure us that the date we had selected to bury Gran suited her schedule. I wondered if she expected us to congratulate Gran when we caught up in the afterlife for dying on a day that was convenient.

'Wait,' Jarrah interjected. 'That's Friday the thirteenth. We can't have it then.'

We all turned to look at Jarrah.

'Why's that?' Dad asked indulgently.

'Because it's an unlucky date,' she said, her eyes bugged as though it should be obvious. 'We can't lay her to rest on an unlucky day.'

'She's already dead, Jarrah,' I snapped. 'I don't think she'll mind. And what's the worst that can happen? It will bring her bad luck?'

Nora turned the page of her diary and tutted quietly as she digested what she discovered overleaf.

'It's just that ...' Nora began before pausing to make a clicking noise under her breath. 'The next few days are quite ...'

'It's fine,' Mum interrupted. 'It's just a date, Jarrah. And Bethie's right; Gran wouldn't have minded. I think Friday is good. It will give us time to get organised without dragging the whole thing out.'

'Well, don't blame me if she comes back to haunt us all,' Jarrah said, crossing her slender arms across her chest in a huff.

For a fleeting, irrational moment, I wished she would haunt us. I would have been thrilled to spend one more minute with Gran, even if she was a poltergeist with a bone to pick.

'So, the thirteenth it is then,' Nora said assertively. 'I think Friday is meant to be nice weather. It will be a lovely day. We'll make sure of it.'

I sensed that Nora was well-practised at placating irrational grieving people.

'Bethie, try and keep an open mind,' Dad pleaded after I shot down Jarrah's suggestion that instead of having a eulogy, we conduct a treasure hunt around the city where people find clues to piece together her life story.

'Don't you think it would be a hoot?' she asked enthusiastically.

'I don't think funerals are meant to be a hoot,' I snapped.

'I know,' she replied. 'But you've already pooh-poohed my idea of everyone contributing to a mural on her coffin, having an ice-cream van at her gravesite and dressing as something beginning with "E". I'm just trying to give her a special send-off.'

'But none of this would be special to *her*,' I retorted. 'Do you really think Gran would be impressed if I scribbled all over her coffin while eating a soft serve cone and dressed as Elvis? If you want to give her a send-off that would be meaningful to her, we should use flowers from her garden in the floral arrangements, scatter some of her ashes at Woodside Ridge, or read one of the poems she liked.'

Silence fell over the table as my family processed the reminder that Gran's funeral was intended to be about her, and not them. We managed to survive the rest of the meeting without adding to the body count. And Nora referred to Gran by the correct name all but once more.

We settled on wildflowers (a 'lovely choice', according to Nora); an eco-casket (a 'responsible choice', according to Nora); and a reading of a Dorothea Mackellar poem (a 'moving choice', according to Nora). We agreed that Mum, Dad, Jarrah and Elijah would perform one song – an improvement on the five originally proposed – and family friends Sharon and Mike would be asked to deliver the eulogy.

Nora left with one of Gran's outfits to dress her in, and her favourite hat, which was to be placed on her coffin for the ceremony. When Mum fetched it from the plastic bag of belongings the hospital had given her, I noticed the hat still had the red-tailed black cockatoo feather, which she'd found when we last visited the orchids together, sticking out of its band. I allowed a new wave of tears to fall as I watched Nora walk away with the hat. It felt like pieces of Gran were already dissipating.

But my mood was buoyed slightly as Nora walked down the path towards the road and one of the local maggies swooped to within about 30 centimetres of her head, clicking its beak loudly. Nora hurried to the safety of the car, and I made a mental note to defy wildlife legislation just this once to toss the maggies a couple of bits of cheese when no one was watching.

Chapter 35

Beth

'Are you going to eat that?' Elijah asked, pointing to the untouched spring roll on my plate.

'Go for it,' I replied, pushing my plate towards him.

Usually, I loved the food we got from the Vietnamese restaurant near my parents' house, but I hadn't felt like eating much of anything since Gran had died. I think I had cried out my appetite. Although it was hard to know where my grief ended and hayfever started.

Over the past few days, Mum and Dad's house had drawn a constant parade of wellwishers, who each arrived with their sincere condolences and a bunch of flowers. We ran out of vases on day one, so had improvised with jars, milk cartons, buckets, jugs, water glasses and empty tins. I despaired at the many thousands of dollars' worth of flowers that were sitting in sullied water on every available surface in the house. There were various takes on three themes: tasteful and sombre arrangements made up of white roses, chrysanthemums and lilies; bright and cheery bouquets with gerberas, sunflowers or coloured daisies; and wildflowers wrapped in burlap and tied with twine.

I had stayed with Gerry at Gran's house each night since she'd died. I enjoyed spending time with her and learning about the Gran that Gerry knew. I also enjoyed hearing Gerry talk about Nick.

Nick and I had been texting and talking whenever possible over the past few days. He had said and done all the right things: listened when I wanted to talk, reassured when I didn't, made me laugh when I needed it, and had organised for a care package full of comfort food and good wine to be delivered. Receiving it had been such a lovely surprise; it was quite possibly the most thoughtful thing anyone had ever done for me.

The time difference seemed to exacerbate the distance between us; eight hours was just long enough that we were at opposite stages of our day. When I was settling into the evening, he was in the busiest part of his morning; and when I was getting up, he was heading off to bed.

'Expecting a text?' Jarrah asked quizzically as I checked my phone for incoming messages after we'd cleared the table and retired to the lounge room.

'What?' I asked absent-mindedly. 'Oh, no. I'm not.'

'Really?' she asked suspiciously. 'Because I've seen you check your phone at least half a dozen times in the last hour.'

'Ha!' I huffed sarcastically. 'You mean you've managed to drag your eyes off your own phone for long enough to notice what's going on around you. Well done, you.'

Her body recoiled slightly from the lash of my sarcasm.

I knew it was a little harsh before I saw the tears gather along her lower lids.

'I lost her too, you know,' she said after a few moments. Her voice faltered. 'I mightn't have been as close to her as you were, but I loved her as well.'

I saw a vulnerability in Jarrah that I hadn't seen before. Her cool, nonchalant confidence had splintered; she looked wounded.

Of course Jarrah had loved Gran. I had found my own grief so all-consuming that I hadn't really given any thought to how Jarrah might have been feeling. Or anyone else, really, except Mum and Gerry.

I imagined what Gran would say in the car after we left if I had been dropping her home.

'Go easy on her,' she would have said. 'You know what she's like.'

And she would have been right. Of course.

I readied myself to apologise – not a grovelling soliloquy, but an acknowledgement that she was hurting too and my last comment was uncalled for.

But Jarrah spoke first. 'Besides,' she said coolly as she crossed her arms over her chest. 'Not all of us had the opportunity to go on a nice little trip to London with her in her final weeks.'

It was my turn to recoil.

'Well, it's true,' she continued. 'Did you ever think that *I* might have liked to come along too? I've spent my whole life watching you and Gran with your special bond and your trips to the bush. You've never thought to invite *me* along.'

'It's not that we excluded you, Jarrah,' I retorted, feeling the heat from my chest rise up my neck and radiate across the lower part of my face in angry red welts. 'It's that you showed zero interest in what we were doing.'

'That's not true.' Her voice carried a whine that stoked my irritation.

'Jarrah, Gran and I shared an interest in the natural world and nature conservation. Those "trips to the bush" were field trips, where we volunteered to collect plant specimens and propagate seedlings. The closest you've ever come to anything like that is going to a bush doof with your friends.'

'Well, it might have been nice to be invited to come along from time to time,' she replied, picking at her fingernails.

'Why? So you could tell us about all the other "like, way more fun" things you had to do instead?' I imitated her delivery, hamming up her ditziness for effect.

'It's not just your trips to the bush, or to London,' she said. The fire inside me was now threatening to jump containment lines. 'I was always left out of your special little duo.'

I stared at her incredulously before laughter erupted from my core. She started backwards.

I tried to quell my laughter, but it felt like my body was necessarily expelling decades' worth of repressed feelings into the ether.

Mum poked her head around the doorway.

'Everything okay in here?' she asked cautiously, her eyes surveying the room for clues of what was transpiring.

'YOU'VE GOT TO BE FUCKING KIDDING ME!' I screamed at Jarrah. 'You honestly have no idea.'

'No idea about what?' she asked, her eyes wide as if assessing whether to activate her fight or flight mode to escape the wrath of a sibling who appeared to have finally lost the plot.

'EXACTLY,' I yelled so loudly the word scratched at the inside of my throat. 'Now you know how I have felt ... MY. ENTIRE. LIFE.'

She looked shocked, which enraged me further.

'I have felt left out of literally everything in this family,' I spat. 'You all share your music, and your art, and funny stories about wild nights and loads of friends. None of that involves me. You all have each other. I had Gran. And now she's gone.'

I was so furious I was breathless.

'Oh, Bethie,' Mum said, having sidled into the room. 'We never left you out intentionally.'

I snorted loudly. 'My whole life, it's felt like it's been "the Dwyer family", and "Beth".' I used my arms to depict the chasm of distance between our two entities. 'I've felt like I'm some sort of appendage that you've had to drag around with you; like you're the headlining band, and I'm just ... a roadie. I mean, just look at our names, for God's sake. Jarrah, Elijah and *Beth*.' I accentuated the plainness of my single-syllable moniker.

'It's Elizabeth,' Mum said quietly. 'Your name is Elizabeth.'

Her calmness, which was in complete contrast to the fury that was raging inside me, shocked me into a moment of silence.

'You know,' she continued, her voice hushed, 'from the moment you were born, you were such a little individual. You had wise, knowing eyes and a staunch, unwavering tenacity. Even the midwives in the hospital commented that you didn't suffer fools and that you would give the world a run for its money.

'As you know, we didn't have the easiest start as mother and daughter,' she continued. 'I had been on bedrest because of complications while I was pregnant, and your entry to the world was dramatic, to say the |least.'

I had been told about my birth in snippets over the years. Mum had never been very forthcoming because she said she didn't want to dwell on it. But, from what I had managed to piece together, I had been delivered by emergency caesarean section, which ended with me in neonatal intensive care, and Mum gravely ill.

What my family *had* shared, with infuriating regularity, was that I was a challenging baby. They had an anthology of humiliating stories to illustrate that I was an unsettled infant and had a fiery temper as a toddler. I hated that they held me accountable for my behaviour from a time when I couldn't control my bowels, much less my temperament.

'You were so different to Jarrah,' she continued. 'She was so placid; she just slept and ate for the first few months. But you definitely turned our world upside down.'

I huffed loudly.

'We did have a different name picked out for you, actually.'

She hesitated as if deciding whether she should continue. Jarrah and I inched our bodies slightly forward in unison.

'Well?' I asked impatiently. 'What was it?'

'Harmony,' she said finally.

'Harmony?' Jarrah laughed. 'Can you even imagine?'

'Really?' I stared at Mum in disbelief.

'You were going to call me Harmony? And then, what, I arrived, and you decided that a name that means peace and tranquillity didn't suit me because I was a difficult baby who nearly died at birth and killed you in the process?'

'It wasn't …' she started.

'Gee, thanks very much, Mum. That makes me feel much better,' I said sarcastically.

'If you'll let me finish,' she continued calmly. 'We decided that you needed a stronger name. A more linear name. One that would serve you well throughout a life that I knew would be filled with achievement and excellence.'

'So you named her after the Queen?' Jarrah quipped. 'Maybe *that's* why you're such a fan of the royal family.'

Mum gave Jarrah her 'you're not helping things but, as always, I have no intention of doing anything about it' look.

'No,' she said, turning back to me. 'We named you after another Elizabeth. It was Gran who suggested it, actually.'

'Who then?' I urged impatiently.

'We named you after Elizabeth Gould,' she replied with a gentle smile.

I was floored. How did I not know this?

'Who's that?' Jarrah asked.

'Elizabeth Gould was the wife of John Gould, a scientist who came out to Australia,' I offered. 'But, more than that, Elizabeth Gould was a brilliant artist. She travelled to Australia with her husband and worked for him as an illustrator. She died young, but her work is celebrated to this day. Including on Gran's wall.'

'Oh yes,' Mum said, nodding enthusiastically. 'You're right. The painting of the finches.'

'Is that the picture of the birds near the toilet?' Jarrah asked.

I nodded.

Mum walked towards me and put her hands on my arms.

'Bethie, my darling, I'm sorry if you've ever felt like an odd man out.' She squeezed my biceps.

'Dad and I have always tried to include you in everything we've done and everywhere we've gone. Maybe I should have tried harder to get you to come along, but you were never that interested, and we never wanted to push you to do anything you didn't want to. Or be anything other than yourself.' Her bottom lip quivered slightly. 'We only ever wanted you to be the best version of yourself. And look at you!'

She took a step back and looked me up and down. 'You're incredible. We're so very proud of you.' A big wet tear cascaded down her face.

'But there was never any room for me,' I said, my voice shaking.

'Oh, Bethie,' Mum said sadly, 'of course there was room for you.'

I searched my mind for examples of when I had been objectively left out. But I could only come up with times that I had said no to joining them. With the exception of family lunches and dinners when I would bring Gran, she had a point. I had rejected their offers to travel to music festivals, refused their invitations to art exhibitions and made up excuses for why I couldn't attend gigs. I had even deliberately made travel plans over Christmas for several consecutive years, so I could avoid spending the holidays and my birthday with them.

'Maybe I should have insisted that we should do more of the things you like doing. I'm sorry I didn't,' she continued. A few times Mum had suggested she come along on a field trip but I'd made excuses for why she shouldn't. I assumed she wouldn't enjoy it, and I wouldn't have been able to handle it if she'd rejected something that was so important to me.

A wave of sadness crashed over me.

'Sorry, Mum,' I said, tears tumbling down my cheeks.

'Don't be sorry, my love.' She placed her hands on the sides of my face. Her hands were cold, but the gesture was immensely comforting. 'I just want you to know that you're never on the outer. We love you. We love you for all the things that make you unique.

'And besides, you *did* have Gran,' she continued. 'The bond the two of you shared was so special. Would you believe sometimes I even felt a little on the outer? You had a connection with her that I never had. And she had one with you that I didn't have either.'

It had never occurred to me that Mum or Jarrah would have felt excluded from the relationship between Gran and me.

'I never realised ...' I started before words failed me.

'Of course you didn't,' Mum cooed. 'And nor should you have. You two were close from the moment you laid eyes on each other. It wasn't like one day you just conspired a partnership to the exclusion of all others; it was something that happened naturally. And even though I wasn't part of your little duo, seeing you together was one of the great joys of my life. I was so comforted to know that you always had someone to turn to when you needed to.' She paused and squeezed my arms again. 'Even if you didn't want to come to me.'

My chest physically ached with the fresh realisation that Gran would no longer be in my life. 'What will I do without her?' I sobbed.

Mum pulled me into a hug and I sank willingly into her chest.

'Well,' she whispered into my hair. 'Maybe you can let me in from time to time. I might not be Gran, but perhaps you can think of me as her apprentice.'

Chapter 36

Beth

When Dad announced that they should rehearse the song that he, Mum, Jarrah and Elijah would be playing at Gran's funeral I instinctively reached for my bag to leave. However, in light of the conversation I'd had with Mum earlier, I knew that doing so would be repeating the pattern of my self-imposed exile.

They had selected 'All I Have To Do Is Dream' by The Everly Brothers – one of Gran's favourites. Mum said Gran played it on the record player so often that she didn't know if there was ever a time that she didn't know the words.

Mum and Jarrah alternated verses, while Dad and Elijah sang back-up harmony and played the bass and acoustic guitar respectively.

As the last of the notes were absorbed by the universe, I became aware of Gerry's quiet sobs. She was clutching a tissue to her face.

'Sorry,' she said through a wet sniff. 'That was so lovely. Would you believe that song came out the year I left Australia? Elise bought a copy of the album and played it nonstop in the college common room.'

Mum walked to Gerry, sat down next to her and placed her arm around her shoulders.

'We don't have to play it if it's too painful,' she said earnestly.

'Oh, you must,' Gerry said, wiping self-consciously at her tear-filled eyes. 'It's absolutely perfect. She would love it.'

Mum, Dad, Jarrah and Elijah played the song through again. I couldn't remember the last time I saw them perform together; usually by the time the guitars were brought out for a family singalong, I was long gone. They were undeniably good, and their rendition of the song was beautiful.

Mum and Jarrah both had the perfect quality to their voice that would have done The Everly Brothers, and Gran, proud. Their voices were so complementary and they blended so seamlessly that it was like listening to the same person singing in a slightly different hue. And Dad and Elijah played with such effortlessness.

But what set this performance apart from all the others I had endured over the years was that it seemed respectfully understated. There was no twirling or dancing, tricky guitar riffs or vocal acrobatics. It was just four gifted musicians singing a song for someone they loved.

'Sure you don't want to join in, Bethie?' Dad asked when they'd finished the song for a second time. 'You could help Elijah and me on back-up vocals, or I'm sure I've got a tambourine somewhere.'

'Ha' I scoffed. 'Baby steps, Dad.'

Gerry and I gathered our things and said farewell to my family.

As I walked down the corridor, Jarrah appeared at my side.

'I'm sorry about before. I really don't want to fight with you, especially about Gran. I know what she meant to you, and you to her. And I never should have put my shit on you. It's just ...' her voice hovered as she searched for the language to describe our new reality. 'I'm just really going to miss her.'

'I know. Me too.' I hadn't expected an apology and was grateful to clear the air.

'She was so proud of you, and I was always a bit jealous of that,' she continued. 'I know she loved me, but she was never proud of me in the same way.'

I had never thought of Gran being proud of me before, but I guess she was.

'I know you think I'm a flake,' she said, spinning her bracelets around her wrist. 'But I am trying. Even though you're younger, you've always been so much more "together" than me. You're so good at managing all the life stuff that I seem to find so hard, and you seem to have it all worked out. Sometimes I feel like I'm floating around at sea, completely rudderless, while you're living your best life on a utopian island. You're an inspiration, actually.'

I couldn't believe what I was hearing. I thought Jarrah intentionally rejected the way I lived my life. I certainly never imagined it would be something she aspired to, and I definitely didn't realise she was struggling so much.

'I don't know about an "inspiration",' I replied. 'I guess we're all just bumbling through the best way we know how. I know I can be rigid and unaccommodating sometimes. And maybe you were right; going with the flow isn't so bad.

'Not with everything,' I added hastily. 'But with some things.'

She smiled as though surprised by my admission.

'The reason I come down so hard on you is because I see that you have so much potential. I just don't want you to waste it,' I said.

Mum arrived in the hallway.

'Everything okay?' she asked cautiously.

'Yes,' I answered, giving Jarrah a meek smile before leaning into her open arms for a hug. 'We're good.'

Mum hugged me tightly as she said goodbye, pulling me back into her embrace as I tried to break it. This time I surrendered and hugged her for far longer than was actually necessary. It was nice.

~

As Gerry and I walked up the path at Gran's place, I spotted a weed that had popped up alongside one of the pavers. I bent down to pull it out, and gave it a firmer-than-necessary tug as if to reprimand it for daring to grow in her garden. The vibrant pink pigface flowers had closed for the evening, and the hum of the insects had quietened as the last of the light had bled from the day. The garden looked more or less like it had a week ago, but somehow the weed I was clutching tightly in my hand was a tangible reminder that Gran was no longer around to care for it.

I wondered what would happen to her beautiful garden and her beloved home. I assumed that in time Mum would sell it, and it would be bulldozed to make space for two or three semidetached units. I shuddered at the thought.

I committed to keeping up with the gardening as best I could in the meantime, but I knew that would be a struggle long-term. The secret of Gran's gardening was that she was constantly doing it. She didn't set aside a block of time every other weekend, or dedicate a week at a time to give it a makeover. Instead, she would 'garden' every time she walked through it; each time she went out or returned home, she'd pull a weed, prune a bush or fix a fallen stake. And she was forever planting cuttings that she'd taken from plants in the neighbourhood when she thought no one was watching. I knew that no one else would have the time to care for it in the same way and that it would never look the same as when she was alive. It had passed its prime.

I peered into the birdbath and noticed it needed refilling. As I fetched the hose and turned it on, I heard the sound of a vehicle pulling up into the space behind my car. I watched to ensure they didn't cause any damage; today was not the day for my new car to get its first dint. And who was turning up unannounced at Gran's house anyway? And at this hour? I hoped it wasn't any of her friends with flowers. Or worse, another casserole.

The back passenger door opened and a tall figure unfolded from the car. 'Hello,' Nick said.

I gasped, dropping the hose, which snaked wildly around my feet.

'What are you ... ?' I stared in disbelief as my heart somersaulted inside my chest. I couldn't recall having ever been more glad to see anyone in my life. The warmth of his smile felt like a tonic for my wounded heart. He gathered his bag and walked through the gate towards me. I rushed into his arms and held him tight.

'Are you going to turn that off?' he said finally, breaking our embrace and pointing to the hose, which was flipping about madly. 'This country is prone to drought, apparently.'

Oh, how I had missed his grin.

The water shut off and I spun around to see Gerry standing at the tap, smiling widely.

'Did you know about this?'

She nodded conspiratorially.

'Oh, sorry. Did you think I was here for you?' Nick shook his head mockingly. 'I missed Gerry so much, I just had to travel eleventy-zillion hours to see her.'

He chuckled endearingly at his own joke as I flung my arms around him again and buried my head in the crook of his neck. I drank in the smell of his skin.

'I hope it's okay that I'm here. I know you said not to come, but—'

'Are you kidding? I'm so happy to see you,' I whispered into his chest. 'Thank you for ignoring me.'

'I'm going to head in,' Gerry said.

Nick and I stood, locked in what felt like our own private oasis, in the middle of the path, in the middle of the most painful time of my life.

'When did you leave London?' I asked, finally releasing him so I could look him over to make sure I wasn't hallucinating.

'Well, that's hard to define with time zones and travel time. I think I left some time before lunchtime *tomorrow*.'

'Why didn't you call? I would have picked you up.'

'What, and miss the opportunity to see you water your shoes?'

I looked down at my new shoes, which were sodden and most likely ruined. I could not have cared less; Nick was here.

'But you've been messaging me all day. How did you do that if you were on a plane?'

'They've got wi-fi on planes now, you know.'

Of course.

'I do have something important to ask, though,' he continued, his demeanour becoming serious.

'What's that?' I urged.

'May I please use the bathroom?'

'Of course,' I said grabbing his hand and leading him up the path and into Gran's house where I steered him towards the bathroom.

'Well, you're a little bit sneaky,' I said to Gerry when I found her in the kitchen filling up the kettle.

'Don't look at me,' she said, grinning widely. 'It was all him. I simply gave him the address.'

She looked very pleased with herself.

'You know, I'll be fine here if you want to head off to your place for the night. The last thing you want is me cramping your style. I'm sure the two of you have plenty to catch up on.' Her voice was thick with innuendo.

She avoided making eye contact with me as she busied herself detangling the strings of teabags that had become entwined in the box. But she needn't have bothered; I was avoiding her gaze too, hoping she wouldn't notice the heat in my cheeks. I knew from my years of staying in the spare bedroom and hearing my grandparents' snoring that nighttime sounds carried in this house.

'Are you sure? I mean, I do need to put some washing on, and I will need to get my clothes for the funeral tomorrow.' It wasn't a complete lie.

'Yes,' she said sincerely. 'You two go and have some fun. Tomorrow will be hard, so you should go and enjoy each other.'

I chuckled awkwardly.

'I mean, each other's company,' she said, quickly.

Nick emerged from the hallway looking more comfortable.

'Oh, that looks good,' he said, gesturing to the cup of tea.

'Funny,' Gerry said. 'Beth was just telling me about all the different types of tea she's got at her place. You should head on back there before it gets too late. I'm going to head to bed now anyway. I'll see you tomorrow.'

She turned and walked out of the kitchen, switching off the light as she left, plunging us into darkness save the tiny green glow from the illuminated numbers on the microwave.

Nick and I moved silently towards each other, guided by an instinctive pull. I stopped just short of him, suddenly self-conscious that I'd misunderstood his intentions. What if I had it all wrong, and he really was just here to see Gerry? Or the quokkas? But as he reached out, drew me in and touched his lips to mine – gently at first and then more wantonly as I kissed him back – I knew that this was definitely something.

Chapter 37

Beth

It seemed wildly inappropriate to wake on the day of Gran's funeral with a sense of contentment. But I felt like my emotions were compartment-alised – my grief over Gran's death wasn't lessened by Nick being here, but adoring him made me happy in a way I had never before experienced. Perhaps I finally understood what Jarrah meant when she talked about filling up your 'love cup'. Having a full love cup didn't empty any of the contents of the 'grief cup', but it was nice to have something else to drink.

I also felt comforted knowing that Nick had met Gran and been witness to her reunion with Gerry. It was important to me that he knew her, since she was such a big part of my life story.

Nick and I ate breakfast at the cafe down the road as I had absolutely nothing in my house to eat. Then we drove to my parents' place via Gran's house to collect Gerry.

The weather was beautiful; it was the type of day that Gran would have described as 'a good day to be alive'. The irony was not lost on me.

I had decided not to forewarn my family that I would be bringing a plus-one to the funeral. *There was no use in drawing out their response,* I had thought. I figured it was best just to turn up with him and let them process it on the spot. It would be like ripping off a bandaid, if the bandaid was decorated with sequins and glitter.

This resolute rationale did nothing to temper my nerves.

We arrived to find the house as chaotic as ever. Dad and Elijah were loading Elijah's van with the equipment they needed for their funeral performance. They were dressed in suits that I didn't know they owned, although judging by the way Dad's pants stretched across his backside, I assumed they had been retrieved from the archives of his wardrobe. Both were chest-deep in the back of the van, swearing and cursing while pushing and pulling. I gestured to Nick that we should slip past quietly. I knew I couldn't control much about Nick meeting my family, but I figured it would be best to avoid it being arse first.

As we stepped onto the porch, we could hear Jarrah and Mum yelling to each other about a misplaced item of clothing.

'Welcome to the madhouse,' I announced to Nick. 'Hold onto your hat.'

At least four more bunches of flowers had arrived that morning and were sitting by the front door – one in an ice bucket, one in a watering can and two in an esky.

'Hello,' I called out as we entered the house. 'We're here.'

'Hi, Bethie. Hi, Gerry,' Mum called out from her bedroom. 'Won't be a tick.'

Jarrah emerged in the hallway, resplendent in just a skirt and a lacy black bra.

'Jesus, Jarrah!' I exclaimed. 'Where's your top?'

'What?' she asked innocently, before noticing Nick behind me.

'Fuck. Sorry,' she said, wrapping her arms tightly around her body, which only accentuated her cleavage. 'I didn't realise you were bringing someone else with you.'

Nick gave her a wry wave.

'This is Nick.'

Her eyes widened, and a huge smile spread across her face.

'Is it now? How nice to meet you, Nick.'

She uncoiled her right arm, which was doing the lion's share of covering her breasts, and extended it towards him.

'Jarrah,' I scolded. 'Go and put on a top. You can meet him properly when you've got some clothes on.'

'Oh yes. Of course. Sorry,' she said, scuttling backwards down the hallway.

'Hi Gerry,' she called out as a wistful afterthought as she disappeared into her bedroom.

'Sorry about that,' I said. 'But you really brought this upon yourself by coming. You were warned.'

'Bethie,' Mum called out from her room. 'Come and help me choose. Should I wear a black feather headdress or a turban?'

I rolled my eyes at Nick.

'Is this a fancy-dress funeral?' he whispered.

'Every event is fancy-dress with this lot,' I replied.

'Mum,' I called out. 'Can you come out here, please? There's someone I want you to meet.'

Mum stuck her head out of her bedroom door. Mercifully, she was fully dressed.

'Mum. This is Nick.'

'Nick? *Oh*, Nick. As in, *Nick*.'

'Yes,' I replied, willing my reddening cheeks to calm.

'A-*ha*. What a lovely surprise that you're here, Nick. Welcome. Did you say hi to your dad on the way in?'

'No – not yet,' I replied.

'THORN.' Her tone was uncharacteristically shrill. 'Can you come in here, please?'

Dad appeared at the front door looking flustered, as Jarrah re-emerged from her room. This had become a 360-degree onslaught.

'Thorn, look! *Nick's* here. You know, Gerry's great-nephew. The Nick that Beth spent time with while she was in London.'

She smiled maniacally.

'Terrific to meet you, mate,' Dad said, extending his hand to shake Nick's, seemingly less phased at his presence than Mum and Jarrah. I was grateful that Dad was behaving as normally as could be expected. 'So you're the reason Bethie returned from London with a smile as big as a Cheshire Cat?'

I willed the ground to open up and swallow me whole.

'Sorry about earlier,' Jarrah said, sidling into the cramped space in the hallway that was filled with far too many people. 'I didn't know we had *company*. It's nice to meet you, Nick. Although now you've seen me in my bra, we can probably do away with the pleasantries.'

'Jesus, what did I miss?' Dad asked.

'Okay, okay,' I hissed, shooing everyone back. 'Let's give him a bit of space. Can we at least invite him into the house before we send him fleeing back out into the street?'

'You're right,' said Mum, looping her arm through Nick's and steering him towards the kitchen. 'Now tell me, Nick, how long are you staying?'

'Mum, go easy,' I pleaded. 'Besides, we have to get going soon.'

Chapter 38

Beth

We had opted to drive ourselves to the funeral, refusing Nora the funeral director's offer to organise a limo. We were perfectly capable of driving ourselves, we thought. And turning up in an ostentatious fuel-guzzler seemed at odds with the environmentally friendly, modest but tasteful farewell we'd organised for Gran.

However, after Elijah discovered he had barely enough petrol to get him to the nearest service station, let alone the funeral, and six sets of keys to three different cars had disappeared from the face of the Earth, we all regretted our decision. When Nora said 'the last thing you want to be worried about is whether you'll get held up by road works or where to park the car', she had obviously assumed my family were capable of first getting their cars out of the driveway.

We loaded as much of the music gear as we could into my car, which Dad and Elijah drove ahead to the cemetery so they could begin setting up. The rest of us followed in an Uber. Wedging Nick in between Mum and Jarrah in the back of a car was definitely a way to expedite the 'getting to know the family' segment of our relationship.

After a tense journey that was indeed delayed by road works, we pulled up to the chapel to find Nora anxiously pacing the threshold.

'Thank goodness you're here,' she said breathlessly. 'We only have an hour before the next funeral begins, and they need time to change over the flowers between services. We have to get moving.'

I scoffed at her lack of compassion.

'They're not my rules, of course,' she offered quickly by way of defence. 'They run a tight ship here.'

We entered the chapel to find a smattering of wellwishers seated already. Dad and Elijah were connecting amps and arranging microphones on the stage next to a giant portrait of Gran that was balanced on an easel. My breath caught in my throat as my eyes landed on her coffin. Of course, I knew it would be there; I had been part of the committee that chose it. But to actually see it, knowing her body was inside it, rattled my already tenuous state.

Seeing her hat perched on the coffin, next to the bunch of flowers that contained some cuttings from her garden, brought me to tears. I felt Nick's hand depress the small of my back as a moist sob escaped my body.

I recognised a few of the people already seated. Some of the other volunteers Gran worked with were huddled together, and two-thirds of a throuple that Mum and Dad had been friends with for years were seated in the back row.

Geoff and Alannah arrived and waved solemnly as they took their seats. I was equally touched they had made the effort to come and grateful they hadn't approached me to chat; small talk felt completely beyond me at the best of times.

People continued to file through the doors at the back of the chapel, every second one clutching an order of service ('one between two,' Nora had insisted; additional copies would have involved an upgraded funeral package).

Jack and Emily approached me.

'G'day, Beth,' Jack said, smiling warmly and holding out his hand to shake my own. I noticed he was holding a brown paper bag in the other one. 'I'm so sorry about Elise. She was one of a kind, that one. A true gem.'

He opened the neck of the paper bag and removed a mason jar half-filled with dirt.

'We went back and collected some dirt from the boundary of the reserve and Woodside Ridge,' he said, handing me the jar. 'Thought she'd like to be cremated with some of her Country.'

I was so touched by the gesture that my heart physically ached. I tried to stop the tears, but they came anyway.

Emily stepped forward and handed me a perfect red-tailed black cockatoo feather.

'And when we got there, we found a Kaarak had left this for her, right where she ...' her voice trailed off.

'Thank you so much,' I managed to splutter before I scurried off to place the feather and precious dirt on top of her coffin. The loud squeal of a speaker interrupted the poignant moment.

Nora touched her mouth on the microphone and, in an excessively breathy voice, announced to those of us still standing that it was time to take our seats. She then instructed us to silence our mobile phones and pointed to the location of the toilets. While I knew it was necessary, it felt like an intrusion of normalcy into a sacred ceremony.

The white-walled chapel was lined with pine beams, and the pews faced large windows, which looked onto a deep garden bed planted with native plants. Wattlebirds and wrens darted in and around the foliage, wholly and blissfully oblivious to the gravity of what was happening inside.

My family and I took our seats in the front pew, while Nick and Gerry sat immediately behind us. I gestured for them to join us, but they both shook their heads, softly, wordlessly communicating they would be more comfortable one row back. I understood completely.

The eulogy was perfect. Sharon and her husband Mike had known Gran and Grandpa since the 1970s. They spoke of her love of her family and of her tenacity and spirit. They also shared a story of when their families went camping. Gran had insisted they go hiking, but no one had packed a map. When they became lost, Gran shared her plans for how they would establish a new society and allocated everyone's roles within it. Apparently, she seemed genuinely disappointed when they stumbled across their campsite a few hours later.

My stomach was in knots as it came time for me to make my way up to the lectern to read the poem 'Colour' by Dorothea Mackellar – one of Gran's favourite Australian poets.

As I read the stanzas that referenced Australia's boundless plains, I thought about how Gran had enjoyed a childhood of freedom and had then returned to a state of liberty when she reconnected with Gerry. The colours of the country that Mackellar described spoke to Gran's love of Australia's bush, and how she cherished her work and being in natural areas.

Mercifully, I made it through the reading without faltering.

Next, the rest of my family rose to perform. And it was perfect.

Jarrah had put together a slideshow of photos that rolled through as the lyrics, and my family's voices, washed over me. Old black-and-white photos of Gran as a girl on Woodside Ridge and one of her and Gerry at uni depicted her full of wonder and optimism. Her marriage to my grandpa and life as a mother were captured in shots of weddings, birthdays and family holidays. Snaps of her in various natural settings, including the one of her and Gerry she'd sent the day she died, spoke of her professional accomplishments. And more recent photographs, where the resolution was crisper and fewer people were blinking, showed her in my favourite of her roles – as grandmother.

As my family reached the song's crescendo, and a photo of Gran I'd taken on my last trip out to Woodside Ridge with her hung on the screen, I allowed my tears to fall.

I felt so proud watching my family. Their performance was perfect, and I understood it was the best way they knew to honour Gran and all that she meant to them.

One by one, those who'd gathered in the chapel took it in turns to place a sprig of rosemary on Gran's coffin. Holding the herb between my thumb and forefinger, I rubbed the spiney leaf with the fingers on my other hand to release the fragrance. The aroma reminded me of Gran's lamb roasts: she would place sprigs of rosemary in the baking tray so the flavour would permeate the meat and the roasted spuds. I willed myself to keep the association of its scent with those fond dinner memories, and not with the time that I farewelled her with Nora the funeral director looking on.

When the celebrant wrapped up the proceedings and invited people to stay for greetings on the lawn across the path ('we'll need to vacate the room since we were late to start,' he added pointedly), I felt relieved the funeral was over.

'That was lovely,' Nick said as I walked with him and Gerry up the aisle, and towards the back of the room and the midday sun.

I nodded, not yet sure I could speak. We wandered up the path and stopped in the shade of a Moreton Bay fig tree. Its magnificent, exposed root system ribboned across the ground for metres.

'So, Nick,' Jarrah said, appearing by my side. 'Tell me all about yourself. I want to hear everything about the person who managed to steal Bethie's heart.'

I scoffed indefensibly. It was true; he had.

'I need to make sure you're up to standard for this one. She's one in a million.'

She flashed me a broad smile before turning to Nick and examining him through narrowed eyes.

'What star sign are you?' she asked.

'I'm a Gemini,' Nick replied.

'I see,' Jarrah said thoughtfully, caressing an imaginary beard. 'A Capricorn and a Gemini ...'

'But I'm not a Capricorn,' I said. 'Remember? I'm now a Sagittarius. Because of the new thirteenth star sign. An Ophi-something.'

'Ophiuchus. No, apparently that wasn't true,' she said, rolling her eyes as though she was disappointed in the universe for providing her with misinformation.

'What?' I squawked.

My mind flashed over the events of the last few months. I thought of Jarrah telling me about the new star sign, and how I'd bought a lotto ticket to prove there's no such thing as fate. I recalled Leo the lotto CEO's big white smile as he congratulated me on my win, which had led to my conversation with Gran when she first told me about Gerry.

'What do you mean there's no thirteenth star sign? You said there was.'

A group of Gran's herbarium colleagues standing nearby looked around to determine the source of my raised voice.

'Calm down, Bethie,' Jarrah said softly. 'Why are you getting so upset? You don't even believe in that stuff.'

I looked at Nick, who was studying me intently.

'Of course I don't. It's just that ...'

My head was swimming as I thought about what Gerry had said on the night Gran died, about her and Gran being star-crossed lovers, and that maybe their relationship had to happen so I would meet Nick.

'NASA tweeted about it,' Jarrah continued with a casualness that belied that she had no idea that her announcement about the thirteenth star sign had set in motion a series of life-changing events.

'Apparently, rumours of the extra star sign surface on social media every few years. You were right about the Babylonians. They did divide the zodiac into twelve segments and lined it up with the calendar. But, according to NASA, it's not that simple; the constellations are different sizes and shapes, and the sun spends different amounts of time lined up with each one.' She traced her foot in an arc in the dirt. 'The sun actually passes through thirteen constellations. Not twelve. But those crazy Babylonians just ignored the last one because it didn't neatly fit with their calendar. It's been there all along.' Jarrah nodded, as if this explanation should settle it once and for all.

My mouth fell open.

'But none of that really matters, does it, Nick?' Jarrah posed, squeezing him in a side hug. 'Sometimes, the universe has a plan for us, whether we like it or not.'

Jarrah wandered off towards Mum and Dad who were surrounded by a crowd of people congratulating them on their performance. This didn't irk me, though; they deserved the praise being showered upon them.

Nick stepped towards me, put his hands around my waist and drew me towards him. And, despite everything that had happened, I felt an unequivocal sense that everything was just as it should be. Celestial even.

Epilogue

Beth

Three months later ...

'Bonjour,' Dad said as he greeted me at the door for lunch on my final Saturday before I left for London.

He was wearing a black waistcoat, had a red scarf around his neck, and he'd drawn a curly moustache on his upper lip; tonight's theme was French, so of course he had.

His face contorted with shock when I stepped into the light of the hallway.

'Bethie,' he gasped. 'You're wearing a beret.'

I pawed at my head. I had seen the beret in the window of an op shop store and decided it might be fun to play along. After all, this would be my last family lunch for a while.

'Très bien,' he whispered as he gave me a huge hug. 'Très bien, indeed.'

When they appeared, Mum and Jarrah both looked like they'd stepped off the stage of the Moulin Rouge. Elijah showed off his Converse: the ultimate French footwear, apparently.

Dad handed me a flute of champagne. 'It's French fizz,' he said proudly. 'Only the best for my daughter's send-off. We thought about making today's lunch English-themed, but warm beer just didn't seem fitting for such an important celebration.'

'You must be excited to reunite with lover-boy,' Jarrah said, before making kissing noises as though she was asking me the question over a water bubbler in primary school.

I rolled my eyes, but it was true. I absolutely was.

On the day after Gran's funeral, when Nick suggested I join him in London to 'see what happens', I told him he was insane. But he insisted I listen to his rationale. He pointed out that Gran and Gerry had been robbed of their relationship due to time and circumstance, so we owed it to them to explore the possibility of what could happen between us. He also reminded me that on the night we spent in the pub in London I had told him travel was in my plans. At the very least, he argued, I could use London as a base to explore the rest of Europe. Then he kissed me passionately and gave me the most compelling reason of all: that he really liked me and didn't want our time together to end. So we'd agreed that he would return to London and I would spend the next couple of months applying for a visa and lining up a job, and tidying up my life, including seeing out the possum bridge project. Then I would fly to London to start the next chapter of my life.

I was looking forward to the next stage in my career. I had secured a job with the local canal and river authority. My role would be to coordinate a project that aimed to better engage with volunteers to help restore the River Thames. The feedback I received from the recruiter was that Geoff had given such a glowing reference that he was suspicious it was made up.

My colleagues at the council had given me a lovely send-off when I left. They had ignored my pleas for my departure to be low-key. Alannah had basically kidnapped me and driven me to a pub for a surprise lunch, which I enjoyed thoroughly. I was presented with an oversized card filled with lovely handwritten messages, including from people who I didn't think knew my name. And I was gifted a eucalyptus leaf pendant on a delicate silver chain. It was exquisite and made me feel guilty for all the times I'd shied away from contributing to office gift collections.

My phone chimed as I sat down at the family dining table, which was covered in a massive charcuterie board, featuring French cheeses and cured meat, olives, veggies and dips. The bakery had been out of baguettes, apparently, so Mum had improvised with some pizza rolls that she sliced and toasted.

I retrieved my phone from my back pocket. The message was from Nick.

Not long now ... I can't wait to see you. x

'Bon appetite,' Mum announced as I slipped my phone away.

'A toast, if I may,' Jarrah said. It wasn't that long ago that her saying this would have evoked immense irritation. I would have assumed she was about to usurp the moment to make it about herself. However, lately, I had found Jarrah to be much less self-absorbed.

I'd finally told my family about the lotto money and my plans to share it with them on the night of Gran's funeral. Jarrah surprised me by asking that I hold onto her share until she knew what she wanted to do with it. She admitted that life admin and, in particular, dealing with money wasn't her strong suit. This, of course, was not a revelation, but I congratulated her for her honesty and capacity for self-reflection.

The following month, she came to me with a very professional-looking business plan that she'd prepared, printed and bound. I could tell she was proud of it. She told me a business idea had come to her as she helped Mum navigate the arduous process of preparing Gran's house to rent out. Many of Gran's collectables were quite valuable, and, while we didn't want to hold on to the majority of them, Mum was reluctant to just hand them over to an op shop where they were at risk of being caught up in the other bric-a-brac. But she was overwhelmed by the prospect of selling them individually on Facebook Marketplace or Gumtree. So Jarrah proposed that her business – Jackalope Treasures – would sell the collectables of deceased estates through popular platforms, rather than at auction like other services, for a small commission.

She used the money I gave her to buy a decommissioned ambulance to cart around the wares, and she developed a website and created some marketing material. Although it turned out she had little need for advertising: since she'd opened for business she'd had as much work as she could manage through referrals she'd received from Nora the funeral director. For Jarrah, Jackalope Treasures wasn't just about the money; she was committed to finding the perfect home for things that had been cherished by their previous owners. Surviving relatives seemed to find comfort in knowing that their loved ones' prized possessions were going to be appropriately appreciated by those who bought them. And the nature of her business meant her work was flexible, which suited her new-found passion: 'forest bathing' (which I had long called 'hiking'). We'd even been on a couple of 'forest bathing' sessions together.

Elijah spent the money I gave him as soon as I transferred it; he and his bandmates used it to lay down an album. I was the first person he called when he found out they'd been chosen to be featured on Triple J.

Mum and Dad refused the money altogether. I insisted I wanted to do something for them – it wasn't like I'd earned it – so we compromised that I would pay for them to come and visit me in London once I was settled.

Now Jarrah stood and raised her glass. 'I think I can speak on behalf of everyone here,' she said, 'when I say that, even though we're going to miss you like crazy, we are so happy for you. We love you, and we adore Nick, and we know the two of you are going to be so happy together.

'And we know how far you've stepped out of your comfort zone to quit your job, sell your new car, rent out your place and move overseas.

But, for what it's worth, I think you're absolutely doing the right thing.'

There was a time that hearing Jarrah say she approved of my life choices would have made me question them intently. But it had been Jarrah who I'd first consulted about my plans to move. I thought I needed a shove in the direction in which I wanted to go, and I knew she was the one to do it. She encouraged me to open myself to new experiences in a way that felt supportive, and not antagonistic like it used to. And, as she pointed out, trying new things had worked pretty well thus far. Although I drew the line at joining a nudist book club in London that she'd heard about.

'Thanks Jarrah, that means a lot,' I said. 'I will miss you all, but I'm excited for the future. Nervous. But excited.' I took a sip of champagne. 'Also I have some other news to share with you.'

Dad slapped the table. 'You're pregnant,' he shouted exuberantly.

Mum gasped.

'Goodness no. No, nothing like that. I got an email today from Emily Lim – the project leader who was with Gran the day she died.' I looked to Mum. 'It turns out that the orchid Gran found was a new species. And they've decided to call it *Caladenia eliseae*, or "Elise's orchid".'

Mum's eyes filled with tears, as had mine.

'Well,' she said, her words choked. 'That would have made her very proud indeed.' She rose from the table and retrieved a package wrapped in green tissue paper. 'We were going to give you this after lunch, but now seems like the perfect time,' she said, passing me the package.

I tore open the paper and looked down at Gran's Gouldian finch print.

'We thought you might like to take it with you,' Jarrah said. Dad and Elijah smiled at me.

I clutched the frame to my chest. The ache of her being gone was still visceral. But, like Elizabeth Gould, Gran had left her mark on science. And, thanks to her, and the twists and turns of fate, the trajectory of my life had been altered, and my heart was open to seeing where it took me.

Acknowledgements

First and foremost, I acknowledge the Traditional Custodians of the land on which I live and work. I wrote this book while on the lands of the Bunurong people, but much of it is set on the lands of the Noongar people in Western Australia. I pay homage to the rich tradition of storytelling that has existed in these places, and indeed across Australia, for millennia, and express my gratitude to First Nations peoples for generously sharing their stories.

While this book shares details about modern conservation, and the work of early European naturalists, I acknowledge that Aboriginal and Torres Strait Islander peoples have been caring for Country for more than 65,000 years.

Put simply, this book would never have seen the light of day if it weren't for my agent Rochelle Fernandez of Alex Adsett Literary. I self-consciously sent a draft to Rochelle for a manuscript assessment and an honest and unbiased indication of whether it was any good. Her words of encouragement, support and work to get it in front of Affirm Press is how *Birds of a Feather* came to be a book, rather than just a file saved in the dark recesses of my external hard drive (which is just as well because my digital filing system is dreadful).

To Kelly Doust, Laura Franks and the entire team at Affirm Press, I thank you from the bottom of my heart for believing in this story and giving me the opportunity to share it with others. I am so grateful for the kindness and patience you've shown as you've led me through this process. Your suggestions and edits have made it a much better book, and I've been honoured that you've held the same affection for the characters as I do.

Thank you also to Sue Tredget, whose friendship and fellowship helped me through the many periods of self-doubt during the writing and editing process. And to Sarah Rood, for indulging me as I shared my ideas for the book in its infancy, for reading an early draft and for providing me with an immeasurable amount of support and encouragement.

A massive thanks to Professor Kevin Kenneally for reading the manuscript to ensure the scientific references were correct and, in the case of those I'd made up, plausible.

Many thanks to the wonderful staff at the Natural History Museum in London, who accommodated me visiting their Reading Room to see the original *Birds of Australia* book. Seeing John and Elizabeth Gould's work was indeed a thrill. Thank you also to the Friends of Kensal Green Cemetery for your help with my early research.

I am so blessed to be surrounded by an army of women who have guided, challenged and supported me as I've transitioned from childhood to adolescence, and womanhood to motherhood, and now to this weird and wonderful time of being middle-aged. To those I've met in workplaces, mothers' groups, at school and university, through my kids, in book clubs and through running and dancing, as well as those I'm related to, and those who just feel like family, I thank you. Every single one of you has enriched my life in some way and added to the tapestry of who I am. And you are all woven into the pages of this book. I am so happy my daughter is growing up at a time when she has strong female role models in the arts, politics, sport and popular culture, as well as in her immediate line of sight.

I am forever indebted to my parents for introducing me to the written word from an early age (*Goodnight Moon* will always hold a special place in my heart) and for your support of everything I've done. By writing and publishing his own fiction books, my dad, Brian Mooney, gave me the confidence to tackle my own. And my mum, Frith Mooney, has shared her love of books with me for as long as I can remember.

Thanks to my siblings, Erin, Sarah and Phil, and their partners and families for supporting and encouraging me, and for always keeping it real. And to my Bonus Mom, Kanani Oberholzer, and her extended family, and my mother-in-law, Rosalynne Sampson, for being part of my treasured intergenerational network.

The biggest thank you of all goes to my husband, Jason, who quite literally keeps the lights on (except when he turns them off when no one is in the room). You are the engine of our cruise ship, and I am so grateful for everything you do for us.

To my beautiful babies, Bailey and Chloe, I love you.

Book Club Questions

1. Early in the book, Beth dismisses the role of fate in determining the trajectory of our lives. By the end, she's open to the idea. Do you believe in fate?

2. What would you do if you won the 'life-adjusting' amount of $264,412.51?

3. Do you ever think about reaching out to the 'one who got away' from your past? If so, what's stopping you?

4. Growing up, Beth identified with Hermione Granger from Harry Potter and enjoyed seeing herself in a popular fictional character. Was there a fictional character who validated the way you felt about yourself growing up?

5. Beth enjoys the history and tradition of London, and appreciates the city's uniformity and formality. Is there a place in the world that you feel suits your personality?

6. The phrase 'birds of a feather flock together' refers to the practice of seeking out like-minded people, as Beth did with Elise, and Elise did with Gerry. How important is it to surround yourself with like-minded people? Can doing so limit your personal growth?

7. In Chapter 24, Elise tells Gerry she felt like she was 'touring this whole new world with a set of old visa conditions'. How do you think it's been for older members of the LGBTQI+ community to adapt to progress and acceptance of their sexuality?

8. Elise holds a mirror to Beth with regards to her relationship with her family and with Nick. Who holds a mirror to you?

9. By the end of the book, Beth gets some clarity around her relationship with her family. Do you think Elise needed to die for this healing to occur?

10. Beth struggles with the decision to give some of her lotto winnings to Jarrah because she considers her financially irresponsible. What are your thoughts about giving gifts you know might be misused? Should you give them anyway? Is it different if the gift is money?

11. Beth can be quite rigid with her family and with others she encounters, but she is warm and empathetic with Elise and, later, with Nick. What is it about the way those two treat her that brings out this other side?